# TOO
# Wilde
# TO TAME

## WILDE SECURITY
## SERIES

Stay Wilde!

# TOO
# Wilde
# TO TAME

### WILDE SECURITY
### SERIES

*Tonya Burrows*

# TONYA BURROWS

Entangled Publishing, LLC
2614 South Timberline Road
Suite 109
Fort Collins, CO 80525
Visit our website at www.entangledpublishing.com.

Ignite is an imprint of Entangled Publishing, LLC.

Edited by Heather Howland
Cover design by Erin Dameron-Hill
Cover art from Shutterstock

Manufactured in the United States of America

First Edition February 2017

**ignite**

*This one's for you, my readers. Thanks for sticking with the Wilde boys and me!*

*This is also for Natalie. You never found your happily ever after in life, so I paired you with the most heroic hero I knew. I think about you often, Nat. Love you.*

# Chapter One

Greer Wilde slumped over his drink like a man who'd had one too many. In truth, he'd been nursing the same glass all night, but he needed to hide his face, and the best way to do that was to pretend he was pissing-himself, couldn't-lift-his-head drunk. The man he was following had been his father's best friend at one time, and he looked too much like David Greer Wilde Sr. to pass as anyone but his son.

Or his ghost.

About an hour ago, he'd purposely let Richard Mendenhall see him. Just a brief glimpse, but good ol' Rich had gone sheet white, which told him a lot about the state of the guy's conscience.

Guilty. As. Fuck.

Probably why the guy was drinking his way through a cheap bottle of vodka right now.

*Does it help? Does the vodka help you sleep at night? Help you look yourself in the mirror after you orphaned five kids?*

The story that his parents were killed in a gas station stick-up gone wrong was bullshit. His father—a career military man, who had spent a good portion of that career in black ops—wouldn't have been taken out by some lowlife punk looking for quick cash.

No. In the deepest part of Greer's soul, he'd always known there was more behind their deaths than he'd been told, but at fifteen, he hadn't been able to do anything about it. He'd been just a kid, and he had four brothers—Reece, Vaughn, Cam, and Jude—all counting on him to keep their family together.

But he wasn't a kid anymore, and if something happened to him now, his brothers would be okay. They had Wilde Security, and Reece, Cam, and Jude were even married to good women who would keep them in line. Vaughn…well, when he'd left home three months ago, Vaughn was struggling, but he'd eventually be okay, too. The rest of the family would take care of him. Which left Greer free to pursue the one thing he'd dreamed about for years, the thing he'd trained himself mercilessly for, hardened himself for.

Revenge.

He lifted his gaze enough to check on Mendenhall. Guy was still drinking and didn't appear to have plans to stop any time soon.

Wincing, Greer shifted positions on his stool and let his body droop forward over his glass again. It wasn't hard to act the part of a drunkard when every cell throbbed with pain. A new trickle of blood leaked from the gunshot wound in his side, sliding in a hot trail down his stomach to soak into the waistband of his jeans.

Damn. Must have popped open the hurried stitches he'd put in.

It was kind of surreal, being back in the States. This hole-in-the-wall bar, where the most dangerous thing was a rowdy drunk, was so far removed from the a war-ravaged country he'd been in less than twenty-four hours ago. In Syria, you couldn't tell the good guys from the bad, and the bad guys from the civilians. He'd spent the last several months sleeping with one eye open and one hand on a weapon, ready to jump into action at the smallest indication of trouble. And still that constant alertness hadn't helped save one of his men. His friend. He'd jumped like he was trained to, and the whole fucking world had crumbled down around them anyway. Nobody had seen the attack coming, and there wasn't much a guy could do when mortars were raining down from the sky except bend over and kiss his ass good-bye. He still wasn't sure how he'd made it out of there...

And wished like hell he hadn't.

No. Greer grabbed the glass in front of him with a trembling hand and gulped down the rest of the contents. He had to shut out all the noise in his head. Had to shut out the recent past and focus on his mission, right here and now. After years of dead ends, he was only feet away from the man responsible for his parents' deaths.

Richard Mendenhall.

At one time, Rich had been a big, happy guy. Always had a quick smile for everyone, and was always up for a touch football game whenever he came to visit, but the man sitting at the end of the bar now in no way resembled the one from Greer's memory. He was stooped and balding and looked older than his sixty-some-odd years. Watching Rich out of the corner of his eye, Greer had to wonder if his father would have aged well or would time have been as cruel to him as it had to this piece of shit?

For years, he'd been so sure his parents' deaths had been because of something his father knew or did with the military. He'd worked his way into the Rangers and then into some of the most secretive black ops units in the world—all hoping to catch a whiff of anything that would point him in the right direction. He never had.

Until the diary.

He reached inside his coat and touched it, stroked a finger over its soft leather cover. His mother had always been writing things down. She'd kept meticulous baby books for all five of her sons, a daily planner, and a personal journal. He and his father had picked out this particular journal—pale blue, her favorite color—for her 39th birthday shortly before her death, and in the months that followed, she filled its pages with her final words.

Words that, after all these years, had pointed her son to her killer.

He checked on Rich again.

The stool was empty.

Shit. Where'd the guy go?

Heart pumping hard, roaring blood through his ears, Greer leapt up and ignored the sharp tug of pain from the gunshot wound in his side. He scanned the bar and spotted Rich's bald head ducking out a side door. Cursing under his breath, he shoved through the small crowd and into the parking lot. If he lost his chance because he was all up in his head and sentimental, he needed an ass kicking. Or another ass kicking, since he'd already gotten a good one in Syria.

This wasn't about sentiment anymore. It was about justice and how there had been none for his family.

He caught sight of his target walking fast across the parking lot toward the street. "Rich!"

The man froze and whirled around, eyes bugging out of his pale face. "D-David?" He shook his head. "No. Can't be. Y-you're dead."

*No, I'm not a ghost, motherfucker. But I'm about to be your judge, jury, and executioner.* He reached under his jacket and set a hand on his gun. "We have something long overdue to discuss."

The attack came from his left—so unexpected he lost his balance and landed hard on the concrete, his gun skidding away from his fingers. He raised his arms, trying to protect his head from the rain of kicks and punches slamming into him from all directions. One connected with his side and the rest of the stitches securing his bullet wound popped open. Blood immediately soaked through his shirt.

There were at least three attackers, and he thought he heard laughter as he struggled to defend himself. Rich's laughter?

Motherfucker. He had this planned all along, and Greer had all but skipped into his trap.

A steel-toed boot glanced off his temple, but he was more concerned about the gleam of a blade that had appeared in one of his attackers' hands. In the seconds after he saw it, he felt the cold slide of it against his neck.

Shit.

He struck out blindly, hoping to knock it away. Got another slice along his arm, but the knife went flying, so that was a win if he'd ever had one. He kicked with both feet, landed a blow to one attacker's groin. The man crumpled to his knees, and Greer got a good look at his face. Short dark hair, wide brown eyes, thin lips under a peach-fuzz mustache. No, not a man, after all. Hell, he was just a kid.

The kid scrambled to his feet, glanced around, and bolted away liked a scared little rabbit. Good. One less punk he had to worry about.

Another steel-toed kick plowed into his temple and he arched in pain, losing track of the kid as his vision flared white then faded to gray. Yeah, that blow did it. He was going to lose consciousness and probably die right here in this parking lot, and there wasn't a damn thing he could do to stop it.

Any other time, he'd welcome the sweet relief of death, but he hated the thought of going out like this—fucking *hated* it—and struck out one last time. Desperate. Imprecise. His groping fingers found the knife on the ground by his side and he swung it up, connected with something solid. He thought he heard a scream of pain, but he wasn't aware enough to know how much damage he'd caused. He was just glad he'd hurt the steel-toed bastard one time before it was over.

His brothers were going to be okay. This would hurt them, but they'd pull through. Hell, they'd be better off in the long run without him. He kept that thought front and center in his mind as his limbs grew heavy and unconsciousness swept him away.

He hadn't planned to live much longer anyway.

# Chapter Two

Last night was endless.

Natalie Taggart groaned as she dragged herself out of her Fiat, then took a moment to stretch in the crisp April morning air. Her midnight to five a.m. on-air shift had gone well enough, despite a couple weirdo call-ins—but that came with the territory when you were the late-night talk DJ. It was after she got off air that everything went to shit. If there was something not broken at the station, it broke on her right then, which had caused some serious timing issues with the morning drive show. Rick and Lou finally got on the air after a full forty minutes of dead airtime.

They were all going to get their asses chewed when the station manager found out.

But that was a worry for later. Right now, all she wanted was to take Jet out for his morning walk, then cuddle up to his one hundred pounds of golden fluff and sleep for a solid eight hours.

Of course, she wouldn't get eight hours. She only had five until she had to leave for the dance studio to teach her evening class, but a girl could dream.

Which class did she have tonight? She scrolled through her mental schedule as she stretched and hoped it wasn't toddler night. She loved those little munchkins, but she just did not have the energy to wrangle them all into something resembling a ballet class.

It was…Friday. Right? So no toddlers, thank all the gods of dance. Tonight was the ten-to-thirteen-year-olds. They could have attitudes, the little prima donnas, but she definitely felt better equipped to handle them than the toddlers. And then she was off for the weekend. Two blissful days of no radio, no dance classes. Just her and Jet and maybe a Netflix binge.

She couldn't wait.

She grabbed her oversize bag out of the car, got halfway to the front door of her apartment complex, and realized she'd forgotten her travel coffee mug in the cup holder.

Dammit. She'd need that when she woke up.

Changing directions, she backtracked to the car and unlocked the door with the fob. She was just reaching in for the travel mug when she sensed a looming presence close in behind her. She started and bumped her head on the doorframe.

"Hey, Aunt Tally. It's just me."

"Andy?" Rubbing the sore spot on her head, she straightened and faced her nephew. Then, for good measure, she punched him in the shoulder. "Don't sneak up on people, you little brat! What are you doing out at this time in the morning?"

Guilt flashed across his features before he ducked his head. He scuffed the toe of his Nike across the pavement. "I… uh, need somewhere to crash for a few days."

She closed her eyes for a moment, gathering strength from her nearly tapped-out reserves. "What did you do now?"

"Nothing!" He actually sounded offended, but going

off past experience, that was an act. He only ever wanted to stay with her when he was afraid the cops were going to come knocking, looking for him because he'd hacked into something else off limits. Like the freaking Pentagon.

"Go home, Andy." She shut her car door and walked toward her apartment complex again.

He was right on her heels. "Can't I just stay for the weekend? You can call Grandma and Grandpa and tell them I'm with you and they'll chill out."

She stopped before keying in the code to open the building's front door and faced him again. He had his hands tucked in the front pocket of his hooded sweatshirt, and he seemed to be anxious—which he damn well should be if he skipped going home last night.

"Where were you?" she asked, point blank.

"I was…uh…uh…"

"Tell me the truth."

He flushed a deep red. "Just…at a friend's house. A girl."

She sighed, and some of the tension seeped out of her shoulders. So it had only been teenage shenanigans for once. "You were safe, right? You used condoms?"

His face got even redder. "Oh, Jesus, Aunt Tally."

"Hey, the last thing you need is a bouncing bundle of joy. Just ask your father. He wasn't much older than you when you came along."

He glanced away. "I don't know where Dad is. I haven't seen him in days."

Natalie's heart squeezed. "Maybe he got a job somewhere."

Andy snorted. "Doubt it."

So did she. Her brother Mathew, Andy's father, hadn't held down a job since he was a teenager. Numbing himself with drugs was more important than trivial things like work or a place to live or caring for his son, which was why her parents now had full custody of Andy.

She studied Andy for another second, then relented. "Okay, fine. But here's the deal. You come in, shower, change, and go to school. You do that, you can stay for the weekend and I'll cover you for last night."

He brightened. "You're a life saver—"

"Ah ah." She held up a finger. "I'm not done. I plan on calling the school every hour to make sure you're still there. If you're not, deal's off. And this weekend, we're going to do some volunteer work."

That brightness dimmed a few degrees, and he grumbled something under his breath she didn't catch.

She shrugged and punched in the door code. "Those are my terms, and you're not going to get better from Grandma and Grandpa. So take 'em or leave 'em. It's up to you."

Andy followed her inside. "I'll take them, but I won't like them."

"It's a start." She didn't bother waiting for the elevator, which was notoriously slow, and took the stairs to her second floor apartment. As she ascended, she dug in her bag for her apartment key. "So...who's this girl? Anyone I know?"

"No," Andy said in the sulking tone only teenagers could manage.

"Have Grandma and Grandpa met her?"

"No." He hesitated a beat. "I really don't want to talk about it. Can we just—" He broke off abruptly and fell into a shocked silence.

"Just what?" Finally finding her key ring, she glanced up from her bag—and dropped everything. "Oh my God!"

A huge man was unconscious on the hallway floor, blocking the entrance to her apartment.

"Oh my God," she said again and hurried to his side, pulling off her jacket as she went. She bundled it up and slid it under his head. His hair was overgrown and a layer of beard covered his jaw, but under all the hair was a handsome, hard-planed face she recognized. David Greer Wilde, Jr.—her neighbor from apartment 211 across the hall, the one who had been missing since January.

They'd never really spoken before he went missing. Or at least, never said anything to each other beyond the occasional awkward hello while passing on the stairway. He always kept to himself. She'd gossiped with her friends about the handsome recluse next door. The only reason she knew his name at all was because she'd been collecting his mail for his brother Reece, who had stopped by several times looking for him. His family was worried sick. Judging by the looks of him now, they had good reason to be. He was bruised and bloody, and wounds on his arms and neck were still bleeding.

"Andy, get my phone out of my purse and call 911." She gently brushed a lock of his dark, overgrown hair from his face. "David, can you hear me?"

He stirred and opened his eyes to slits but gave no indication that he'd understood her, or even that he was fully conscious yet "Help..." he rasped.

"It's okay." She soothed more hair back from his face. "You're okay now. We'll get you to the hospital. I'll call your brother, too. Your family has been so worried." She started to turn away to see what was taking Andy so long, but a huge hand shot up and clamped around her wrist. She gasped. He stared up, his nearly black eyes focused intently on her face. Definitely conscious now, but possibly also delirious.

"No. Hospital," he gritted out between bloody teeth. "No brothers."

"What?"

"I don't want...hospital. Or—my brothers."

"Why the hell not?"

"Please." His grip loosened as his eyes rolled back. A moment later, he was unconscious again. She sat back on her knees and stared at him.

The guy was crazy. Completely nutso. He very obviously needed the hospital. Possibly a psych screening. And of course his brothers deserved to know he was no longer missing. How cruel to keep that from them.

She shook her head and turned to her nephew. "Andy! Phone! He needs—" She broke off, shock freezing her to the bone. Andy clasped something in his bruised and bloodied hands, but it wasn't her cell phone. He had a gun. A freaking gun! Her heart bungeed into her stomach. "What are you doing?"

"He's supposed to be dead."

She glanced from him to her unconscious neighbor and back. "Oh, God. Tell me you didn't do this."

"Get out of the way, Aunt Tally. I need to finish the job."

"No." She stood and positioned herself between the gun and David. "Think about what you're doing. If you kill him, your life is over. Completely. There's no turning back from that."

He shook his head. "There's no turning back now."

"Fine. If you really think shooting him is your only option, do it. But you'll have to shoot me, too, because I will not let you get away with this. I'll go right to the cops."

The gun wavered in his hand. "You don't understand."

"No, I don't! What the actual fuck, Andy?"

Tears filled his eyes, and the gun shook harder in his grip.

She chanced a step closer. "This isn't you. Put the gun down and let's help him. Please. Do it for me."

"I can't." Andy whirled and ran down the stairs like the worst demons hell had to offer were nipping at his heels.

Natalie sagged with relief even as her heart thundered against her ribs. She scrambled over to the spilled contents of her bag on the floor and found her phone, dialing 911 with shaking fingers. But she didn't hit send. She glanced over at her neighbor, then at the stairs. If she called an ambulance, the cops would show up, and she'd have to tell them what she knew. She didn't want to do that until she talked to Andy and found out what the hell was going on.

She gazed back over at David. He'd said no hospital, so by not calling she was honoring his wishes, right? But she couldn't leave him lying here, and taking him across the hall to his place wasn't an option. For one thing, she didn't have a key.

So. He'd have to stay with her. Just until he was on his feet again. Hopefully that would give her enough time to convince him not to press charges against her wayward nephew.

Cursing under her breath, Natalie got to her feet and stepped over him to unlock her apartment door. Jet was waiting there on the other side, but instead of his usual wagging tail and sloppy so-glad-you're-home grin, he was lying on the floor, big head resting on his paws, brown eyes fixed on the door. He jumped up as soon as she had the door all the way open and bounded to David's side, snuffling at his hair. Empathetic creature that he was, he'd sensed that someone was in pain on the other side of the door, and going by the claw marks in the wood, he'd tried to get through it to help. Sweet thing. She couldn't even be mad at him for ruining any chance at getting her deposit back.

Jet gently licked David's face, then looked up at her with concern shining in his eyes when he got no reaction from his patient.

She chuckled softly and rubbed his head. "He'll be okay, buddy. We just have to get him inside." She walked into her apartment, set her cell phone down on the kitchen counter, then went into her bedroom to find a sheet. She could roll him over onto it, then drag him inside.

When she returned to the living room, she found him standing in her doorway, swaying like he was on the deck of a ship in stormy weather. "Oh." She hugged the sheet to her chest. "You're awake."

"I-I need…" He stumbled forward, gripping the wall as he went, and made it to the half bath in the hall only seconds before she heard him gag.

She looked at the ceiling and said a little prayer of thanks that her apartment was the exact same layout as his. Otherwise, she doubted he would have been able to find the toilet in his condition, and she really didn't do well with vomit.

When the bathroom went silent, she crossed over and peeked inside. He was leaning over the toilet, head bowed, eyes squeezed shut.

"Are you okay?" she asked, and then mentally kicked herself for it. Stupid question, considering he just prayed mightily to the porcelain god and was currently bleeding all over her bathroom floor. "I mean…are you sure you don't need the hospital? You, uh, probably have a concussion."

"No shit," he snapped.

She straightened her shoulders. "Excuse me? I'm trying to help you, but if you're going to act like that, I'll drive your ass to the hospital, dump you there, and call your brother."

He gazed up slowly, and if she wasn't mistaken, there was shock in his eyes before he hid it. "I don't need the hospital. I'm fine."

"You look it."

"Just…need to sleep it off. Gotta get to my apartment—"

She thought about her nephew and her stomach dropped. What was to stop David from calling the cops? "No!"

He looked at her again.

*Dial it back, Tally.*

"You can't be alone if you have a concussion," she added, all reason. "You should stay here on the couch."

He said nothing for a moment. She stared at him, hands on hips. He glowered back with red-rimmed eyes. Finally, he grumbled an agreement. He seemed to do that a lot. Grumble.

Then again, she'd never been beaten up like he was, so maybe she'd grumble in his situation, too. He pushed himself to his feet but had to grip the sink to keep upright as he twisted on the faucet and rinsed out his mouth.

"Um," she said. "I have a first aid kit. We should probably clean up those cuts."

He gazed at his reflection in the mirror over the sink and—well, he didn't quite wince, but his lips tightened. "Already did." He turned away from the sink and wobbled on his feet.

"Whoa." She darted forward and grabbed him before he fell, because once he went down, she wasn't going to be able to get him back up. "Hang on. Let me help."

He grunted. Jeez. She knew he wasn't much of a talker from past experience and, granted, he was hurting, but couldn't he try communicating at least a few evolutionary steps above caveman?

Shoulder wedged under his arm, she led him to the couch. He didn't make a sound as he lowered himself to the cushion, but she saw pain in the way his jaw hardened and creases fanned out from his eyes.

He needed more medical attention than she, with her rudimentary first aid knowledge, was able to give, but she'd do what she could. She sat on the coffee table opposite him and opened the kit, found an antiseptic pad. Then she hesitated.

"You should probably take off your shirt."

"Probably." But he didn't move.

"Do you…need help?" *Please say no. Please say no. Please—*

He ground his teeth together in obvious frustration. "I can't lift my arms."

Oh, God. What had Andy done to him? And why? She just couldn't wrap her mind around it.

Swallowing hard, she stood again and helped push his arms

through his sleeves. As gently as she could, she pulled the shirt off over his head. His chest looked worse than his face, bruises blossoming in deep purple splotches all along his ribs. There was already one dirty, bloodstained square of a bandage low on the left side of his chest. She hesitated, then gently pulled it off. The wound underneath was not new, having already been closed with a line of rudimentary stitches, some of which had popped open. It was angry and red and looked a hell of a lot like a bullet hole.

He'd been shot. But not tonight. This wound was a couple days old, at least.

She breathed out softly in shock and touched it without thinking. He hissed through his teeth. She snatched her hand back.

"Sorry." She went to work with the antiseptic pads, cleaning some of the smaller cuts. "What happened to you?" Maybe he could fill in the blanks for her. Andy couldn't have shot him, but her nephew's bruised knuckles did point rather ominously to a recent fight. Though she still had trouble believing it. None of Andy's actions tonight jibed with the crazy-smart, sometimes mischievous, but never outright bad kid she knew her nephew to be.

There had to be an explanation, but all Greer said in response to her question was, "I got mugged."

Yeah, sure. A big guy like him? She was tall—five-nine, which had at one time been the bane of her dancing career—and he still towered more than half a foot over her. He must have been close to six-five, all muscle, and she'd seen him leave his apartment in an Army uniform on more than one occasion. Intimidating wasn't a strong enough word to describe him—not exactly the kind of guy most muggers would look at and think, "Now there's an easy mark."

There was more to this story, but she had a feeling she would get answers out of Andy before him. He had the strong and silent thing down to an art.

Once she cleaned his cuts, she re-bandaged the bullet wound. "Are you in pain?" she asked and began picking up the trash. "I'm afraid I don't have anything stronger to offer than ibuprofen."

"I'm fine. I'll live."

"Okay." She closed the first aid kit and stood. "I'll toss your shirt in the wash if you want."

"Don't bother. It's beyond saving."

Did that mean he was going to lie here on her couch half naked? "Um, okay." Uncertain of what to say or do next, she rocked back on her heels. "I'll get you a pillow and blanket."

"I'm fine. I'll go home and—" He tried to stand and didn't make it to his feet. He fell heavily back to the couch. Dropped his head into his hands and groaned. "Fuck."

"Are you going to puke again?" What a stupid thing to ask. If he was about to, he wasn't going to answer her with a polite, *Why, yes, I think I might. Would you mind terribly if I did so in your trash can?*

Yeah, this guy didn't do polite on his best days.

She grabbed the trash can from under her desk and dumped the papers in it onto the floor. She took it back to him, and he dry-heaved over it for a few minutes. Finally, exhausted and pale, he leaned back against the couch and closed his eyes. She waited a moment more, then gently pulled the bucket from his hands and set it on the floor next to him.

"I'll get that blanket and pillow," she murmured. He said nothing in response. She had the feeling he despised his current situation, and probably her, too, because she was part of it. She made it halfway across the room but stopped and turned back. "David—"

"It's Greer. David was my father." He peeled one eye open and squinted at her. "How'd you know my name?"

"Oh. Uh, I've been collecting your mail for your brother.

Reece."

He closed his eye and turned away. "He can't know I'm here."

She frowned. "Why not?"

Both eyes opened this time and pinned her with a dead serious look that chilled her to her core. "Because he'll try to stop me from killing the man who killed our parents."

# Chapter Three

Greer's eyes felt glued shut, and it took several tries to pry them open. Everything was blurry—unfocused splashes of an unfamiliar setting. He didn't remember falling asleep and didn't know where he was. Syria? Was he still lying in a pile of rubble, bleeding out from a bullet wound, waiting for death? Or, no. He vaguely remembered pulling himself out of the wreckage of the former CIA safe house, stitching himself back together, and catching a ride on a cargo jet to the States.

Yes, that was right. He'd come home because he had a mission. He couldn't die without avenging his parents.

Christ, he was hot, as if he was baking in an oven. In Texas. On a hundred and ten degree day. Sweat poured off his forehead, beaded on his upper lip, and he threw off the blanket covering him. Cool air kissed his bare chest, but it wasn't enough.

Why was it so hot?

Maybe he was in hell. Not Syria, which had been very hell-like, but the real deal. Fire and brimstone and all that. If he wasn't there yet, then that had to be where he was headed.

Why else would he be so fucking hot?

Abstract splotches of color and shadow moved around him. He turned his head, focused on one swirl of pink and gray, spinning, spinning, spinning. He watched until it stopped moving, and before his eyes it took on the shape of a woman. A ballerina in a pink leotard and gray tights, all long lines and grace as she flowed through the movements of her dance.

He stared, mesmerized. Couldn't remember ever seeing anything so beautiful.

Yes, he must be dying. It was the only thing that made sense. He was dying and this was his angel, sent by his mother to collect him. He wasn't a good man, didn't deserve heaven, but Mom must have pulled some strings to make it happen. Why else would his angel of death arrive on ballet slippers? Mom wanted him to know it was all okay and he didn't have to fight anymore. He didn't have to be afraid.

And for the first time in recent memory, he wasn't.

He'd seen so much bad in this world, had witnessed the horrible things people did to each other when they believed they were right and everyone else was wrong. So much hatred and blood. He'd lived more than half his life mired in that darkness, sometimes so deep he thought he'd never see light again…

But the woman dancing in front of him sparked with light and color.

His angel.

She'd take him home, and he'd see his parents again. He no longer had to worry about avenging them. He'd tried and failed and he was tired. So very tired.

He reached for his angel, wanting nothing more than to touch her, absorb some of her light into his dark soul. If he could just get to her, she'd save him…

• • •

*Crash!*

Natalie stumbled a Grande Jeté, nearly twisting her ankle as she landed. She spun toward the noise and found her neighbor sprawled on the floor. He was conscious, his hard face flushed an unhealthy red, his eyes glazed. He kept muttering something that sounded like "angel," but she couldn't be sure.

"Hey. Shh, you're safe. You're going to be okay." She shut off her iPod and hurried to his side, clasping his outstretched hand. His skin was on fire. She didn't need a thermometer to know he had a fever. A high one, at that.

Dammit. He needed a hospital, but he'd been so adamantly opposed to going she hated to betray the trust he'd put in her by taking him. Then again, that trust wouldn't matter a whole lot if he died on her living room floor.

She had to do something.

She all too easily pried her hand from his grip and scrambled to her feet. She'd put his brother's card in the ceramic dish on the kitchen counter where she kept bills waiting to be paid. She shuffled through the papers, found the card settled at the bottom of the pile, and picked it up.

Reece Wilde.

She'd call him and wash her hands of this whole mess. After all, living next to Greer didn't give her the right to make decisions about his medical care. His family needed to know.

She picked up her cell phone and dialed the number on the card, but never hit send.

Except…there was Andy to consider. She hadn't been able to get a hold of him in the last twenty-four hours. Nor had she found him when she checked his usual hangouts. And she still had no idea how he was involved in all this. If she called Greer's brother, the police would investigate and… well, neither of them wanted that. Sighing, she set the phone down and looked over at her patient. He'd once more lost consciousness.

If he died…

No.

She grabbed the phone again and called the only person she could think of—Raffi, her best friend from her days at Juilliard. His older brother was a top-secret soldier-slash-spy or something like that. Raffi would know what to do.

"Hey, Tally," Raffi answered after two rings with a smile in his voice. "Funny, I was just talking about you and the time you got stuck in the pumpkin carriage during our first performance of *Cinderella*."

She smiled a little at the memory. Her "horses" had dragged the carriage too far into a narrow hallway offstage, and she hadn't been able to get the door open. She would have missed her next cue if Raffi hadn't rescued her. "You've always been my knight in shining pointe shoes, Raf." She glanced over at her patient and winced. "And I, uh, could actually use a little help now."

"Girl, don't tell me you're stuck in a pumpkin again."

"No. This is…" She searched for a way to explain, came up blank. "God, this is so far above my pay grade, I don't even know where to begin."

"Natalie?" The humor faded from his tone, replaced with real concern. "Are you in trouble?"

"Honestly? I'm not sure. Yesterday morning, I came home from work and found my neighbor unconscious in front of my door. Someone had beaten him up badly. He's also been shot, but he refused to go to the hospital and—" She decided not to tell him the part about Andy pulling the gun on Greer. "And, well, now he's passed out on my couch. Or on the floor in front of my couch. He's running a fever. He woke up delirious a few minutes ago."

Silence stretched on the other end of the line for several beats.

"Wait," Raffi said finally. "Which neighbor?"

"The one I told you about over lunch last week. The one that's been missing—"

"Fuck." Raffi dragged the word out. "Greer Wilde?"

She started. "How'd you know?"

"I know the Wildes through my brother. Gabe's worked with them before."

She gripped the phone tighter and stared at her neighbor. "So Greer's like…black ops?"

"I don't ask Gabe for details. I just know they have a working relationship."

"Can Gabe come help?"

A beat passed. Then another. "No. He was almost killed on a mission back in January. He's out of the hospital finally, but he's going to be recovering for a long time."

"Oh my God, Raffi. I'm so sorry. Why didn't you tell me?"

He hesitated. "It's…complicated. A lot of shit went down with my family after he was injured and, to tell you the truth, I'm still trying to cope. It's not something I've felt like talking much about."

Her heart ached for him. She knew he was close with his brother, and if Gabe had nearly died, Raffi must have been a wreck. "When you do feel like talking, you know you have me, right?"

"I know." A smile returned to his voice. "Saint Tally, always wanting to right the world's wrongs." Before she could scoff at that, he added, "Let me call the guys on Gabe's team, see if I can get Greer some off-the-grid help. I'll get back at you within the hour."

She nodded even though Raffi couldn't see her and the line had already gone dead. This was unbelievable. And Raffi was talking about it like it was just another day in the life. Who knows? Maybe it was for him. She'd always thought he was on the periphery of his brother's top-secret world, but now she wondered. Was he more involved?

No. She shook her head. No way. This was *Raffi* she was thinking about. The guy who liked fashion more than she did and who changed his hairstyle every other week. He didn't conform, so there was no way he could be some super-secret soldier-spy like his brother. That was just ridiculous.

Then again…

She glanced at Greer. Her neighbor was apparently a super-secret soldier-spy, so at the moment anything seemed possible. If eighty-year-old Mrs. Chan two doors down suddenly revealed she moonlighted as a topless dancer, Natalie didn't think she'd bat an eye. She was that far down the rabbit hole.

And what in God's name did Andy have to do with any of this?

Since the phone was in her hand, she tried her nephew again but didn't get an answer. Not that she'd expected one. He was in full-blown avoidance mode. She tried her brother but wasn't the least bit surprised when she didn't get an answer there, either. If Matt was on a binge, he'd be out of touch until he came down from whatever substance was his current favorite fix-all.

Worry gnawed at her belly. This wasn't like Andy. He was a computer nerd, not a gangster. And he certainly was not a killer. She had to find him, but she honestly had no idea where to start looking.

She started to set the phone down, but it rang again, Raffi already calling her back.

"Good news," he said when she answered. "The team's medic is in town to check up on Gabe, so I gave him your address. He's headed over now."

The back of her neck prickled. Was she okay with letting a complete stranger into her home to care for the semi-stranger currently unconscious on the floor in front of her couch? Better question, did she have a choice? "How will I know him?"

"For one thing, he's probably the only guy in DC wearing a cowboy hat. At least he's the only one who can pull it off without looking ridiculous." When she wasn't able to muster the laugh he'd obviously been aiming for, Raffi's voice gentled. "He's good people, Tally. You can trust him. If you want, I'll drive down—"

"No." She shook her head at herself. She was being paranoid. "I can't ask you to do that."

"You weren't asking. I was offering."

Tempting, she had to admit. She'd love to see a friendly face right now, but Raffi worked on Broadway and was gearing up for opening night of a new show. She knew how hectic that could be and didn't feel right about monopolizing his time. If he said she could trust this medic, then she shouldn't need more reassurance.

"No," she said more firmly. "I'll handle this."

"All right. But if you need me, I'll be there."

"I know. And I appreciate it."

Twenty minutes after she hung up with Raffi, there was a knock at her door. She didn't usually bother with the peephole, but this time, she felt it was warranted. Sure enough, the man on the other side was wearing a cowboy hat. Raffi was right—he could pull it off.

She opened the door a crack. "Raffi sent you?"

"Yes, ma'am." Oh, he even had the drawl to complete the sexy cowboy package. He swept his hat off his head before holding out a hand in greeting. "Name's Jesse Warrick. I'm a...colleague of Raffi's brother. And a friend of Greer's. May I take a look at him?"

She eyed Jesse. He didn't look like a James Bond spy type. His dark hair curled at the collar of his leather coat, and his face had a rugged edge to it, shadowed with a couple days worth of scruff. Despite his modern clothes, everything else about him screamed authentic cowboy, like he'd just stepped off the range. He looked more like a rodeo star than a medical professional, and suddenly she wasn't so sure about letting him near Greer. "Are you a doctor?"

His easy smile remained in place, but she noticed a tightening around his eyes. "I don't have the MD after my name if that's what you're askin'. Never got around to med school, but I was a combat medic in the Army. I've treated Greer on multiple occasions."

At the news, she relaxed a bit. "So he'd be okay with you examining him?"

"Hell no," Jesse admitted and grinned. "Because like so many of the guys I treat, he's a stubborn bastard who hates admittin' he's not invincible."

Natalie decided right then she liked this guy. His words had a ring of truth to them. A lie would have been faster, and she appreciated that he hadn't glossed over her concerns. Honestly, she wasn't even sure why she still had concerns. Raffi had vouched for Jesse, and on any other occasion, that would have been enough, but she was feeling very mother bear protective over Greer for reasons she couldn't begin to name.

She opened the door wider to let him in. "Greer's on the floor in front of the couch. He fell off and I can't lift him."

"I'll get him." Jesse set aside his hat and the bag he'd been carrying, then knelt down next to Greer. "Hey, buddy. What the hell happened to you?"

She watched him effortlessly lift Greer into a fireman's carry and deposit him back on the couch. "He said he was mugged."

Jesse snorted, which only confirmed her original suspicion that the mugging story had been a lie. He straightened, grabbed his bag, and fished around until he found a forehead thermometer.

After a beep, he frowned at the small screen on the device. "Jesus. He's burnin' up. I'm thinkin' he got an infection from one of these gashes or…" His eyes widened as he pulled off the new bandage square she'd placed over the gunshot wound. "Dayam. That'll account for it."

"I cleaned it with antiseptic pads."

"Yeah, might not have mattered. Infection already had its hooks in him by the time you got to him." He studied the hole for a moment, probing it gently with his fingers. "It's a fairly clean entry wound. That's good."

Jesse seemed to be talking more to himself than her, so she remained silent.

"Small caliber, not enough punch to go all the way through him or cause much damage. Looks like he already dug the bullet out."

"Wait." She stared at the angry wound and bile surged into the back of her throat. "You mean, by himself?"

"Mmm," Jesse said. She wasn't sure if it was an affirmative answer until he straightened away from the couch and added, "He did a fair good job stitchin' it up, too—at least until the stitches popped open. He probably didn't have clean tools handy when he did it and that's where the infection came from, I'd wager. I'll start IVs for fluids and antibiotics. He'll be right as rain after a massive dose of both. Until then, we need to get his temperature down before he fries." He nodded toward the dining room space in front of her bay windows, which she had converted to a makeshift dance studio with several mats and freestanding ballet barres. "I see you're a dancer. I assume you have ice packs for injuries?"

She nodded.

"All right. Get 'em, wrap 'em in washcloths, and put 'em under his arms. It'll help bring his temp down."

They worked in silence for several minutes, her with the

ice packs, him with the IVs. He then tended to the gunshot wound, closing the hole with a neat line of stitches. When he finished, he hung the IV bags on a lamp, then stood and stared down at Greer, hands on his slim hips.

"Now what?" she asked.

"Now we wait." He aimed a smile in her direction. "I'd like to stick around for a bit if you don't mind. Make sure those antibiotics are doin' the trick. He might need another dose."

"Oh, sure. Of course." She cringed at the thought of having to make small talk for the next couple hours, but he was probably right to stay. If the antibiotics didn't work, she'd need his medical expertise. She got up from her seat on the couch beside Greer and headed to the kitchen. "Would you like anything? Coffee, tea?"

"Coffee would be great," he said with a suppressed yawn. Only then did she notice how exhausted he looked, how shadowed his blue eyes were.

"Long day?"

"Long year." He started packing up his medical kit. "And, Jesus God, it's only April."

"April Fool's Day," she said.

"Yeah, well, this whole year's been a prank, and I'm not laughin'."

She measured out the grounds from a canister on her counter, then closed the lid of the coffeemaker and started the drip. "Raffi just told me about his brother. Will Gabe be okay?"

"Yeah," Jesse said on a sigh. "It was touch and go for a while, but he's a tough bastard. He'll be back on his feet. Might take a while, but he'll get there."

"That's good. Raffi would be devastated if he lost Gabe."

"As would we all. Gabe's a good friend. A good leader." As he spoke, he checked the IVs one last time and watched Greer with the assessing eye of a medical professional. He blew out a long breath and shook his head. "I wish my friends would stop tryin' to get themselves killed. It's gettin' old."

How did she ever doubt his credentials? Because right now he looked very much like an overworked doctor frustrated by his patient.

"You've known Greer for a long time, right?" she asked and grabbed two mugs from a cupboard.

He left Greer's side to join her in the kitchen. "About twelve years now, yeah."

"Can you..." She hesitated, unsure if she was overstepping her bounds. Then she figured what the hell, the man was unconscious on her couch and she'd seen him puke. They were way past normal neighborly boundaries at this point. And she needed information if she had any chance of figuring out how Andy was involved. "What can you tell me about his parents?"

Jesse shifted on his feet and shot a glance back toward the couch. He seemed to carry on an internal debate, then apparently came to a decision and sat down on one of the stools at her breakfast bar. "I don't know much, except that they were killed when Greer was 15. He applied for emancipation from the state of Virginia, won it, and spent the next several years taking care of his brothers until Jude was a senior in high school, then he joined the military."

Oh. The poor kid. No wonder he'd turned into such a hard man. He'd had no other choice. "He protected them."

"Yeah. He does that. Protects," Jesse added when she looked a question at him. "It's hardwired into him."

How could that be true? It didn't jibe with the man she met yesterday, the one who seemed so dead set on getting revenge. Though, now that she knew a bit more about him, she couldn't blame him for wanting it. Still didn't agree with it, but couldn't blame him.

Heart in her throat for the kid Greer used to be, she turned to pour the coffee. Last thing she wanted was for Jesse to see how upsetting she found the image of Greer as a lonely, frightened teenager left to raise his brothers. She handed Jesse his coffee. "Do you know how his parents were killed?"

He waved away her unspoken question about cream or sugar and took a drink. "No. It's not somethin' he's ever talked much about."

She glanced over at the couch. The event had obviously scarred him. How could it not have? She couldn't imagine not having her parents while growing up. And she knew a thing or two about protecting one's siblings. She'd been trying to protect Matt from himself for most of her life.

She sure hoped Greer had been more successful protecting his brothers than she had hers.

"Jesse?" She looked at him. "If Greer ever found the person responsible for the deaths of his parents, would he have it in him to kill them?"

Jesse's brows shot up in surprise. "Why do you ask?"

She hesitated. Should she tell him about Greer's plan? No, she decided. It wasn't her place, and she didn't know for sure that it hadn't been his injuries talking. But now that she'd cracked open this can of worms, she had to say something. "He's, uh, talked a little in his sleep, and I just get the feeling he would if he had the chance."

Jesse watched her for several seconds. He didn't believe her half lie. She saw it in his eyes.

"It's just a hypothetical question," she added.

"Yeah, sure it is." He muttered a curse and took a drink from his mug. "*Hypothetically*, if Greer found the person responsible, he could and would kill them."

Natalie's heart plummeted. That had not been the answer she'd wanted to hear. She looked at the man so peacefully unconscious on her couch. "What should I do, Jesse?"

"Truthfully?" He set his mug down and met her gaze. "If I were you, I'd stay the hell out of his way."

# Chapter Four

Where the hell was he?

As consciousness flooded back, Greer bolted upright and glanced around. This definitely wasn't his apartment. Too much color and light and…girly stuff. It was a very female living space. He didn't recognize it…and yet he did. The apartment's layout mirrored his own.

"Oh," a female voice said softly from the foot of the couch he was lying on. "Hi. You're awake."

He snapped around toward the voice, and his head spun. Whoa. Too fast. Way too fast. He closed his eyes, breathed through the dizziness.

"Are you okay?" the woman asked again.

He opened his eyes and focused on her again. Short dark hair—a "pixie cut" it was called, though he didn't know how the hell he knew that—framed dainty features. She was curled up in an oversize armchair with a book balanced on her knees and her feet tucked under a large gold dog, which took up more of the chair than she did. She wore a long-sleeve T-shirt over leggings and had a gray shawl wrapped around her shoulders. The fringe on the shawl whispered as she unfolded from the chair and moved toward him like one would approach a cornered animal.

Where did he know her from?

Had he picked her up somewhere, spent the night at her house?

But, no, that wasn't his usual M.O. He never stayed. For him, sex was just another basic bodily function, like taking a piss or eating when hungry. Nothing more than a need that occasionally had to be fulfilled in the quickest, easiest way possible. It was all wrong for him to be waking up in a woman's house, feeling like he had a massive hangover. This was more like something his youngest brother Jude would have done before he was married.

"Are you okay?" the woman asked again. "How are you feeling?" She wasn't acting like they'd spent a night together. In fact, she looked like she was tucked in for a cozy weekend home alone.

His neighbor, he realized slowly. It was starting to come back now. The clusterfuck that had been Syria, getting jumped in a bar parking lot by three kids while chasing down Richard Mendenhall. He didn't remember how he'd gotten home but did recall she'd helped him when he'd collapsed in the hallway. He searched more of his memory but couldn't come up with her name.

Had he ever known it? Probably not. Although he'd lived in this building for five years between deployments, he preferred to keep to himself. He didn't know any of his neighbors except for the old Korean lady next door, Mrs. Chan, who insisted on babbling endlessly every time she bumped into him.

This woman was definitely not Mrs. Chan. Thank Christ.

She was watching him, waiting for an answer, so he mumbled something along the lines of, "Not good," which was the understatement of the year. Everything in him ached, and his head felt stuffed with cotton. And he was pissed at himself for being so focused on the man he suspected had killed his parents that he let a group of punks get the jump on him. If he ever got his hands on those kids—

"I bet," his neighbor said, breaking through his thoughts. "You took quite a beating…and, uh, by the looks of things, you were already pretty badly injured."

He blinked. "Huh?"

"The…" She hesitated and her gaze dropped to the fresh white bandage taped to his chest. "The bullet wound in your side."

*Incoming!*

The memory hit with the same force the bullet had.

Position compromised. Firing from the window at the tangos swarming the dirt road around their building. The bullet hitting him. He hadn't felt the pain at first because he was more focused on one of the assholes outside aiming mortars at them. The first fell short, blasting out a chunk of concrete, rocking the building. He'd glanced over at Dustin Williamson and had seen the knowledge of death on the guy's dirty, bearded face.

*"Been nice knowing you, Wilde."*

Air stalled in his lungs. His chest was frozen, and he gasped, but got no oxygen.

He'd made it out. Somehow. He'd fucking made it out of that building, that country, and he shouldn't have. Dustin sure as hell hadn't.

"Greer?"

The sound of his name broke the icy hold panic had on him, and he sucked in a lungful of sweet, feminine-scented air.

His neighbor stared at him, worry furrowing her brow. "Are you okay?"

He nodded and managed a choked, "Hurts." He just

wasn't about to tell her it was his memories hurting him, not his battered body.

"I know it does." She winced. "Jesse said you'll be hurting for a few days, but you should make a full recovery."

Wait. Who?

Greer blinked against the sunlight streaming in through the windows. The words she was saying made sense, but they were all wrong. "Jesse?" He must not have heard her right, his brain scrambled from one too many blows in too short of a time.

"Your friend, Jesse. The medic? He gave you antibiotics and—"

"Warrick?"

"Yeah, that's his last name. I hope it's okay he examined you. You refused the hospital and didn't want me to call your brother, so I didn't have many other options. If it's not okay… well, tough shit. He probably saved your life."

He shook his head. Maybe if he rattled things around enough in there, this would start making some fucking sense. "Why was Jesse *here*?"

"To make sure you weren't dying. I thought you might have been, so I called for help."

Dread prickled along his spine. How the hell did she know Jesse? Unless she was a plant, a sleeper operative put here by the powers-that-be to keep an eye on him.

He bolted to his feet and drove her backward, pinning her against the wall. He didn't have a weapon to defend himself, but he damn sure wasn't about to be caught unaware again.

Behind him, the dog barked, but he paid it no attention. "Who the fuck are you?"

She blinked several times, and her complexion lost all color. "I'm…uh, your neighbor. Natalie. I've lived across the hall from you for three years. Don't you remember?"

"Of course I fucking remember. Who are you working

for?"

"What?"

"Who. Are. You. Working. For?"

"I-I don't understand. I work for a radio station." Her eyes were wide, but it seemed to be more out of surprise than fear. Probably because she could feel his strength waning and knew he wasn't much of a threat in his current condition. Damn it. He'd just have to convince her otherwise.

He tightened his grip and shoved her against the wall again. "Bullshit."

The dog lunged, but she made some kind of hand motion at her side, and it stopped short, its barks subsiding into a low throat-rumble of a growl.

"Let me go, Greer." Her voice was surprisingly calm, considering her situation.

"Not until I get some goddamn answers."

She suddenly dropped out of his grip. He had her one second, and she was gone the next. Stunned, he looked down to see she'd done a perfect split. She rolled between his legs and came up behind him, hands planted on her hips, a scowl on her pretty face.

*Pretty?*

The thought brought him up short. Yeah, with those dainty features, porcelain skin, and melted caramel eyes snapping annoyance, she was very pretty.

She shoved at her short cap of hair. "What is *wrong* with you?"

Now that he was looking, it dawned on him that she was more than pretty. *Gorgeous* was a better description. Tall and slender, all legs.

And, holy hell, that split? It gave him all kinds of erotic ideas, none of which he wanted in his head.

He clenched his teeth. "Who are you working for? Who's paying you to keep tabs on me?"

"Oh my God." She flopped her arms, and her tone was one of complete exasperation. "I told you, I'm not working for anyone. I'm not spying. I'm. Just. Your. Neighbor. And a 'thanks for saving my life' would be nice right about now."

He ignored the snark in her tone. "How do you know Jesse Warrick?"

"I don't. Yesterday was the first time I ever laid eyes on the man, but apparently we have a mutual friend. Raffi Bristow?"

Raffi. Gabe Bristow's younger brother. And Gabe was the commanding officer of HORNET, where Jesse served as team medic. The pieces were starting to fall into place, and he could relax because the picture they showed him seemed to be more coincidence than machination. But, damn, he hated coincidences. They made his skin crawl with unease. "How do you know Raffi?"

She crossed her arms over her chest. "We attended Juilliard together."

A half memory, something hazy like from a dream, played through his mind. *An angel in ballet slippers…*

"You're a dancer?" He could barely choke the question out past the tightness in his throat.

"I was until a knee injury ended my career. Now I teach part-time." She cocked her head at him. "Are you okay?"

That was the question of the day. And no. No, he was not okay. In fact, he had to get the hell out of her apartment, get as far away from her as he could. Because she was too damn pretty. And she was a dancer.

His mother hadn't sent an angel of death in ballet shoes to collect him. Oh, no. Instead, she was playing matchmaker from beyond the grave.

Which was so much like Meredith Wilde, it left a bittersweet ache behind his ribcage.

But he didn't need a complication like Natalie the pretty

next-door neighbor in his life right now. Or ever. "I have to go."

. . .

Natalie watched him leave, her head spinning. She'd known he was reclusive, so why did it surprise her that he was paranoid to boot?

Jet still sat in the exact same spot he'd plopped down when she'd given him the hand signal to sit. He stared at her with worried brown eyes.

"You're right," she said to the dog. "I don't need his brand of weirdness in my life. I will not meddle. I've done a good job of keeping that resolution this year, haven't I? Why break it now? And for him of all people?" She turned away but stopped before taking a step. She didn't need his weirdness, but Greer was obviously struggling with some demons. She knew a thing or two about demons. Maybe he needed someone like her in *his* life.

And Andy. It kept coming back to that. She couldn't overlook the fact that Andy was somehow involved in what happened to him. Her nephew was part of the reason Greer had been so badly hurt.

Would Greer hurt Andy in return?

She closed her eyes, heaved out a sigh. God help her, she just couldn't leave it alone. She spun on her heel and marched across the hall. She didn't bother knocking on his door—they were well past pleasantries like that at this point—and shoved it open.

"The least you could do is say thank—" She stopped short. He stood in the center of his living room, staring at the empty space in silent shock. "—you," she finished stupidly.

"Where's all my shit?" he demanded.

Dammit, she'd completely forgotten. She cursed herself

for letting him walk in here without preparing him first. "Your apartment was ransacked a few weeks ago. I saw two guys go in and called your brother. By the time Reece got here, the men were gone and everything was ripped apart, destroyed."

For a second, his big shoulders seemed to sag. But only for a second, because then the anger came.

"Motherfucker," he said under his breath. He faced her, and she took a step back at the expression on his face. Not rage, like she'd expected. Not grief. Just…emptiness. Like he was already dead inside and his body just hadn't gotten the memo yet.

On impulse, she reached out and touched his cheek because he seemed to need the human contact. She half expected him to feel cold, but he didn't. He was still a bit too warm. Although his fever had broken, it hadn't completely vanished.

A muscle jumped under her palm before he brushed her away. "Where are my car keys?"

She dropped her hand back to her side. "I don't know."

"They were in my jacket."

"I'm sorry. It was ruined beyond repair. I emptied the pockets before I threw it out. All you had was a wallet, a leather notebook, and a few other things. I didn't see any keys, but everything's in a Ziplock bag on my kitchen counter. You can—" She motioned behind her, intending to say he was free to go look, but he was already shouldering past her.

Oh, this boorishness of his was getting old.

She gave herself a minute to rein in her impatience before following. He'd had one shock after another lately, and that was the only reason she was letting his attitude problem slide for now.

In her apartment, he'd already found the bag, dumped it out, and was now sorting through the stuff. He smacked the counter and cursed. "I need to borrow your car."

"Are you serious?" Dumb question. He didn't look like the kind of man who was often unserious. "Uh...no. I don't think so."

"I'll pay you." He pulled a stack of bills out of his wallet and counted off a couple hundred.

Her eyes bugged. Who carried that much cash nowadays? Even weirder, the brightly colored bills he returned to his wallet were definitely not American. If she wasn't mistaken, she thought she saw Syria printed on one of them. "And risk never getting my car back?"

"You'll get it back."

"Answer's still no."

He ground his teeth, stuffed the cash back into his wallet, the wallet into his jeans. "I'll take a cab."

"Good luck with that." He hadn't had a shower in several days and looked the part of a contagiously ill homeless man. No cabbie in his right mind was going to take him anywhere.

He gave her a look over his shoulder that could only be described as a nonverbal *fuck you,* and continued toward the door.

"Bastard." She should let him go. No, she would let him go. She was sick of his nasty attitude, and if he thought she could be bullied, he had another thing coming.

But...

Andy.

*Dammit.*

"Wait." She hurried to block his path, ducking under his arm. "I'll take you wherever you want to go. On one condition," she added when he gazed down, one eyebrow raised in question. "You need to shower first and let me wash your clothes. I'm not taking you anywhere until you look human again."

# Chapter Five

Greer pressed his hands to the tiled wall, dropped his head forward, and let hot water stream down his back, washing away the vaguely mint-scented suds from Natalie's soap. The shower may help him look human, but he still didn't feel human. That stain on his soul was an entirely separate problem that no amount of soap and hot water would cleanse. At one time, he had been as innocent as Natalie was. He was sure of it, even though he couldn't recall what that felt like.

Jesus, he was being a jerk to her. He knew it but couldn't seem to stop himself. Every time he opened his trap around her, all the anger he'd kept bottled up inside him for so many years came spilling out.

She didn't deserve it.

He should apologize and thank her for all of her help.

Or, better yet, he should slip away while she wasn't paying attention. Asking to borrow her car had been a boneheaded move. He should have taken the damn thing by force. Scaring her was better than getting her involved in the disaster that was his life. The place he had to go was the very last place on earth he wanted to take anyone he cared about.

Whoa. Cared about?

He had to dial that shit back. He didn't even know her. Yeah, there had been times when he'd seen her out walking her dog or passed her in the hallway that he'd entertained the fantasy of a quick and dirty with her—she was a beautiful woman and he wasn't blind—but fantasy was all it ever was.

He shook his head. No, he didn't care about *her*, specifically. But he did care about innocent people getting hurt, and she was an innocent. She'd almost certainly end up injured or worse if he involved her in his world.

Greer shut off the shower and stepped out, wrapping a soft towel—pink because of course it was—around his hips without bothering to dry off. He cracked open the bathroom door, glanced up and down the hallway. Her apartment had the exact same L-shaped floor plan as his. The front door opened to a hall and on the left was the guest bathroom and second bedroom. Straight ahead, the hall widened into a kitchen that overlooked the combined living and dining areas, which made up the shorter side of the L. The master bedroom was to the left of the dining area. The laundry room was a narrow utility closet tucked in the corner just beyond the master bedroom's currently open door.

The set-up sucked.

Unless she was in the master bath with the door closed, there was no way he could get to the laundry room, grab his clothes, and sneak off with her car keys without her noticing.

And force wasn't an option, even as much as he wished it were. He was an asshole, but he wasn't the kind of asshole who hurt women.

So he'd just have to suck it up and ask her nicely. He hadn't been too polite about it the first time. If he calmly explained why he needed her car and somehow guaranteed she'd get it back, he'd be able to keep her out of harm's way. That was it.

He'd march his ass out there and be the gentlemen his mother had always hoped he'd be.

But then he walked into the dining room and saw her sitting in the bay window, staring out over the postage stamp of a park behind their apartment complex. Across that little spit of mud was the former strip mall that now housed Wilde Security and a bunch of empty stores.

Greer froze.

How many times had she sat there, looking at Wilde Security?

How many times had he stared out the grimy little window in his office at this building? Or at her as she'd walked her dog through the park? Too many to count.

She was only sitting there, long legs pulled up to her chest, not doing anything the least bit suggestive, but his reaction to the sight of her was visceral. His stomach clenched and his cock stiffened. The sexual need he'd repressed for too long roared to life, demanding he do something about his recent stretch of celibacy.

And not just any woman would do. Nope. He wanted this woman. His neighbor.

All thoughts of being a gentleman flew out the window. He didn't want to want her and it pissed him off that he did.

He clenched the towel tighter around his hips and cursed the terrycloth for not offering more cover. "Where are my clothes?"

"I told you—" She looked at him and her eyes widened, but she didn't blush or glance away like he expected. Instead, a distinct spark of interest lit her caramel-color eyes as she unabashedly ran her gaze over him. He swore he felt it like a caress down the length of his body.

Maybe the girl next door wasn't so innocent after all.

And, damn, that thought did nothing to help the situation happening behind his towel.

Natalie uncurled from her seat. "I told you I was going to wash them. I just put them in the dryer. They're not done yet."

"What am I supposed to wear until then?"

She gave him another up-down and grinned. "The towel looks good on you."

*It'd look better on the floor. Along with your clothes.*

Jesus. He turned away, annoyed that his thoughts had gone there. He had a mission and he wasn't going to be distracted from it by the promise of a good fuck.

It would be good, too. Somehow he knew it right down to his bones. She was the perfect height for him, and they'd fit together like a goddamn puzzle, with her long legs wrapped around his hips...or his shoulders...or—

No.

He needed something more to wear, something that gave him a bit more coverage before he did anything he'd regret. "Were all my clothes destroyed?"

"I don't know. Your brothers boxed up the few things that were salvageable and left them in your bedroom."

His brothers had been in his place after the cleaners had finished the job of erasing him. Just the thought of it gave him chills. All of these years, he'd been so careful to keep his black ops world a secret from his brothers. He hadn't wanted them anywhere near the dark part of his double life.

Jesus. If one of them had stumbled into his place while the cleaners were working? He'd have one less brother now. Which was exactly why he had to keep away from them. And exactly why he should distance himself from Natalie, ASAP.

He strode down the hall, flung open the front door, and came face-to-face with the old Korean lady who lived in the apartment next to his.

She eyed him up and down, then raised a bushy salt and pepper brow.

He blew out a breath. "This...isn't what it looks like."

She smiled. She was missing several teeth. "I'm eighty-two years old. I know a walk of shame when I see one, young man."

"Hi, Mrs. Chan," Natalie said from directly behind him.

"Hi, Natalie. Did you have fun last night?"

"Hardly," she said, and Greer felt her glare boring into his back.

Jesus. She was not helping.

"I need to…" He motioned in the vague direction of his apartment, and Mrs. Chan stepped aside.

"Yes, run away," the old woman called after him. "If you haven't learned how to please a lady yet, there's no hope for you."

Just before his door shut, he heard Natalie's snort of laughter join Mrs. Chan's delighted cackles. And the sound the old woman was making was a cackle, too—no other way to describe it but full-on witch. If he didn't know any better, he'd almost think Natalie and Mrs. Chan had planned that little run-in for their own amusement.

He leaned against his door and willed the heat to drain out of his face. He couldn't remember the last time he'd blushed, and it pissed him off that he was now.

Grumbling to himself, he followed the hall to the master bedroom and found a stack of cardboard boxes against one wall. His bed frame was still in place, but the mattress and box spring were gone. His dresser was still there as well, though a little dinged up. Then again, he'd had the thing for as long as he could remember, so the dents and scratches might have been it showing its age and he'd just never paid any attention to them before. He crossed the room in three long strides and pulled open the top drawer, relieved to see several pairs of boxers there. Someone had folded them—probably Reece, because he couldn't see any of his other brothers taking the time to fold underwear. He grabbed a pair at random and pulled them on, discarding the towel.

Thankfully, his run-in with Mrs. Chan had deflated his erection. He didn't have time to deal with annoying bodily needs right now.

In one of the other drawers, he found T-shirts and one pair of cargo pants, also folded. Jesus, Reece was anal-retentive. But at least some of his clothes had survived.

Once dressed, he checked the boxes. He hadn't had a whole lot in the way of possessions to begin with, but anything personal had been destroyed. All that was left were the most innocuous knick-knacks of daily life. His coffeemaker sans pot, because of course he might have drank straight from the pot and left his DNA. A few more small kitchen appliances, but no other dishes or flatware. Some books he'd been meaning to read and had never gotten around to, but none of his movies because DVDs held fingerprints. Anything that could have been used to potentially identify him was gone. The paranoid bastards he worked for had done a complete erase.

He found an old duffle bag and packed his few remaining clothes. Unfortunately, it looked as if all of his shoes had also fallen victim to the apartment cleansing, so he had to face Natalie again. His boots were still in her apartment.

No set of spare keys. Damn.

Not that he'd be locking his apartment—there wasn't anything left to steal—but it'd be great to have the keys to his Jeep and Harley. It'd also be great to know where both vehicles were. He usually stored his bike for the winter, but the people who did this to his apartment would have gone to his storage unit, too. The bike had probably been chopped up and sold for parts.

And he didn't want to think about that because it pissed him off. That bike had been his only luxury.

As for his Jeep, he must have driven it home after he'd

been attacked, but he couldn't remember for certain. It was possible he'd dropped the keys somewhere between the parking lot and the spot he'd collapsed. If that was the case, he probably wasn't going to find them. It'd be faster to just buy a new car. He'd been meaning to anyway, since the Jeep was on its last legs.

He finished searching the boxes and, finding nothing else useful, he grabbed the duffle. Took one more look around.

This. Was. Bullshit.

He stormed across the hall and started to enter Natalie's apartment, but thought better of it and rapped on the door.

She opened it a minute later and tossed his boots at his feet. "Are you done moping now?"

*Moping?* He didn't fucking mope.

He ground his teeth together and stuffed his feet into the boots without lacing them up. "I need your car."

"Yeah?" She propped a hand on her hip. "That's unfortunate because I'm not giving it to you. I told you I'd drive you wherever you needed to go."

"No."

She started to shut the door in his face. "Then I guess you're not going anywhere."

"Natalie—" He stopped the door with his foot and tamped down his impatience. What was it about this woman that got his back up? "Please."

She whistled. "Ooh, that hurt didn't it?"

That's it, he decided. The sarcasm was what did it. And the fact that he was used to having his orders followed—even his brothers listened to him, usually after much bitching and moaning, but they always did as they were told. Not Natalie. She. Didn't. Follow. Orders. And it drove him crazy.

"Jesus. I'll take the bus." If he caught the very next bus, he could make it to the airport before rush hour and rent a car. Either way, he was getting to Virginia today.

Natalie said nothing until he was halfway to the stairs.

"Dammit. Greer. Wait." She chased after him. "Jesse said he doesn't want you driving for a few days until your concussion heals."

The mention of the word concussion made his head pound in beat with his heart. He swallowed back a sudden surge of nausea. "I'm fine."

"No, you're not. You just turned green." She sighed. "I'll take you where you need to go."

"You can't."

"Why not?" she shot back. "It's not like you're going to some top-secret military base."

Wow, she'd nailed that one on the head. He clamped down on the surprise and thought he'd done a good job of hiding it from his expression, but her mouth dropped open in shock.

"Holy cow. You are?"

"I can't talk about it." He sidestepped her. "And you're not taking me."

She ducked past him and blocked the stairway with her arms and legs outstretched. "Then you're not going. Jesse said no driving."

"I don't give a flying fuck what Jesse said. Now either move or I'll move you."

"You will not—" Before she could finish the sentence he picked her up like a recalcitrant child and set her aside. She gasped in outrage. Feeling rather smug, he ignored the pain from his wounds and reached for the push-bar.

"Fine. Leave," Natalie said behind him. "But I'm calling Reece and telling him you're not missing anymore and that you're purposely avoiding him because you plan to murder someone. How do you think *that* will go over?"

He swung around. She already had her cell phone in hand, and he snatched it away. "There's a difference between murder and getting a bit of long-overdue justice." He took the battery from her phone and pocketed it. "And I'm protecting my brothers by staying away. I'm trying to protect you, too, but you're making it fucking impossible."

Her lips parted in a soft, "Oh." She stepped into his space, stood on her toes, and cupped his cheeks in her hands. "Jesse said you do that. Protect people. But, Greer, who's protecting you?"

The gesture was so unexpected he didn't know how to react. For a solid five seconds, he just stood there, staring down at her, trying to convince himself he didn't want to kiss those lips and failing. He leaned down, caught himself.

Cursing, he stepped back, away from her reach. "I don't need protecting."

"Says the man I found unconscious in front of my door a few days ago." Features set in stubborn lines, she crossed her arms over her chest and glared.

For the first time in his life, he realized this wasn't a battle he'd win. If he left her behind, she'd do something stupid, like call Reece or follow him. Might as well keep her close until he found a way to shake her off his tail.

"All right." He held up a finger when she gave a bright, triumphant smile. "But you're only driving me as far as I tell you to, and then you'll turn your pretty little ass around and go someplace safe. Do you understand?"

Some of the brightness faded. "What kind of trouble are you in?"

Greer shouldered his duffle and shoved into the stairway. "I don't know yet."

# Chapter Six

He made Natalie drop him a mile away from the base. She hadn't liked it. Had liked it even less when he waited and watched to make sure she'd pointed her ridiculously tiny Fiat back toward DC, before finally hiking it the rest of the way to base.

Stubborn woman. She just didn't get it. She absolutely did not want to land on these people's radar. They fucked up lives. They certainly had his.

The guards at the gate knew him by sight and surprisingly didn't act shocked to see him. Then again, they wouldn't have the kind of clearances to know he'd most likely been decommissioned. They let him pass without so much as a blink of suspicion, and he stalked to the administration building, where the man he'd come to see kept an office.

Sergeant Major Jeremiah Revly dropped a stack of folders when Greer entered the room. "Holy shit. You're alive."

He ignored the man and shoved into Lieutenant Colonel Bruce Chambers's office.

"Greer?" Eyes wide, Bruce half-rose from behind his

desk. The same place he sat when he made dumbass decisions that more often than not nearly got his operatives killed. Decisions that had nearly killed Greer not all that long ago.

As a matter of fact, Bruce kind of looked like a ghost had just walked into his office. "Good lord," he whispered. "You're alive."

"You sent cleaners to my apartment."

Bruce and Revly exchanged a glance.

"Well, yes," Bruce said. He waved Revly away, sank back into his seat, and scrubbed his hands over his face. "It's SOP when an operative dies, and you fell off the radar after Syria. What else was I supposed to think?"

"You expected me to die there," Greer said.

"No, I expected you to do the job and come back like you always have. When you didn't…" He dropped his hands and stared at Greer for a long moment. "I mourned for you, son. I mourned for your brothers, too. I thought about going to them, telling them what I could, giving them a little bit of closure, but…"

Greer's heart bungeed in his chest. "We had a deal, Bruce. You get me, and you don't go anywhere near my brothers."

Bruce held up his hands. "A deal I upheld. I've never talked to them, even after I thought you were dead. They still think you're missing."

"Good." And he wanted to keep it that way, since he very likely wouldn't survive much longer, one way or another. It was just easier if they never knew what had happened to him. Or what he'd done to make sure they'd survive.

"What happened to you in Syria?" Bruce asked. "You completed your mission and then just…vanished."

Greer shook his head. It wasn't something he was ready to talk about. Now or ever. He held out his arms. "As you can see, I'm not dead."

"What about Williamson? Is he with you?"

A wrench tightened around Greer's chest, and he dropped his arms. "Sergeant Dustin Williamson didn't make it out."

"Shit," Bruce said softly. "Did you make sure his remains couldn't be identified?"

"He took a mortar straight to the chest. There was nothing left of him to identify. Sir," he added belatedly, bitterness coating his tongue. He suddenly hated this man, who sat behind this desk with an entire ocean between him and the horrors of war, and so blithely talked about desecrating a human body—a friend's body.

Bruce rested his elbows on his desk and templed his hands in front of his tight lips. "Greer, we have a problem here. Technically, you're a deserter."

Yeah, right. "You gonna court-martial me and explain to the world just what the hell I was doing in Syria?"

Bruce said nothing more for a solid minute. And then another. Greer waited. If the guy thought silence would intimidate, he really didn't have a fucking clue about the monster he'd created.

There would be no desertion charges, and they both damn well knew it. Most of the regular Army wouldn't approve of the things they'd done—the general population definitely wouldn't approve—and Bruce wouldn't take the risk of it all becoming public knowledge.

"I should," Bruce said finally. "This isn't the first time. That whole mess last year when you sent mercenaries to rescue Zak Hendricks in Afghanistan? I'm still taking heat for that."

Greer's fists rolled into balls at his sides. "I wasn't leaving him there. He's alive today only because I went against orders."

"He's alive because your mercenary friends got lucky. And in the process, they all but handed a nuclear device to our enemies. It could've ended much, much worse."

"They handled it." And Bruce was trying to distract him.

"Look, we both know you're not going to court-martial me, so let's cut the shit. I need leave time before you put me back in the field."

Bruce's eyes narrowed. "For what exactly?"

*Revenge.* "Shits and giggles. What do you think? I haven't seen my brothers in months."

"Good," Bruce said, which startled him. He'd been expecting a fight, but the guy was nodding with approval. "I was going to suggest a leave. You have it coming and, honestly, you look like you could use it." He indicated Greer's battered face. "Do you need medical attention?"

"I've already been tended to by the best in the business. Prognosis is I'll live." *For a little while longer, anyway.* He changed topics. "I need a new set of wheels. Thanks to your cleaners, my bike was sold for parts and I don't have keys to my Jeep."

"Your bike's fine." Bruce cracked a smile. "I put it in my garage."

The news left him dizzy, almost happy, though he didn't let the emotion show on his face. Why he cared so much about the damn Harley when he hadn't cared about much of anything for months, he didn't know. Maybe it was just the concussion screwing with his brain. Or maybe because the bike was the one indulgence he'd allowed himself in his entire life. Whatever the reason, knowing it hadn't been chopped up was a huge relief. "I want it back."

"Of course. I'll make the arrangements."

"Thanks." With that, Greer turned to leave the office.

"We really thought you were dead," Bruce said behind him. "You could have walked away from all this, disappeared, and we'd never have known. Why didn't you?"

For one thing, he had a killer to catch. For another…

He faced the man who was equal parts mentor and devil in his mind. "You would have known. Eventually. And

I'd have spent the rest of my life looking over my shoulder, waiting for you to show up and drag me back."

Bruce closed his eyes as if the words pained him. "Listen, son—"

"I'm not your son."

"No, you are your father's son." He winced. "You're a great soldier, Greer—but, I'm sad to say—David was the better man."

The words were like a knife straight to the gut. "I'm exactly what I needed to be. Exactly what you made me."

"Yes, I know." Bruce heaved a breath, opened his eyes, and nailed Greer with a look that was full of regret. "I didn't mean that the way it sounded. But your father never let his loved ones go without knowing he was safe. You need to talk to your brothers, Greer. They're worried about you. Don't leave them hanging."

Greer didn't bother with a response. He was almost to the door when the intercom on Bruce's desk buzzed.

"Yeah?" Bruce answered.

"Sir, patrol spotted an unauthorized vehicle loitering near our perimeter," Revly said.

"All right. Have the guards detain the occupants. I'll be there in a minute."

Greer swung around. "Is it a woman?" There was only one person stubborn enough—or possibly stupid enough—to hang out near a top secret base without prior authorization.

Bruce relayed the question and got a response in the affirmative.

Greer punched his thigh for lack of a better thing to punch. "Goddamn it."

"Do you know her?" Bruce asked.

"She's my neighbor."

"Greer, Jesus. Are you out of your mind bringing her here?" His chair scraped back as he jumped to his feet. "Get her the hell out of here."

"I didn't bring her. She dropped me off and was supposed to go back to DC."

"Obviously she didn't."

"It's on me. I should've known she wouldn't listen."

They both reached the door at the same time, and Bruce held it open. "Yeah, it is, son. Get her out of here and make damn sure she knows she needs to forget anything she's seen."

"Yes, sir."

• • •

Natalie glared at the two guards currently holding her captive in a room that looked like something out of *Zero Dark Thirty*. Did they torture people in here?

No, never mind. She really, really didn't want to know.

It had been stupid to circle back to the spot she'd dropped Greer off. She knew it, accepted it, but Greer still had her phone's battery in his pocket, and her phone was her only link to Andy at the moment. What if Andy decided to reach out, ask for her help? She needed her phone intact in case he did. She'd turned back hoping to catch Greer, and the next thing she knew, her car had been surrounded by guards.

How did she get herself into these things? She hadn't even been meddling this time. She'd only wanted her phone back in one piece. That was it.

The door flung open, banged against the concrete wall. A huge shadow filled the frame, and her guards snapped into salutes.

"Sir," they said in unison.

"I'll take it from here." At Greer's voice, she relaxed in the hard metal chair they'd cuffed her to.

"Yes, sir." They filed out.

"Thank you," she said earnestly when they were gone.

Greer didn't make a move to uncuff her. "Are you suicidal or just stupid?"

She jerked upright. "Excuse me?"

"I told you to go back to DC. Go somewhere safe." He finally stalked across the room and dipped a hand into his pocket, pulled out a key. Her cuffs released and clattered to the floor. "So what did you do? You turned around and followed me. Jesus."

Rubbing her wrists, she whirled to face him. "I didn't follow you. I tried to catch you because you still have my phone battery."

"So buy a new one."

"Do you think I have a magical money tree in my apartment? I'm working two jobs and can barely afford my rent. I don't have $100 to fix the phone that *you* broke."

He dipped a hand into his pocket and shoved the battery at her. "Now get the hell outta here."

"Gladly." Except she hesitated, her conscience not allowing her to wash her hands of this mess. Greer was going to murder someone. Whether or not that person killed his parents—well it didn't matter because she firmly believed the whole "eye for an eye makes the whole world blind" thing.

She couldn't let him do it.

"Greer, are you really going to mu—" She stopped short. She had no idea if they were being monitored, but just in case, she chose the rest of her words carefully. "—do that thing you said you were going to do?"

"It's none of your business."

"It's wrong."

"And you're the morality police, is that it?" He wrapped one huge hand around her arm and dragged her toward the door.

"No, but I try to be a decent human being. Something you obviously struggle with."

He jerked her around and glared down. "I don't need a moral compass. I need you to leave me the hell alone and forget everything you've seen here."

"Forget everything I've seen?" She snorted and glanced around her prison. "Four concrete walls and my guards, Tweedledee and Tweedledum. It's not like I saw any national secrets."

He stared at her a beat, then turned away. "We're leaving."

"We?" She followed him out the door and down a hallway as plain as her prison had been. Another soldier waited at the end of the corridor, and she experienced a flash of recognition. She'd seen him somewhere. At least, she thought so. Maybe? Greer pulled her by the man too fast to focus and place a name with his semi-familiar face.

Greer pushed through another metal door and the late afternoon sun momentarily blinded her. She blinked against it. "You're going with me?"

"I'm making sure you go back to DC this time." He nodded to the two soldiers huddled together at the front gate. Both gave her curious looks before one disappeared inside and the gate rattled open. Her car waited on the other side.

Greer pulled open the passenger side door. "Get in."

"No."

He cast his gaze skyward as if asking a higher power for patience. "Natalie, I will pick you up and throw your hot little ass in this car if you don't—"

She held up a hand, cutting him off. "I'm totally on board with leaving this place, believe me. But I'm driving. Jesse said—"

"Jesus. Christ," he gritted out and slid into the seat himself.

Satisfied, she circled the hood and climbed in behind the wheel. She'd just started the car when there was a tap on her window. One of the guards stood there. She rolled down the window.

"Ma'am, your purse," he said with a barely suppressed smile and handed it to her. There was something different in his tone now. Almost something like…respect?

Weird.

Then he saluted Greer and his smile broke into a grin. "Sergeant."

Greer saluted back, but he only used one finger. The guard laughed and backed away from the car.

Oh, boy. Greer did not look happy. Of course, she'd never actually seen him happy. Did he even know the meaning of the word?

She winced as she pulled the car out onto the road. "I'm sorry if I undermined your authority."

"Fuck that," he muttered and stared straight ahead. "I don't have any authority in that place."

"What…exactly is that place?"

He gave her a desert-dry look. "You're supposed to forget you ever saw it, remember?"

"Right. Forgetting." She switched on the radio to her station and recognized Jay's voice. He was a nice guy, a college student who thought he wanted to get into DJ-ing and currently hosted a Saturday night jam session that featured local bands.

Which meant her weekend was half over already. Where had it gone?

She glanced over at Greer. Oh. Right. Her weekend had gone to taking care of her sick, grumpy neighbor.

God, how did she get herself into these messes? And what exactly was she going to do about it now that she was in it?

She couldn't let Greer out of her sight, lest he commit murder, and she still had to track down her nephew and find out what the hell was going on. Just another exciting day in the life of Natalie Taggart.

Not.

She glanced over at Greer again. "So…now what? Are we going home?" She didn't see how he could since he no longer had any furniture to speak of.

"You are," he said. "You're to go straight back to your place after you drop me off in Alexandria."

"What's in Alexandria?"

"Just—" He raised his hands in front of him, closed them into fists like he wanted to strangle something, then dropped them back to his thighs and heaved out a breath. "Can you just drive and not talk? I'll tell you where to go."

Natalie bit her lip. Yeah, it was probably better to keep her mouth shut for the rest of the drive. Frustration rolled off him in waves, and if she said the wrong thing, he might strangle her instead of air next time.

After all, he had told her he planned to commit murder, and Jesse had said he was more than capable. And yet she just couldn't picture it. Sure, he wasn't the most pleasant person she'd ever met, but a murderer? It didn't jibe. A man so bent on murder wouldn't care to protect his brothers, and he certainly wouldn't give two damns about her safety.

She slid him a glance.

Complicated. That was Greer Wilde in a nutshell, and she couldn't help but want to figure him out.

# Chapter Seven

Greer's head pounded. Whether the headache was from his concussion or the frustrating woman sitting beside him was anyone's guess, but he was inclined to think the latter. Natalie had a way of getting under his skin, and he didn't like it one bit.

But soon it wouldn't matter. He'd had her turn off the highway, and they were approaching his old neighborhood, just a few blocks down from the house he'd grown up in. He'd stay in the old Colonial until he figured out what to do about his apartment—which had the added benefit of keeping him an entire city away from Natalie. If he stayed right across the hall from her, he might end up doing something he'd regret.

"I know this neighborhood," she said suddenly. He didn't respond, and she rambled on. "My parents live in the next neighborhood over from here. It's a nice place. Good schools, friendly people, next to no crime—well, my mom did mention there was an arson recently that had shaken everyone up, but I believe they caught the person who did it. Oh. There." She pointed. "That must be the house—"

Greer straightened in his seat. "Stop the car."

His heart clawed into his throat, and he shoved open the door almost before she had the car completely stopped. The old brick Colonial usually sat up on a small hill, tucked away from the road, but it was gone. So was the tree out front where his father had hung a tire swing. He used to climb that tree to get some peace from his younger brothers—or at least he had until Vaughn tried to follow once and broke his arm. Dad had nailed a "no climbing" sign to it after that.

But the tree was gone.

Everything was gone.

Nothing left but a pile of ash.

Oxygen stalled in his lungs, and he turned away, propped his hands on the hood of her car. He told himself to breathe. Told himself to fight down the icy surge of panic. Just breathe.

He finally managed to pull in some oxygen and exhaled in hard pants. "Jesus."

Natalie touched his back. "Is this the house you were coming to?"

"It was my parents'. All we had left of them." His throat was so tight that forming words was painful. He faced her. "You said arson?"

"Maybe. I don't know for sure. That's just from the local gossip…"

He was starting to have trouble breathing again until her arms circled his waist, and she pressed her cheek against his back.

"Oh, Greer. I'm so, so sorry," she whispered.

The hug anchored him and his lungs opened, filling with cool air. Having her touch him like this was…comforting. And he didn't want it to be. He shrugged her off. "When did it happen?"

She stepped back, hugged herself. "Uh…my mom told me about it sometime in January. I'm sorry I don't know the exact day."

Right around the time he'd been sent to Syria. That couldn't be a coincidence.

He grabbed the car door and yanked it open so hard the hinges protested. "Take me to a hotel."

Natalie didn't move. "Which one?"

"I don't fucking care. Just pick one and I'll stay there."

After another second, she walked around the car and got behind the wheel again. She was saying something, but he wasn't in the mood to chat. He shut her out.

Jesus. His childhood home was gone.

What had losing it done to his brothers? What had it done to *Reece*? He'd spent tons of money on upkeep over the years and had been more attached to the house than any of them. Greer had expected Reece to move in with his wife Shelby. They'd settle in, raise their own family, and the place would be a home again.

But the house was gone.

Bruce was right. He should call his brothers, go see them. But...he just couldn't bring himself to face them. Not after Syria. And definitely not after failing to take down their parents' killer—though he planned to rectify that as soon as he was able.

Thoughts racing too fast, emotions all kinds of jumbled up, Greer didn't notice where Natalie had pointed the car until she pulled into the parking lot of their apartment complex. "What the hell? I said take me to a hotel."

She shut off the engine and turned in her seat. "You're staying with me."

"No." A jolt of pure terror injected adrenaline into his system. Holy fuck, no. He couldn't stay with her. The longer he was around her, the more he wanted to touch her. She was nothing but a distraction he didn't need.

"Yes," she insisted. "I have a perfectly good couch, and

we already know it's big enough for you to sleep on. You can stay at my place and order new furniture for yours. That way, you'll be right here when it arrives and can just move back across the hall."

"I don't want new furniture."

She blew out a breath that lifted her sideswept bangs. "Okay, now you're just being stubborn."

Yes, he could be stubborn. His father had often said it should have been his middle name. But this time, he was only being truthful. He didn't want to buy new furniture because he wasn't envisioning the kind of future for himself where he'd need it.

"Besides," she added, "you were extremely ill less than twenty-four hours ago. You shouldn't be alone yet."

He opened his mouth to protest but closed it again without uttering a sound. He was just too damn tired to fight her on this. "I'll stay tonight."

She smiled and opened her door. "It's a start."

· · ·

Well, she'd convinced him to stay… but what did she do with him now?

Once they were closed up together in her apartment, she hesitated. How exactly did you entertain a grumpy neighbor who had been shot and concussed, who was probably involved in black ops, and was the man your nephew recently threatened to kill?

And when had her life gotten so complicated?

She tossed her keys into the little dish on her kitchen counter. "Uh, are you hungry?"

He grunted.

She exhaled slowly to expel the surge of annoyance. Really, she shouldn't be surprised. She hadn't known him long, but she already knew grunting was so very much a Greer response.

Screw it. The weekend was over, and she hadn't taken any time to decompress. Tonight, she was going to follow through with her original plan for her days off and Netflix it. If Greer didn't like it, he could entertain himself. He could feed himself, too. His comfort wasn't her responsibility.

She turned to tell him exactly that but stopped before opening her mouth. He was pale, the bruises on his bearded face standing out in stark relief. Only the force of his immense will held him upright.

And, dammit, there was that tug to take care of him. A familiar sensation, one she'd dealt with her entire life. Raffi had always jokingly called her "Saint Tally" because she just couldn't stand to see anyone in pain, either physical or emotional. At one time, she had spent so much energy taking care of the rest of the world, she often forgot about herself—a flaw she was very aware of and actively tried to counteract.

But, God, she hated to see someone struggling and Greer obviously was.

She softened a little. After all, he'd been shot, beaten, and had just discovered his family home was nothing but ashes. If anyone deserved a pass for being rude today, it was him.

"Hey," she said gently and waited until he met her gaze. "I was going to order a pizza and watch TV, but if you want to sleep, I can take my laptop into my room."

His implacable expression eased. "Pizza sounds good. I can contribute some cash." He dropped his bag beside the couch and grabbed his wallet from his jeans pocket. Again she saw a flash of colorful bills that definitely weren't American and curiosity got the better of her. She plucked one from his hand before he could stop her.

"What kind of money is—" She froze and gazed up at him again. "What were you doing in Syria?"

He scratched at his chin through his beard but didn't appear angry like she thought he'd be. No, it was more an expression of resignation, maybe a hint of sorrow. He took the bill from her and replaced it in her hand with an American twenty. "Nothing you want to know about, angel."

A chill scraped down her spine. This was a very dangerous man, and she couldn't shake the feeling she was tempting fate by having him in her home. Even so, a not entirely unwanted spark of heat flared in her belly at the term of endearment.

Angel.

He'd called her that once before, but she'd thought it was the fever talking. And maybe it had been then, but this time it was a deliberate word choice and not the ramblings of a very ill man.

Angel.

Why would he call her that? Did it mean he was attracted to her? He didn't strike her as the kind of guy to go around calling women by sugary pet names, but he also didn't seem to notice or care that he'd called her something that sounded... intimate. So maybe he was that type of guy. Or maybe—

She was way overthinking this.

She shook her head at herself. Okay, so he was hot. She'd remarked on that fact more than once to her friends since she moved in across the hall from him, and they'd poked fun at her because the sexy, broody, reclusive god of a man next door, whom she'd never even spoken to for more than a few sentences, always managed to rev her engine just by passing her on the stairs. Even now, as bruised and battered as he was, it was impossible not to notice the cut edge of his jaw or those piercing dark eyes or the hard-planed body that put even the hunkiest of A-list actors to shame.

But she had to lock down her ridiculous physical response to him. He wasn't attracted to her. Or if he was, he had more on his mind right now than sex. As he should.

So why couldn't she get her mind off doing the dirty with him?

She realized she was standing there, staring at him with a twenty in her hand. "Uh, I'll order that pizza. I'm a carnivore, so I usually get the meat lover's. Is that okay?"

He offered a tight smile. "A woman after my own heart."

Yeah, no. His heart was definitely not what she wanted. His body on the other hand…

She spun away a bit too fast, made herself dizzy.

*Focus, Tally.*

She dug in her purse for her phone and placed the order with her favorite pizzeria, watching as Greer started pacing circles around her living room like a caged wildcat. She could almost hear the gears in his mind working overtime. There was so much going inside that head of his. She wished he'd open up a bit and at least tell her how he'd ended up bleeding and broken on her doorstep, but she had the feeling she'd need a crowbar to pry information out of him. Or better, the Jaws of Life.

She set her cell phone aside, propped a hip against the kitchen island, and crossed her arms over her chest. She watched him pace for a few more minutes and finally decided it was time they had a conversation. She needed a better grip on the situation so she'd know what to do about Andy. And right now, Greer was the only string she had to unravel the mystery of her wayward nephew.

"I know you weren't mugged," she said, and he stopped moving like he'd hit a brick wall.

"Yeah, I was." He dragged both hands through his overgrown hair and winced. "I was jumped by a bunch of kids outside a bar. I was already injured, and they got the better of me."

Dread coiled around her insides. Had Andy really…? But why? It didn't make sense. "There has to be more to it than that. What did they want?"

"Fuck if I know. My wallet?"

Oh, he knew. She didn't exactly see the knowledge written in his expression because the man had a poker face to beat all poker faces, but something about his sarcasm told her he was evading. "They didn't take it, though," she pointed out.

"Jesus," he muttered and finally spun to face her. "I think they were paid, all right?"

"Paid?"

"By the man I plan to kill."

Another scrape of dread down her spine. She dropped her arms and stepped toward him. "You're not going to kill anyone, Greer." Not if she could help it. And especially not if the person in his line of fire was her nephew.

The look he gave her was so dark, so unemotional, she stopped before touching him. He was hurting, and not only because his body had taken a beating. He was emotionally wounded and, dammit, she wanted to help. Someone had to or this man was going to self-destruct. She could all but see the bomb ticking down to zero in his eyes.

"It won't help," she added in a whisper. "I know you think it will slay whatever demons you're struggling with, but spilling blood will only feed them."

He held her gaze for a moment before looking away and staring down at his hands like he'd never seen them before. "What the fuck do you know about spilling blood?"

She couldn't just stand there when he so obviously needed some kind of comfort. She closed the remaining distance between them and folded both of her hands around one of his. "I know it has never, in the history of mankind, solved any problems."

His gaze lifted briefly to hers again, then dropped to her lips. He was going to kiss her. For a heart-stopping moment, she was sure of it. And, God help her, she wanted it, despite all the perfectly logical reasons she shouldn't.

But logic had never been her strong suit.

Jet wiggled his big body between them and jumped up onto Greer, tongue lolling out of his mouth.

Greer sucked in a sharp breath and backed a step away. He looked at dog. "Jet, right?"

Natalie crushed down the surge of disappointment at the interruption and plastered on a smile. "Yep," she said a little too cheerfully and grabbed Jet's collar to pull him down. "You'll have to forgive him. He failed puppy school. He's not all that bright."

"He doesn't look like he's all that fast, either. Why Jet?"

"I originally named him Jeté…uh, it's a kind of leap in ballet," she added, realizing that was probably a term he wasn't familiar with.

The corner of his mouth kicked up in something that might have been a smile. "I know what a jeté is."

That took her by surprise. "You do?"

"My mother was a dancer. She made me and my brothers take lessons right up until she died."

That info clicked together several pieces of a puzzle she hadn't even been aware she was working on inside her head. She held up a hand. "Wait. Was her name Meredith LaGrange?"

"That was her maiden name," Greer confirmed.

"But it was the name she used when she danced?"

"Yes." His brow creased. "You knew her?"

"Knew of her." She'd read an article in a children's dance magazine recently about Meredith LaGrange. It was all about how she had encouraged her five sons to dance. There had even been photos, and now she wondered if any had included Greer. She'd have to find it again. "Your mom was good, and the ballet community is a small one. Her death hit everyone hard, especially my teacher. Larissa Schafer?"

He shook his head.

"Oh," she said, surprised he didn't recognize the name. Then again, Greer had only been a teenager at the time, and kids that age often didn't realize their parents were more than just parents. She sure hadn't appreciated that hers were real people with lives outside of their children until she reached adulthood. Greer probably didn't know most of his parents' friends. "Well, Larissa was devastated. She dedicated that year's recital to your mom. She owns the dance studio I teach at. I'm sure she'd love to meet you."

He appeared distinctly uncomfortable at the idea, which only cemented in her mind that it needed to happen. She doubted his parents would want this revenge rampage he was so intent on—what good parent would? Maybe reminding him of them, making him see them as something other than victims, would change his mind about seeking justice. Bonus: it'd keep her nephew from becoming his next target. *If* Andy had truly been paid to mug him, that was.

God, she wished she could talk to the kid, but he wasn't answering his phone, and her parents—bless their naive hearts—thought he was staying with her for the weekend.

"How long for the pizza?" Greer asked abruptly, yanking her attention away from thoughts about her nephew and back to the conversation.

She smiled a little. He was definitely trying to change the subject. All the more reason she should engineer a meeting between him and Larissa. "They said twenty minutes, but that's what they always say. My guess, it'll be more like forty."

He squeezed his eyes shut and pinched the bridge of his nose. "Mind if I lie down until it gets here?"

"No, go ahead." She watched him cross to the couch and sit down, one hand pressed to his side. He didn't make any sound to indicate he was in pain, but he didn't have to. His face had lost color as they stood around making awkward conversation, and sweat now glistened on his forehead.

"Here." She went into the kitchen to fill a glass with water, then found the bottles of medicine Jesse had left. One was a painkiller. The other, an antibiotic. She shook out the proper dosage of each and took them over to Greer with the water. "These will help."

He eyed the pile of pills in her palm like she was offering him anthrax. "I'm okay."

"Jesse said you'd say that. He also said if you refused to take them, I should call and he'd come force feed them to you."

Greer grunted.

She waggled her hand, making the pills clink against each other. "Yeah, you act all big and tough now, soldier, but the shape you're in, I'm thinking that hot cowboy could hogtie you without much effort."

He scowled and grabbed the pills. "Jesse's not hot."

Leave it to the male ego to focus in on that after everything else she'd said. "Of course you wouldn't think so. But Raffi and I agree, the cowboy look works for him. So do his Wranglers."

"He's no good for you. Sucks at relationships. Been divorced three times."

"Who said anything about a relationship?" She grinned as Greer's scowl darkened. "Besides, if he's divorced, that means he's unattached. Sounds like a perfect partner for some horizontal dancing."

He grumbled and tossed back the pills, then snatched the glass of water out of her hand. "Find a different partner."

A little thrill danced through her heart, and she drew a deep breath to calm it. Even though he was trying to brush it off, he didn't like the thought of her with Jesse. Was he jealous? She should take pity on him and tell him he had no reason to be—yes, Jesse was hot, but he wasn't the neighbor she'd been crushing on for the last couple of years.

Except…

She kind of liked that he was jealous. Nice to know she wasn't the only one to notice the tug of attraction between them.

Feeling bold, she asked, "A different partner? Like you?"

Well, he didn't spit out his water. That was a good sign. He swallowed the gulp he'd taken, then slowly lowered the glass to the coffee table. For a handful of seconds, he watched her, considering. Lust burned in his gaze as he swept it down her body. He was clearly playing out that horizontal dance in his mind's eye.

But then he shook his head. "You're too complicated."

She planted her hands on her hips and glowered down at him. "Oh?" She laced the word with as much sarcasm as she could fit into one syllable. "*I'm* complicated?" She wasn't the one with Syrian money in her wallet, a bullet hole in her side, and a connection with a top-secret military base. "How's that?"

If he was at all fazed by her snark, he didn't show it. "You're too close."

"To what?" she demanded.

"To me." With that, he lay down on the couch—or, really, it was more of a collapse—and gave her his back.

She wasn't at all ready to drop the conversation, but as she moved around the couch to face him again, she realized arguing was a moot point. He wasn't feeling well, so even if she did convince him they'd rock together in bed, they weren't going to try it tonight. She braced her arms on the back of the couch and gazed down at him. "Greer."

He didn't open his eyes, but she could tell he wasn't asleep. He tensed ever so slightly at the sound of his name.

"You're only getting a pass because you're not well, but we're not done with this conversation. I think you might need some complicated closeness in your life."

His eyes finally opened. "No," he said so softly she wasn't even sure he'd spoken at first. "That is the very last thing I need."

# Chapter Eight

*The house was exactly as Greer remembered it. The oversize floral slipcover on the sofa and matching valances over the window, family pictures hanging on the sponge-painted wall of the stairway, the huge, boxy TV he and his brothers used to fight over after school. Everything untouched, a frozen tableau of his childhood. He smiled a little as he ran his hand over the faded ink marks on the wall between the living room and dining room. His mother used to line him and his brothers up once a year and commemorate their growth spurts with a marker. He'd always been the tallest. He still was, though the twins weren't very far behind him.*

*He could hear the twins. Not as the men they were now, but as little boys. And he saw them, like ghosts, chasing each other down the stairs, through the living room, the dining room, the kitchen, and circling back. One of them was probably going to fall and get hurt—because one of them was always falling and getting hurt.*

*"Twins! Knock it off!" He put the bite of command in his voice, and the two little boys skidded to a stop in front of him.*

"He started it," they said at the same time, each pointing at the other. Then Cam stuck his tongue out at Vaughn and they were off again.

"Wait for me!" Ten-year-old Jude came bolting down the stairs and chased after them. That kid was always bouncing off the walls and tonight, he was especially hyper after sneaking over to a friend's house and bingeing on candy as they watched Jurassic Park.

No, Greer thought. Christ, no. Not this night. Any night but this night.

He watched a younger, ganglier Reece catch Jude by the back of his dinosaur pajamas. "You're going to be in so much trouble when Mom and Dad get home."

Jude squirmed. "I didn't do anything."

No. No, no, no, no.

Greer knew he was dreaming and tried to open his eyes, wake up, but he couldn't. He was trapped and silently panicked as his dream self moved across the living room to pull Reece and Jude apart. His body felt different, not quite as big, and his voice was younger, not quite as deep. "Reece, leave him alone. Go get the twins back in bed. Mom and Dad will never trust us to stay home alone again if we let them destroy the house."

Reece grumbled, but did as he was told and chased after the twins.

"I didn't do anything," Jude said again, pouting.

Greer crouched down in front of him. "Yeah, you did, little man. You snuck out and really scared Mom and Dad." He hoped they came back soon so he could tell them Jude was safe. Mom had been worried sick for her youngest son when they left.

"You sneak out all the time," Jude pointed out.

Greer winced. "That's different. I'm older." And not setting a very good example for his brothers, he realized.

"So when I'm older, I can sneak out again?"

"That's…not how it works."

"Why not?"

"Just…because."

"But why?"

He pushed out a sigh and wracked his brain for a response, because Jude wasn't going to let it drop until he got a satisfactory answer. "Because I'm oldest and the oldest always gets special privileges."

"That's not fair."

"Well, the youngest gets special privileges, too."

Jude perked up at that. "Like what?"

"Well…uh, when the twins graduate high school and go to college, you'll have the whole house to yourself. Just you, Mom, and Dad."

Jude's face scrunched up as if he couldn't comprehend it. "I get Mom and Dad all to myself?"

"Yup. The rest of us will all be away at college."

"Huh. How old will I be?"

"You'll be seventeen. A senior in high school."

"How old will you be?"

"I'll be twenty-two."

"You'll be old."

"Yeah, I will."

"How old will you be when I'm twenty-two?" Jude asked and Greer groaned inwardly. Once the questions started, they didn't stop until you either fed the kid to shut him up or he fell asleep. And he definitely didn't need any more sugar tonight, so the only other option was to bore him to sleep.

"Do the math. I'm five years older than you, so what's twenty-two plus five?" Greer asked.

Jude didn't have to think about it. He'd always been good with numbers. "Twenty-seven. You'll be really old then, Greer. Almost as old as Dad." The doorbell rang and Jude jumped. "Who's that?"

*Reece reappeared in the archway between the living and
dining room, the twins right behind him.*

*"Is it Mom and Dad?" Vaughn asked.*

*Reece rolled his eyes and pushed his slipping glasses up his
nose. "They wouldn't ring the doorbell, knucklehead."*

*"Then who is it?" Cam asked.*

*Greer gave Jude a gentle shove toward Reece, then moved
over to the door and peeked out the window. "It's…the cops."*

*As soon as the words left his lips, he knew. Somehow,
without even opening the door, he knew his parents were dead
and Jude would never have his year alone with them.*

Suddenly, Greer had control of his body again. He was no
longer his younger dream-self stuck in a time-loop. He was an
adult, and he sure as fuck wasn't going to open that door and
ruin his brothers' lives. He spun toward them, and they grew
before his eyes. The house changed too, fire leaping up around
them in licks of yellow and orange, blackening the walls, the
ugly sofa, the family photos. The height chart peeled away,
exposing the wall studs underneath. Fire leapt from Jude to
Cam, then to Vaughn and Reece, but none of them moved to
escape it. They just stood there, staring with hatred in their
eyes as they burned.

"You were wrong," Jude said. It strangely wasn't his adult
voice, but still the voice of a ten-year-old. Fire crawled up his
body and in the seconds before it engulfed him, he pointed an
accusing finger. "This is your fault. We lost our home because
of Syria. What you did. What you are. It's. Your. Fault."

· · ·

Greer burst from sleep gasping like a man who had been held
under water too long. It was a familiar dream, one he'd had
many times before.

And still, it got to him. Every. Fucking. Time.

Rosy morning sunlight streamed through the sheer curtains over the bay window. Last thing he remembered was that awkward conversation with Natalie while waiting for the pizza. He'd taken those pills, stretched out on the couch, and had dropped into unconsciousness. By his estimation, he'd slept for well over twelve hours before the nightmares decided to torture him.

That had to be a new record for him. Most nights, he was lucky to get more than three hours.

Sitting up, he raked shaking hands over his face and through his hair. He locked his fingers around the back of his neck and breathed deep, forcing oxygen into his constricted lungs.

He often dreamed of the night his parents were killed. Sometimes it was a painfully realistic blow-by-blow replay of the night's events. Sometimes it was a horrific reimagining. Sometimes, like last night, it was a mix of both. But last night, the dream's ending had been a new one. Never before had the house caught fire. He could only guess that came from seeing the burned-out ruins yesterday.

"Greer?" Natalie's voice floated across the apartment and settled over him like a soft blanket. Warm. Comforting.

Complicated. So damn complicated.

He looked toward her bedroom.

She leaned in the doorway, backlit by the soft yellow light of a lamp. Like a halo. His angel.

"Are you okay?" she asked.

"Yeah," he managed. "I'm fine." Which, he realized, was the truth. Despite the lingering adrenaline rush from the nightmare, he felt better than he had in days.

"Are you sure?" She was wearing her shawl again. When she closed the distance between them, the fringe whispered against her legs. She propped a hip on the arm of the couch by his feet. "Because you didn't sound fine a few minutes ago.

You kept shouting 'no' over and over again."

Jesus, she'd heard him? "A dream," he muttered.

The corners of her mouth tilted into a frown. "It sounded like a bad one."

"It's not the worst." While dreaming of his parents was always emotionally traumatic, it wasn't the sheer horror he faced in some of his other nightmares. But why did he tell her that?

She was too close. The thought kept bouncing around in his head. Too damn close.

Her frown deepened. "Do you talk to anyone about these nightmares?"

"You mean a shrink? Hell no."

"Typical." She huffed out a breath and slid down the couch's arm to the cushion. "It might help, you know."

He snorted.

"Well, if you won't talk to a professional, you could…" She hesitated. "Talk to me."

And bring her in closer? Not a chance. He sent her a sidelong glance. "I thought you were a dancer."

"I was. Am," she corrected. "But I also have a masters degree in psychology."

Okay, he hadn't seen that coming. When he found out she was a dancer, he'd just assumed that was all she was. Like his mother and his high school girlfriend—dance had been their lives and neither of them had gone to college in the traditional sense. "You have a masters degree?"

"Don't sound so surprised." Natalie picked at a loose thread on her shawl. "My dance career ended when I was only nineteen."

"That's young." At nineteen, barely out of high school himself, he'd been responsible for his four teenage brothers. He'd also had an anvil hanging over his head in the form of Bruce Chambers and the promise he'd made to keep his brothers together and safe.

Natalie nodded. "I was very young and I didn't have a back-up plan. Dance was all I ever wanted to do from the time I was four years old. I sacrificed so many of the normal childhood experiences—I was even homeschooled so I could spend more time at the studio. Then one wrong landing during rehearsal…and bam! It all ended. All those years of work, and it was just over."

Something his mom used to say came back to him in a whisper of memory. "Dancers die twice. The first time is when they stop dancing."

A ghost of a smile played over her lips. "It's true. I was so depressed after my injury, I didn't even want to live anymore."

His stomach cramped. He knew what that was like. That pull to just end it all. He lived with it every day. "How did you deal?"

"Lots and lots of therapy. Eventually, my doctor convinced me my life hadn't ended with my dance career, and he urged me to go to college. I originally thought I'd be a physical therapist like the ones who helped me after my injury, but I found psychology much more interesting."

"But you still teach dance."

"I enjoy it. It was such a huge part of my life growing up. I'd never be able to just stop doing it. But I can't do as much as I once did because of my bum knee, so I use my degree, too." She smiled over at him. "I'm Tally from *Talk to Tally*. The call-in radio show?" she added when he showed no hint of recognition.

He tilted his head back against the couch and shut his eyes. "A radio shrink. Even better than a regular shrink."

"Hey!" She swatted his arm. "I like helping people. Even if it means I only act as their sounding board. And, technically, I'm not a shrink. I stopped school after getting my masters. Might go back for a doctorate someday, but for now, I like what I'm doing. Teach dance in the evenings, do the radio thing at night, sleep during the day, weekends off unless I volunteer for a suicide hotline…which is usually every weekend."

"When do you date?" He regretted the words as soon as they left his mouth. What did it matter to him? It shouldn't matter. He had other things to worry about than his neighbor's sex life, dammit.

But it did matter. Like it or not, he was interested in this woman as more than just a neighbor.

She frowned slightly. "I don't. Not really, at least. I'm focusing on me. But I'm not lonely or anything," she added quickly. "I have lots of friends and family. It's a good life."

It did sound nice. Quiet. Stable. Worlds away from the violence that was his own. Would he have lived that kind of life under different circumstances? He liked to think so.

When he was fifteen, his career goals hadn't included a life of military servitude. He certainly hadn't thought he'd end up being what boiled down to a hired gun for the government. He'd wanted to go to college but couldn't recall if there was anything he'd had his heart set on studying. He'd enjoyed football, figured he'd end up coaching when he had kids of his own someday. But at fifteen, his world had been so narrow. He hadn't thought much beyond the next homework assignment, the next football game, the next school dance, getting his driver's permit on his next birthday. Adult life had been so far away, no more than a hazy eventuality—until his parents died and adulthood had smacked him in the face. He'd had to grow up fast out of necessity, and he never had the chance to be anything more than what he now was. So why was he dwelling on the might-have-beens?

"You're thinking awfully loudly," Natalie said. She shifted on the couch, drawing his gaze to her long legs as she curled them up underneath her.

Lust hit hard and fast. His heart suddenly pounded

against his ribs, and his mouth went dry. He didn't want to think anymore. There was only one thing he wanted at the moment—those legs wrapped around him while he pounded into her until he couldn't think at all.

Too complicated, he reminded himself. Too close.

His angel.

But maybe that was exactly why he should give in to the urge. If he got her out of his system, he'd be able to put more distance between them. As long as she was an unknown, she'd be an enticement, a distraction, but once he had her, she'd fall from the damn pedestal he'd placed her on and he could get on with his mission.

Mind made up, he faced her. "Do you want to fuck?"

Laughter burst from her in a disbelieving huff of air. "Wow. That was romantic."

"I'm not talking about romance. I don't do romance. I'm talking about hot, hard, down and dirty fucking. No strings, no emotions. Just you, me, and an itch that needs scratched."

"Oh." Her breath hitched. "Oh, you're serious."

"I'm rarely not."

"That's a shame. You'd look good with a smile." She studied him from across the length of the couch, and the heat in her eyes sent blood rushing to his cock. He didn't bother hiding the bulge growing at the front of his pants. No point since she already knew what he wanted. The ball was in her court now. What happened next was all up to her.

"I thought I was too complicated," she said finally.

"You are."

She stayed silent for another long beat, and he saw the exact moment she made her decision. Her breathing quickened, and color bloomed across her cheeks. "If I say yes?"

"If you say yes…" He leaned over and tugged on her feet peeking out from under her nightshirt. He pulled her legs straight, traced his hands up her firm calves to her knees. She had a scar on her left kneecap about three inches long. He leaned over and dragged his tongue along it as he pushed her legs open. "I want these legs around me."

His hands continued northward, tracing the soft flesh of her inner thighs. She wasn't wearing underwear, but he stopped just short of touching her. "If you say yes, I'll fuck you until you can't walk. And then when you come screaming, I'll flip you over the back of this couch and do it all again from behind."

She groaned and lifted her hips to meet his hand. "Oh, God, yes."

# Chapter Nine

She shouldn't be doing this.

Shouldn't be, but her body so didn't care about all stop signs and warning bells her brain was throwing out.

Except for one.

She covered his hands with her own. "Are you okay for this?" He'd slept so long last night, not even waking when the pizza arrived. She'd worried he was slipping into a fever again, but his skin was cool to the touch.

He grabbed her wrist, guided her palm to his erection, and pressed. "What do you think? Do I feel okay?"

He felt hard and huge. Definitely okay. More than okay. Dampness pooled between her thighs. She wanted to peel away the layers of clothes between them and touch his bare skin, see him in all his naked male glory.

Oh, what the hell. If he hurt himself, that was his problem.

With a flick of her wrist, she unsnapped the button on his jeans.

"No." He caught her hand. "You strip."

Her breath snagged in her lungs. "I don't follow orders."

He tightened his grip on her wrist, just enough to be a little painful. A warning before he released her. "You'll follow mine. Strip."

Oh, that commanding tone shouldn't affect her like it did. Shouldn't make her ache with want. But it did. It so worked for her.

She whipped her nightshirt off over her head. She never wore underwear to bed and she'd never been gladder for it than when she saw his sharp intake of breath. He cupped her waist, skimmed his hands reverently up to her breasts, then back to her hips. His touch left a trail of tingling heat in its wake.

Oh. God.

He'd barely touched her, and she might combust before he really got down to business. "Greer…"

"Yeah, I like the sound of my name on your lips." His breath fanned her inner thigh as he settled between her legs. "Say it again."

That tone. The smug command of it. Part of her wanted to fight it, but the rest of her was powerless to resist. "Greer."

"That's it, angel. Keeping saying my name, and I'll give you what you want."

"Greer…" When his mouth touched her, she shivered at the pleasure of it. Her nipples tightened, becoming so sensitive even the caress of air over the buds was too much. He cupped one breast in his hand, circled the nipple with his thumb, and she arched off the couch, his name ripping from her throat on a moan.

He lifted his head, his lips wet from her, his eyes almost black with lust. "Open wider."

She did, dropping her knees to the sides. Later, she'd worry about her status as a strong, independent woman who didn't want a man telling her what to do. But right now, she was helpless to do anything but follow his commands.

He growled, delved his hands under her butt, and lifted her hips to meet his mouth. His tongue explored, dipping into her sex before tracing her cleft northward to the bundle of nerves throbbing for his attention. He flicked his tongue over it, circled it, sucked it into his mouth. He knew exactly what he was doing, and backed off just as she started to peak, drawing out the pleasurable torture.

She was definitely going to combust if he didn't…let her…

The orgasm tore through her. She dug her hands into his hair and held on as he continued to lick her through it. Even as she came down, she felt the tension start to curl inside her again.

He was aiming for a two-for. And judging by the way her legs began to shake, he was going to get it. She was already there again, and if he just kept up that delicious back and forth flick of his tongue —

*Bang bang bang bang.*

Someone knocked loudly on her apartment door and Greer bolted upright. The lust in his eyes disappeared in an instant, replaced with weariness. "Who the hell visits at seven in the morning?"

"I don't know." She scooted away from him and scooped up her clothes on the way to the door. Her heart began to pound, and not because of the exquisite orgasm she'd been about to have.

What would she do if it was Andy on the other side of the door? She'd have to play it cool, tell him to hide until she could get Greer gone, and hope her nephew did nothing stupid. Except if he was in trouble, she couldn't turn him away. The walk to the door only took a few seconds normally, but it felt endless this time, a bit like she was slogging through mud in slow-mo.

Mouth dry, she checked the peephole…and breathed an internal sigh of relief. Not Andy, but a man. Tall, lean, with dark hair and hazel eyes. Now that she'd spent time with Greer, she recognized the family resemblance. "It's Reece."

"Fuck," Greer said under his breath. "Get him out of here. And don't tell him I'm here."

She yanked on her nightshirt and pulled her shawl over her shoulders before opening the door a crack. "Hi, Reece. Is everything okay?"

"Yeah. Shit." He winced and gazed down at his watch. "I'm sorry it's early. Did I wake you?"

"Uh, no. It's fine. I was up." More than up. She'd been flying high in orgasm. She glanced over her shoulder. Greer made a shooing motion with his hands. She drew a breath and stepped out into the hall, closing the door behind her. "I'd invite you in, but I've been busy and the place is disaster."

"No problem. I just stopped by to…" Reece trailed off and looked across the hall at the door of Greer's apartment. "Have you seen anything out of the ordinary since I was last here?"

Besides Greer's extraordinary body? All those muscles, and abs, and… God, the sinful things that man could do with his mouth and tongue…

She hugged her shawl tightly around her, very aware that she was naked underneath her nightshirt and that Greer was mostly naked on the other side of her door. "Uh, no. I'm sorry. I haven't."

Reece swore softly. He looked tired, less polished than the first time she'd met him back in January. He'd lost the tie and endless stream of business suits—which, if you asked her, was for the better—but his hair was starting to get a little too shaggy and worried shadows darkened his eyes.

"Thanks anyway," he added.

"Why do you ask?" she blurted, then mentally kicked herself. She wanted him to go away so she and Greer could pick up right where they left off. Which, yes, was selfish of her. Especially when Reece was so obviously worried for his brother.

Reece rubbed a hand across his stubbled jaw. "There's stuff missing from his place. I know I folded the few of his clothes that weren't destroyed and put them away, but now they're gone. Several of the boxes have been opened, too. I thought maybe..." He trailed off and his shoulders slumped. "Maybe he'd come home."

"If he had, I would've—" The lie stuck in her throat, and she couldn't finish it.

Reece nodded. "I know. You would have called. Just wishful thinking on my part. We keep hitting dead ends searching for him. It's like he dropped off the face of the earth—a decade ago." He exhaled a soft, cynical laugh. "Apparently, he ceased to exist the day he joined the military."

She wasn't surprised. That place he'd gone to yesterday wasn't your run-of-the-mill military base. Not with the way they'd locked down when she showed up.

"How could a guy just up and disappear for nearly four months?" Reece rubbed at one eye under his glasses like he had a headache. "He's been keeping secrets from us."

And now she was, too. She opened her mouth but couldn't figure out what to say and closed it again.

"Anyway," Reece said on a sigh. "Thanks, Natalie. For everything." He started toward the stairs and her stomach knotted. He looked so anxious for his big brother, and she couldn't let him walk away without saying...something.

"Reece."

He stopped, glanced back.

"Greer's okay. He'll turn up soon. I'm sure of it."

A line formed between his brows. "Yeah," he said, dragging the word out. Then he shook his head slightly. "Yeah, I hope you're right."

She waited until he disappeared down the stairs before

opening the door to her apartment. Greer stood there, hands on his hips, gaze to the floor, emotions warring over his face. He looked sexy and mussed, his pants undone, the bulge of his erection still prominent…but she'd lost her appetite for sex.

She hugged her shawl around her and leaned back against the door. "Lying to him didn't feel good, Greer. It's not fair to keep him in the dark like this."

His shoulders moved as he sighed, and for one shining moment, she thought he would do the right thing and have her call Reece back. Then he looked up and his eyes were hard, his features set in determination. "You will not tell him."

She straightened, not liking the snap of command in his tone one bit. "I'm not one of your soldiers. You don't get to order me around."

The corner of his mouth lifted in a sneer. "You were taking orders just fine a few minutes ago, angel."

"You bastard." Heat flooded her face and an acrid mix of embarrassment and anger seared her throat. She didn't need this. Hell, she didn't want it. Even as much as she craved Greer's body, she wasn't about to put up with him being a jackass solely for the sake of a good roll in the sheets. She pointed at the door. "Get out, and don't come back until you learn to treat me with some respect."

He opened his mouth, but she held up a hand, stemming any protest. "No. I don't want to hear it. I'm not the kind of woman you can push around just because we've had sex, and I will not accept you speaking to me the way you just did. Especially when I've done nothing but go out of my way to help you."

His scowl darkened as he snapped up his shirt, grabbed his duffle bag, and stuffed his feet into his unlaced boots. He said nothing until he was standing beside her again, hand on the doorknob. "I never asked for your help."

"Actually…" Her voice wobbled. Dammit, she was not going to cry. She straightened her shoulders, lifted her chin, and met his angry gaze without flinching. "You did. That's the first word you said to me. Help. So I did, and I don't deserve to be treated like a throw-away lay."

His jaw tightened and a muscle ticked under his eye. He yanked open the door, stepped through, but caught it before it slammed behind him. "Natalie." A beat passed. "I don't think of you as a throw-away anything."

With that, he softly shut the door.

Natalie stared at the door a long time, a few tears escaping despite her determination not to cry. She'd been doing okay until his parting words. If he didn't think of her as a slam, bam, thank you ma'am, then why had he been so cruel?

The man had a lot of mean in him. She'd only caught glimpses, but it was all she needed to know she didn't want that in her life.

Good riddance.

Disgusted with herself, she swiped at her face and gazed down at Jet, who sat by her side. He looked up at her, then at the door. For reasons unknown to her, the dog liked Greer. Had from the moment Greer collapsed in front of her apartment. She could see Jet's confusion at Greer's sudden departure and reached down to rub his head reassuringly. "Your taste in men isn't any better than mine, buddy."

Jet's tail thumped on the floor twice, and she leaned over to kiss his big, soft head. "Good boy. Let's get you breakfast, huh?"

As she walked into the kitchen, she couldn't help but glance over her shoulder at the door again. Part of her—the silly, hopeless romantic who loved sappy movies—wanted him to come back with an apology and grand gesture to show he meant it. The realist in her knew there was no chance in hell of that happening.

Like he said, he didn't do romance.

She shook her head at herself and resolved to put him out of her mind for the rest of the day. After all, she had more important things to worry about—like her nephew and whatever he'd become tangled up in. She had to find Andy as soon as possible...

And Reece Wilde was going to help her.

• • •

It wasn't the first time Greer had been ordered out of a woman's apartment, and probably wouldn't be the last. So why did those two words hit like a one-two punch to the gut? Even now, he couldn't get the picture of her—hair spiked, cheeks pinked with anger, nipples peaked against the soft fabric of her nightshirt—out of his head. And, fuck, he still wanted her.

He'd lost his goddamn mind in there. Sex hadn't even blipped on his radar for months—maybe it was even closer to a year at this point—but now that he was so close to his goal, his cock suddenly decided to come out of hibernation.

Was that why he'd been so snarly with her?

This powerful attraction to her had completely KO'd him. He was still reeling from the blow and imagined he had little cartoon birds circling his skull. It was so unfamiliar, this off-kilter sensation he'd had since feeling her come so magnificently on his tongue. In that moment, his chest had fully expanded for the first time in years, and his head had cleared of all the noise. Watching her tremble with her eyes all soft and her lips parted in an enticing little *O*, he'd wanted nothing more than to spend his every waking moment for the rest of his life pleasing her.

And he didn't like the feeling one bit. Because wanting anything for the rest of his life implied he planned to have one after he ended Mendenhall. Which he didn't. All he wanted was for it to be over already—the nightmares, the flashbacks, the persistent heaviness weighing down his chest. He wanted it all gone, and already had one foot in the grave as far as he was concerned. If he wanted the other one to join the first, he had to keep away from Natalie Taggart. He'd already let her too close, already cared too much about her when he hadn't cared about any-damn-thing in a long time, and feared he might have inadvertently given her the power to pull him back from the edge.

He didn't want to be pulled back.

Did he?

He reached the parking lot and wind sliced through the thin material of his T-shirt. Winter wasn't ready to give up the city just yet, despite the bright morning sunshine's best efforts at springtime. He'd have to break down and do some shopping today, get a few essentials. A jacket, some quick food, a sleeping bag—no furniture because that would be nothing but a waste.

No, he decided, he absolutely didn't want to be pulled back.

His brothers didn't need him anymore, and he couldn't shake the memory of Syria or the profound sense of relief he'd experienced in those seconds before the mortar exploded, when he thought he was dead. He wanted—needed—that relief again. He just had to do this one last thing for his family.

He had to find Mendenhall and end it.

But first, he needed wheels.

He grabbed his phone out of the side pocket in his bag and dialed. When Bruce Chambers answered, he said without preamble, "I need my bike."

A pause, some shuffling. A door closed in the background before Bruce responded, "I'll meet you with it, but I'll need a couple hours."

"All right. Two hours. My usual spot." He hung up and started toward the nearest bus stop. It was two hours more than he wanted, but he'd use the extra time to get those essentials.

He also had to come up with a plan of attack. He'd drive by the flophouse where Mendenhall had been staying, but he doubted the guy was still there, and he had no idea where to start looking.

Except...

The kid. The one who had run away during the mugging. He'd gotten a good look at his face, would recognize him if he saw him again. Find that kid, and he had no doubt he'd have a direct line to Mendenhall.

# Chapter Ten

This was probably a very bad idea.

Oh, God. Scratch that. It was definitely a bad idea. Being here, she was just asking for more trouble with Greer...but it was the only idea she had at this point.

Greer's brothers knew how to find people, and she needed Andy found. Just call her desperate.

Natalie drew a breath and pushed through the glass-fronted door marked WILDE SECURITY in black lettering. A small bell overhead chimed with her entrance. The office was a long rectangle with several nice wood desks on one end and a comfortable seating area under the window on the other. On the back wall were two doors, a small fridge and countertop between them. The smell of coffee was strong in here, but the pot on the counter was empty and didn't look as if it had been used in a while. A handful of photos decorated the wall behind one of the desks, and someone had written "Wall of Internet Shame" on a sheet of paper and taped it in the center of all the photos. Other than that, there wasn't much in the way of decoration.

The man seated at one of the desks gazed up at the sound of the bell and scowled. She hadn't met this particular brother yet, but he resembled Greer even more than Reece. Similar square face shape, same nose, same eyes—except his eye color was a stormy blue-gray rather than the deep brown of his older brother's. He wore his dark hair long and wavy and had it pulled back in a little stub of a tail.

He pushed out of his seat. "Where's my brother?"

Okay, she didn't know him, but he apparently knew her. Her heart leapt into her throat, and she had to swallow it down before she could speak again. "I-I don't know where Greer is."

"You're lying."

No, actually it was the truth. She really didn't know where he'd gone after she ordered him out of her apartment this morning. Which was troubling and part of the reason she was here now.

She straightened her shoulders. "I am not."

The door opened behind Natalie, and a brunette with the kind of body that belonged on the cover of a magazine came through. "Vaughn, stop it." She carried two steaming coffee mugs and started to hand one to Vaughn, but she snatched it away before he took it. "Only if you play nice."

He snaked an arm around her and drew her into his side, planting a hard kiss on her lips. "I never play nice, vixen."

"I know. It's one of the things I love about you." The woman returned his kiss, then extracted herself from his arms and shoved the mug of coffee into his hand. "But scaring away new clients is bad for business."

"She's not a new client," he muttered into his mug before taking a sip. "That's Greer's neighbor."

"Oh," the woman said and smiled. "We haven't met yet." She set her coffee down and held out her hand. "I'm Lark Wilde. Vaughn's wife."

"Natalie." She accepted the handshake. Lark was far more approachable than her husband. Plus, she didn't feel like the other woman could see right through her like Vaughn could. "I was looking for Reece."

"Do you have news about Greer?"

Yes, so much. And if she were smart, she'd come clean. She shook her head. Well, she'd never claimed to be smart. But there were just too many unknowns right now, and until she could guarantee her nephew's safety, she was keeping her lips sealed. "No. I'm sorry."

"She's lying," Vaughn said matter-of-factly. Lark elbowed him in the ribs, but it didn't deter him from boring holes into her with his eyes.

"Ignore him." Lark sighed. "He was born without manners. It's an unfortunate genetic defect with no known cure."

Yes, Natalie decided, she liked this woman. "Is Reece around? I'd hoped to talk to him. Not about Greer," she added quickly. "This is…something else."

"Yeah, he's here, but he's helping out at the coffee shop next door."

Ah. So that explained the strong smell of coffee.

"His wife, Shelby, owns the place," Lark explained before Natalie could ask. "A barista went home sick, so he's filling in until the replacement arrives. Shouldn't be too much longer if you want to wait for him."

Wife? Huh. In all the months she'd known Reece, she hadn't known he was married. Although he was a handsome man, he'd never sparked her interest like Greer, so she hadn't paid any attention to whether or not he wore a ring. "Thank you. I'll do that."

"Or," Vaughn said and pointed at her with the hand still holding his coffee. "You could tell me where my brother is."

Lark huffed out a breath in exasperation. "Vaughn.

Enough."

He shook his head, his features softening the tiniest bit when he looked at his wife. "You won't get me to back off this, vixen. I know she's lying. Reece knows she's lying. There's something about Greer she's not telling us."

Lark's pretty blue eyes, narrowed with suspicion, turned in her direction. "Why would you lie?"

"I'm not." The words came out strangled. Reece knew she was lying? How was that possible? She straightened her spine, forcing all uncertainty from her posture and voice. "I'm not."

"Then why are you here?"

Yes. Subject change. She breathed a soft sigh of relief and strode forward, digging in her purse for her phone. "I want to hire your husband and his brothers to find my nephew." She held out the phone, showing them the most recent photo she had of Andy, snapped during his birthday party two months ago. "That's Andy. Andrew Taggart. He's sixteen."

Lark took the phone and studied it, a crease forming between her perfectly manicured brows. She passed the phone to Vaughn. "How long has he been missing?"

Now for the tap dance. She had to give them enough information to find Andy, but not enough to implicate him in any wrongdoing or expose Greer. "I last saw him Friday morning. He showed up at my place after staying out all night and wanted to hide from my parents—they're his legal guardians, and he was afraid they'd ground him for breaking curfew."

"If they are his legal guardians, why haven't they reported him missing?" Vaughn's tone still dripped with suspicion, but there was definitely something different in his demeanor as he sat down behind his desk. Was that a hint of concern she sensed under the suspicion? Oh, she hoped so. She did desperately need Wilde Security's help.

"My parents don't know yet. I told them he's been with

me all weekend." She bit her lower lip. She so hated lying to them, but they had been through enough distress while raising her brother, and if there was a chance she could spare them that this time around, she would. "I'd hoped to find him before worrying them."

"So he's a runaway?" Vaughn asked. "You don't suspect foul play?"

"No, he's definitely—" When he plugged her phone into his computer, her heart hit her stomach with a cannon ball splash. She hurried around the desk to see his screen. "What are you doing?"

God, was there anything incriminating on the phone? She didn't think so—she didn't have Greer's cell number, so there was no evidence of communication between them—but she really didn't want to take any chances. Vaughn was suspicious enough to look and it appeared he had the skills to do it.

He lifted a brow at her, then went back to keying in commands. "I'm downloading your nephew's photo and phone info. If he has it on him and it's active, I can ping it and find out his location."

She stared as he pulled up a map on screen. "Just like that?"

"Yup. Just like that." Lark perched a hip on the edge of the desk and watched him work. She smiled in a conspiratorial way. "He's the absolute best at finding people."

"You would know, huh, vixen?" Vaughn spared her a quick roguish grin, then went back to his work. "But if Andy's battery is dead, I won't be able to find him. It's a starting point, though."

Yes, this was a bad idea. If he was the best at finding people, she had no doubt he was also scouring every data byte on her phone for information about Greer even though she couldn't see him doing anything but looking for Andy. She tucked her hands into her pockets to keep from snatching the phone away from him.

Breathe. He wouldn't find anything. Just breathe and act normal.

Ugh, she sucked at lying. Why was she even bothering? It was so freaking stressful, and after the way Greer treated her this morning he deserved to have all of his secrets spilled.

But, dang it, she hated to betray his trust. Even now.

She shifted on her feet. Stared at the computer while Vaughn expertly guided it through the search. Lark offered to treat her to a coffee at the cafe next door, but she declined, too worried by the prospect of leaving Vaughn alone with her phone. After that, Lark gave her husband a quick kiss and wandered away.

Natalie waited several more minutes, her anxiety growing with each tick of the clock. "How much longer will this take?"

"Why?" Vaughn asked casually, not lifting his gaze from the computer. "Have a hot date with my brother tonight?"

She thought she kept her face impassive, but something must have given her away because he turned away from the computer and faced her. Had she drawn in a sharp breath? Or maybe he had super-sonic hearing and had caught the loud, stuttering *ba-bump* of her heart at his question.

Vaughn's gaze was serious as it locked on hers. "What do you have to gain by lying?"

"I-I'm not."

"Yeah, you are. Reece said the last time you spoke, you referred to Greer as Greer. Up until then, you always called him by his first name, David—the name on his mail. Process of elimination, sweetheart. None of us told you he goes by his middle name, so the only person who could have corrected you is him."

Well, shit. So much for her super-secret spy skills.

She searched for a response, came up with nothing. It didn't matter anyway, because Vaughn steamrolled right over any weak excuse she might have given. "Where is he?"

She drew a breath, let it out slowly. "I can't tell you. I promised him I wouldn't."

For the first time, something other than suspicion darkened his eyes. Hurt. "Why doesn't he want to see us?"

She just shook her head. "I won't betray his trust."

"Dammit. I wish you weren't such a decent person." He looked back at the computer screen, and his voice softened. "Is he okay? We've been worried."

"I know you have," she said just as softly. "And I wish I could tell you yes, he's fine. But honestly, I don't think he is."

Vaughn closed his eyes for a second, and she stayed quiet, letting him have the time to collect himself.

"All right." He placed his hands back on the keyboard. "Let's find your nephew."

"You're not mad?"

"Oh, I'm pissed." He offered her a surprisingly gentle smile for such an imposing man. "But not at you. You're only doing what he asked you to. I get it."

She wanted to tell him not to be angry at Greer, but the plea would fall on deaf ears. Vaughn needed his anger right now, but she hoped when Greer finally came out of hiding, Vaughn would realize his brother needed him more than his anger.

• • •

Greer's "usual spot" had at one time been a gas station. Now the pavement was cracked, the pumps were gone, and colorful splashes of graffiti covered the boarded-up building.

Apparently murder was bad for business.

He'd had to hoof it from the nearest bus stop three blocks away, and his bike was already there waiting on a flatbed trailer behind Bruce's truck.

Bruce climbed out of the driver's seat when he approached and looked distinctly uncomfortable with this whole meeting. "Why do you torture yourself by coming here?"

Greer glanced down at pavement that had been splattered with blood the first time he'd seen it twenty years ago. He wasn't about to tell Bruce this place reminded him why he was the man he'd become, and of all the things he'd done for his family. And he sure as hell wasn't going to tell Bruce he felt closer to his parents here, where they were murdered, than he did at their graves, where they rested. No need to let the whole world know he was a sick fuck.

"It's just an easy place to meet." Which was the truth. It was halfway between his apartment and the base, so it made for a convenient rendezvous. He jumped up on the trailer and started undoing the ratchet straps holding his bike in place. "Help me with this."

Bruce climbed up and lowered the ramp, then dealt with the straps on the other side.

Once the bike was free, Greer swung a leg over the seat and took a moment to savor the familiarity of it before easing it backward off the ramp. "My helmet?"

Bruce jumped down from the trailer and went to the passenger side of his truck. The helmet sat there on the seat.

"Hey," Bruce said and tossed the helmet to Greer. "I know you requested a leave, but there's some shit going down in Nigeria. A war brewing with the wrong people poised to take power. With Zak Hendricks permanently out of the game and Dustin Williamson gone, we're low on men. Your country might need you."

Yeah, sure. His country. As if he cared anything about patriotism when he was just trying to convince himself to live another hour, another day.

His stomach dropped like on the first hill of a roller coaster at the thought of another mission. No. He couldn't do it all again. He'd lose whatever of himself was left. If Bruce canceled his leave, he'd have little choice but to go AWOL. Having his file slapped with a deserter label wouldn't matter to him in the long run, but it'd hurt his brothers, and the last thing he wanted was to hurt them any more than he already had.

Greer deliberately took his time putting on his helmet to give himself a chance to modulate his voice before he spoke. "Are you ordering me to go?"

"Not yet. Just giving you a heads-up." Bruce watched him closely.

He schooled his features into a mask. No way would he let it show how desperately he didn't want another mission. "Consider it given."

"Uh-huh. You're not going to do anything crazy are you, son?"

"Define crazy." Without waiting for a response, he snapped the visor down over his face and started the bike. Bruce called his name, but the engine's rumble drowned out the protest as he opened the throttle and careened from the parking lot.

Now that he had wheels again, he had work to do.

His first stop was the bar where the kids had jumped him. Since it was so early in the day, at least as far as bar hours went, the place was a ghost town. The bartender leaned on the scuffed oak bar, chatting with a few guys who probably had permanent stools there, and glanced up when the door opened.

He sized Greer up, then lifted his chin in a gesture of recognition. "You're the guy from the parking lot the other night."

So this bartender had been on duty that night. He didn't recall much from the hours surrounding the mugging, probably due to his concussion, and the guy's hangdog face wasn't ringing any bells.

"Look," the bartender continued. "You should know I filed a report with the police. They know you ran off before help arrived. The bar's not responsible for your injuries."

"I'm not going to sue you." Greer slid onto a stool and did his best to appear non-threatening. Not an easy task for a hulking six-foot-five man. "But I am looking for the kids who jumped me."

The bartender's eyes rounded. "Kids?"

"At least three. One looked to be about 15 or 16. Dark hair, brown eyes." He drew his finger across his upper lip. "The start of a mustache. Sound familiar?"

"Nope." The answer came fast, and a little too casually. A lie.

Greer leaned over the bar. "I just want to talk to the kid, that's all."

The bartender rubbed his stubbled chin and glanced over at the bar's two permanent residents, who were watching the exchange with rapt attention.

"Sounds like the computer kid," one of them said.

Greer turned toward them. "What computer kid?"

"Dunno his name," the second guy said and lifted his glass to his mouth. His speech was already slurring despite the early hour. "He fixes computers and things."

"Yeah," the first guy chimed in again. "Weren't he just in to fix the registers, Max? He was really happy to get paid as I recall."

Bingo, Greer thought. The kid wanted money. Now the question was did he want it desperately enough to mug someone?

He turned to Max, the bartender. "This computer kid. He match my description?"

Max hesitated a beat, then nodded. "It does sound like him, but that description could fit lots of other guys, too. Andy is a good kid. Smart. He hangs with some lowlifes, but he's not the kind of boy who goes around mugging people."

"How long has he been hanging around here?" If he was a regular, this bar had to be where Mendenhall had met him.

"A few days. No more than a week."

Greer raised a brow. "And you let him play around with your computers?" Having grown up with Reece for a brother, the king of computer nerds, he knew exactly what could be accomplished by someone who knew what they were doing with a keyboard and internet access.

Max shrugged. "I have a sense for people. Andy's a good boy."

"Do you have cameras in the parking lot?"

"Usually, but they're not working now. Andy was going to fix them for me next time he stopped in."

Yeah, this Andy kid had fixed them all right. He'd gained access to the bar's computer system and had no doubt erased all video evidence of the mugging. Smart move. "Does Andy have a last name?"

"I'm sure he does, but I don't know it."

The door opened and everyone turned to look at the newcomer.

Shock coursed through Greer and he stood. "Natalie?"

Her head jerked up at the sound of his voice, and her expression ran the gamut of emotions all the way from "oh, shit" to "play it cool." A poker player she was not.

He closed the distanced between them. "What are you doing here?" It couldn't be a coincidence. This bar was nowhere near their apartment complex.

"Uh…" She scrambled to hide her phone from his view, but he was faster. He snatched it away and held it out of her reach. He studied the picture she had pulled up on the screen, and for the second time in less than a minute, his blood ran cold with surprise. Dark, hot anger followed, chasing the cold away.

The kid with the barely there mustache.

He stared at Natalie in disbelief. She might as well have the word "guilt" stamped across her forehead for all the waves of the stuff she was throwing off. But she couldn't be involved in this. No matter how many times he tried to fit the pieces together, he didn't see a logical way she could be.

Except, she had a picture of his mugger on her phone. And she was here now.

What the fuck?

This wasn't a convo he planned to have in front of Max and the two bar rats, so he gripped Natalie's arm and marched her outside. After the dank interior of the bar, the bright sun blinded him, and it took several blinks to clear his vision.

"Greer—" she started, but he didn't give her the chance to lob some lame explanation in his direction.

He shoved the phone at her. "Who is this kid and how do you know him?"

She dragged her teeth over her lower lip and, damn his body all to hell, he shouldn't notice how sexy she looked when she did that. But, yeah, his cock stirred. He hadn't gotten enough of her this morning to flush the need out of his system, and he silently cursed Reece for his shitty timing. The whole point of this morning was to minimize his distractions, and now he couldn't keep his gaze off her lips.

"Who is he?" he demanded again.

"Andy," she said softly after a beat, and her shoulders slumped a little. "My nephew."

"You knew your nephew was involved in my mugging?"

She shook her head. "I didn't for sure, but he ran off when he saw you in the hallway that night, and I haven't been able to find him since. I got information that this was the last place his phone was active."

"Information from where?"

She ducked her head. "Your brother. Vaughn. He helped me."

Greer paced away several steps, digging his hands into his hair. "Do they know I've been with you?"

"I think so. Yes."

Jesus. All his carefully laid plans started crumbling in large chunks around him. "You just can't keep your mouth shut, can you? Talk show DJ. Should have figured."

"There you go being a complete ass again." She jammed her hands on her hips and glared at him, anger sizzling in her eyes. "For your information, I didn't tell them. They guessed. They're not idiots, Greer."

"You shouldn't have gone to them in the first place."

"I needed help!"

"Then you should've asked me!" And more than anything else, that was why he was pissed off. She'd needed help and had gone to his brothers instead of him. Not that he'd given her much reason to confide in him, a small voice chided in the back of his mind. But still, he owed her for helping him out when he was incapable of taking care of himself. Finding her nephew would settle the score with the added bonus of leading him to Mendenhall. He gentled his voice. "Let me help you."

"Why?" She stalked forward and shoved him. "So you can kill Andy, too?"

He let the verbal blow land, felt it all the way to the core of his being. It killed him that she thought so low of him, but he'd done nothing to deserve better than her scorn. "I wouldn't hurt a kid."

"But you'll hurt an adult?"

"It's what I do."

She scoffed. "Well, give him a few more years, and he'll be eligible for your hit list. Will you go after him then?"

He gripped her arms and tried to make her face him.

"Natalie—"

"Don't." She broke out of his grasp, and he let her go, only to get a finger jabbed into his chest. "I don't need your help. I'll find my nephew on my own and do whatever it takes to keep him safe from you. So if you want to hurt him, you'd better be willing to go through me."

He watched her storm away, more than a little befuddled. Whenever he'd passed her on the stairs these last three years, she'd always smiled and said a cheerful hello. She'd always given him the impression of sweetness and innocence. The sweet, bubbly girl next door. It was an impression he'd hung on to. He'd liked the image.

But she wasn't sweet or bubbly. She had claws, and she had no problem using them to swipe at him like a mama bear protecting her cub.

Her nephew.

He rubbed a hand over his face. The kid with the peach-fuzz mustache, his only link to finding Mendenhall, was her nephew.

Fuck.

The news wasn't going to stop him from locating Andy or finding out what he knew, but now he'd have to rethink his approach. He'd never planned to hurt the kid but would have done whatever it took short of that to get the information he needed. Now he had to be careful. He didn't want to hurt Natalie.

Swearing under his breath, he walked back into the bar, left his phone number, and told the bartender to contact him if Andy showed up again. Then he jumped on his bike and headed to Mendenhall's house, just in case the bastard had returned.

Nope.

Natalie's nephew, he thought again as he pulled on his helmet. Jesus.

# Chapter Eleven

Frustration rode Greer hard for the rest of the day. He circled back to Mendenhall's several times, checked in at the bar, and got a fat load of nothing. He was out of places to check, leads to follow. Dead end after dead end after dead fucking end. It was infuriating.

The argument with Natalie played over and over again in his mind. He couldn't blame her for wanting to protect her nephew, but the kid had done something wrong. Andy and his friends had meant to kill him. The only reason they hadn't was because Andy lost his nerve and Greer had gotten a hold of that knife.

Shit. The knife. He'd forgotten about that. He'd definitely stabbed one of his attackers. He needed to check hospitals — which he couldn't do without asking his brothers for help. Hospitals didn't freely give out information about patients, so he'd need to hack into the patient records. Which he couldn't do. He was hopelessly incapable with a computer. Always had been, but now he was wishing he'd spent more time listening when Reece and Vaughn spoke computer geek to each other.

He could really use their help now.

No. Dammit, he didn't want them involved in this. There had to be another way to find the guy—or kid? Christ, he hoped not—that he'd stabbed.

As darkness approached, he finally conceded he wasn't going to find Andy or Mendenhall today, but he didn't want to go home. Natalie would be there, and he had no clue what to say to her. He supposed he could stay in a hotel, but that idea reeked of cowardice to him. He had to talk to Natalie sometime. They both wanted the same thing—to find her nephew—so they should work together. It only made sense to help each other out. So he'd pony up, go home, and face her.

Soon. Ish.

He drove aimlessly, just taking the time to enjoy the roar of his bike, the feel of all that power underneath him, all the freedom it offered. How tempting it was to point the bike west and just go until he hit the opposite coast. Just lose himself in the countryside and forget about…well, everything.

He scoffed at the thought. Nothing but fantasy. A wild, thrilling fantasy. But he could never take off like that. Bruce would hunt him down. So would his brothers. He had too many responsibilities, too much weight resting solely on his shoulders. For him, there was no escape from that crushing weight in this life.

No, his only escape would be in death.

He suddenly couldn't breathe. Hyperventilating inside his helmet, he pulled off the road into a parking lot and yanked the thing off his head. He set it on the bike in front of him and leaned over it. Told himself to breathe. Just block everything else out and breathe. Cool April air filled his lungs. He welcomed the wintry bite of it and gulped it in like a man trapped underwater for too long. It took agonizing minutes, but finally his lungs expanded and his head stopped spinning. His pounding heart slowed to a more reasonable rhythm. At least it was no longer threatening to burst from his chest.

Panic attack. Goddamn things were happening more and more frequently.

He sucked in several more breaths before slowly straightening and glancing around to get his bearings again. He was in the parking lot of a large brick building, a turn-of-the-century firehouse that had been converted to retail spaces after World War II. He knew this building. The top floor used to be the dance studio his mother taught at. He and his brothers had spent a good portion of their childhoods here, taking classes or just hanging out while Mom taught. His subconscious must have brought him here, seeking...

What? Comfort?

There were a lot of good memories here. And not-so-good. At fifteen, he'd thought ballet was stupid and uncool for a boy. Shortly before her death, he'd fought with Mom over going to class. He'd been nasty to her in the way only a disgruntled teenager could be and regretted the things he'd said to this day.

He'd never had the chance to apologize.

Was this place still a dance studio? He turned off the bike's rumbling engine and looped his helmet over the handle bar. He climbed off and walked around to the front of the building. The stores on the lower floor had changed. One was a coffee shop and bakery, the other a Thai restaurant, both doing brisk business for dinner. He gazed up. The huge windows upstairs spilled yellow light to the sidewalk below. The plain white sign underneath them read simply DANCE ACADEMY in cursive lettering, just as he remembered.

So it was still here.

He pulled open the glass door and walked up the staircase that seemed much narrower than he remembered. The old wood steps, worn nearly white by decades of little dancers and their parents, creaked under each footfall. He used to race Reece up and down these stairs when they were boys. Now they wouldn't fit shoulder-to-shoulder in here.

At the top of the stairs, a harried mother corralled her daughter into a bright blue coat. It wasn't until they started down and the mother spared him a curious glance that it registered he had no reason to be here. He stood to the side and let them pass, and waited until they were out the door. Then he just stood there, halfway up the steps.

He should leave.

He glanced to the top, saw no other kids or parents. A class didn't appear to be in session, though pop music floated down from the studio. He continued up, drawn by the solemn notes of a love song. It wouldn't hurt to have a peek into the studio, take a moment to reminisce. His mother's spirit was all around here. She infused the air, the wood, even the music, and he felt closer to her than he had since before she'd died.

The room at the top of the stairs had changed from his memory. It used to be small and narrow, with a row of lockers at one end and a few uncomfortable plastic chairs along one wall. The other wall had been a window looking into the studio. The room was bigger, the dented lockers now tidy cubbies, and the plastic chairs replaced with cushy leather. Framed photos and magazine covers decorated the walls, and he wasn't prepared for the gut punch of seeing his mother smiling out from many of them. There she was on one of the magazine covers, mid-leap, head thrown back, lost in the music. The headline read: *Meredith LaGrange: From Prodigy to Artist, Teacher to Mother.*

"She's so pretty."

Greer started. He'd been so absorbed in memory he hadn't noticed the little girl sitting in one of the chairs. She scooted out of her seat and joined him.

He gazed down at the top of her neat little bun. "Who?"

"Meredith LaGrange. She used to teach here but..." A

small frown tugged at her mouth. "She died."

"How do you know that?" The girl was far too young to have known his mother.

"Miss Natalie told us about her."

Something like nerves fluttered in his belly. "Natalie Taggart teaches here?"

The girl pointed at the window. He turned slowly, stared through the glass at the woman dancing across the studio like she was floating in water, each movement precise and yet effortless. She wasn't Natalie anymore, but an extension of the music. Watching her, a quietness settled over him and his mind stilled for the first time ever. In that moment, he wanted to watch her dance for the rest of his life—if for no other reason than she brought him peace.

"Miss Natalie is pretty, too." The girl sighed and gazed up with earnest brown eyes. Her lower lip poked out in a pout that hit him square in the gut. "I'll never be as good as she is."

Attention fully on the girl now, he faced her. "Why do you say that?"

"I'm black. Black girls don't dance ballet."

"Well, that's the stupidest thing I've ever heard. The color of your skin has nothing to do with how well you dance. Who told you that?"

Her shoulders hunched up around her ears. "My mom. My dad's white, but she said it doesn't matter."

Some mother. A parent should never undermine their child's self-esteem like that. If his mom were still alive, she'd make damn sure this girl never once felt inferior for any reason. "Nah, she doesn't know what she's talking about. You're here taking classes, aren't you? I bet you're just as good, if not better, than Miss Natalie." She didn't look convinced, so he crouched down to her level. "What's your name?"

"Annalise."

"Okay, Annalise. Can you plié?"

"Yeah…" Her expression was full of *duh*. "Do you even know what that is?"

"I used to dance, too."

Her eyes bugged. "You?"

He motioned to the magazine cover on the wall. "That's my mom."

He didn't think it was possible, but her eyes got even rounder. "Meredith LaGrange is your mom?"

"And she insisted her children had to know how to dance. It's been a while, but…" He called up an image of his mom drilling the moves into him and his brothers, pressed his heels together, bent his knees halfway, then wobbled straight again. It wasn't pretty, and he couldn't decide whether Mom would be impressed that he remembered after all these years or rolling her eyes at his poor execution.

Annalise giggled but muffled it behind her hand.

"C'mon, kid, it wasn't that bad."

She snorted. "It wasn't good."

Kid had sass, that was for sure. In some ways, she reminded him of a younger version of Reece's colorful wife, Shelby. He liked her. "Okay. Show me how it's done."

She hesitated a moment, then dropped her bag and pliéd perfectly.

He inclined his head, graciously accepting his defeat. "Yeah, that looked good. What else you got?"

Flashing a toothy grin, she went up on her toes and kicked out a leg in a move he didn't have a name for. Hell, it had been a stretch to recall the simple plié. Annalise did a few leaps, landed softly, and took a bow.

Showing off, he thought. Good.

And because he liked her and wanted to hear her laugh again, he copied her. Mom was probably looking down and shaking her head in abject horror at his form, but it was worth it to hear Annalise's giggles. He hadn't allowed himself to let

go, to be goofy, since he was a teenager, and it was…freeing.
When Annalise collapsed into a fit of giggles, he laughed, too.
A real laugh, from deep in his belly. The first in a very, very
long time.

• • •

Laughter rose up over the music, and Natalie stopped
dancing to watch Annalise bound gracefully across the floor
at the other side of the studio. The girl was a natural—no
surprise since Larissa, her grandmother, was practically dance
royalty—but it took more than natural talent to make it in
ballet. It took drive, dedication, and a deep yearning to dance.
Annalise had it all. Within the next couple years, she'd be
ready to compete at the Youth America Grand Prix, where
ballet companies pick up much of their young talent. She'd
go far as long as she didn't let her good-for-nothing mother
talk her out of it. Unfortunately, she'd already heard the girl
repeating her mother's mantra of "black girls don't dance
ballet." Which was bullshit.

A man followed behind Annalise, clumsily copying her
movements and sending the girl into fits of laughter. His laugh
boomed in the high-ceiling room. This must be Annalise's dad,
Larissa's son. She'd heard a lot about him, but he traveled for
work and she'd only ever seen pictures of him.

Smiling, Natalie wiped sweat from her eyes and scooped
up her water bottle as she crossed to them. "You look like you
could use some lessons…" He turned, and her mouth went
dry despite the sip of water she'd just taken. "Greer?"

He was the absolute last person she'd expected to find
here. And goofing around, no less. This was the first time
she'd even seen him smile—really smile like he meant it. It
softened his features, crinkled his eyes, and carved dimples
in his cheeks. He looked younger, and so much more like

his brothers. It was like peering into an alternate reality and getting a quick glimpse of the man he would've been had his circumstances been different. A glimpse at the kind of father he'd have been.

And, dammit, the wall she'd spent the afternoon constructing around her heart began to crumble. She crossed her arms over her chest as if that would keep the pieces in place. "What are you doing here?"

That beautiful smile started to fade, replaced by wariness. "Honestly, I don't know."

She opened her mouth, intending to tell him to leave, because she didn't want to soften toward him. She didn't want to care about him or his mission. She didn't want to worry because the shadows in his eyes seemed to have deepened since she last saw him. She didn't want to care, period. He was out to hurt her nephew, so he'd made himself an enemy.

Except she couldn't send him packing. As much as she didn't want to, she did care.

Larissa hurried in, saving her from having to say anything. Maybe she wouldn't have been callous enough to tell him to go away when he looked so lost, so in need of a friend, but she was glad for the interruption. Now she'd never have to find out.

"I'm so sorry I'm late, baby." Larissa bent over to kiss her granddaughter's head. "Thanks for staying with her, Tally. There was an accident on the freeway, and they were detouring everyone off at one of the exits. Traffic is a nightmare right now." She straightened and finally noticed Greer. Her smile of greeting faltered, and she slapped a hand over her mouth. Her eyes widened behind her square-frame glasses. "Oh my God. You're one of Meredith's sons. You're her oldest? Greer, right?"

"Yeah." Greer looked as if he'd rather gouge out an eye than have this conversation.

"Look at you! All grown up and as big as your daddy was." Larissa enveloped him in a hug. Next to him, she was as thin and petite as a sapling branch, but Natalie knew from experience the woman was stronger than she looked. Decades of ballet had honed her muscles, and she was in better shape than a lot of twenty-year-olds.

Greer didn't move.

"Oh." Larissa stepped back and offered a watery smile. She wiped at her damp eyes with shaking hands. "I'm sorry. You probably don't remember me. I'm Larissa Schaffer. Your mother and I opened this studio together. She taught while I was touring and vice versa. Last time I saw you, you were… oh, barely a teenager, I'd imagine. All gangly, hadn't grown into your feet yet. And look at you now. You're the spitting image of your daddy."

Finally, Greer showed a flicker of emotion. "You knew my parents?"

"Well, of course. Meredith was one of my very best friends, but I didn't see much of her in those last few years before she died. Life got in the way. We'd known each other since we were little more than kids. I was a bridesmaid in her wedding. At the time, I wasn't happy about it. I thought she was throwing away her career. But, oh, she loved your father. Then you boys came along…" She smiled, but it was tinged with sadness. "I still remember going to the hospital right after you were born. I'd never seen her happier. She was so proud of you."

"I know," Greer said, voice tight.

Good. This was good. Larissa just had to keep talking and remind him of the kind of people his parents were. Good people, who wouldn't have condoned his revenge scheme.

"When we lost her…" Larissa shook her head. "It tore out a piece of my soul. I can't imagine how hard it was for you boys to cope."

"We managed."

"I sent money to you, donated food and clothes, whatever I could manage. I hate that the person responsible was never caught."

"He will be," Greer said, implacable as stone again, all hint of emotion gone.

Larissa blinked and took another step back. "What?" She glanced over at Natalie, then to him again. "Are they reopening the case?"

"It was never closed. It just went cold."

"So they're investigating again? Is there new information?"

Greer gave one of his noncommittal grunts. This conversation was devolving fast, but luckily Annalise spoke up before it had a chance to continue.

The girl tugged on her grandmother's hand. "I'm hungry."

"Okay, baby. Go get your coat and we'll stop somewhere for dinner." She gave Annalise a gentle pat on the back and waited until the girl was gone before returning her attention to Greer. "Please keep me updated? If there are any breaks in the case, I'd love to know."

Another grunt from Greer. Neither a yes nor a no, but Larissa must have taken it as agreement, because she nodded and followed her granddaughter out. Their footfalls creaked on the old staircase. Annalise chattered happily until the door cut her off.

Silence fell. Despite the large size of the studio, it was suddenly too tight, too close, Greer's big body taking up too much space. Natalie put distance between them on the pretense of gathering her purse and change of clothes from the little office where she'd locked them before class started.

What was she going to do about him? She couldn't stay away, but she genuinely feared for her nephew's safety if Greer got to him first. So she'd just have to convince him working together was the best option for both of their causes.

Yes, that's what she'd do. Then she'd be there when he found Andy and could play referee.

When she returned to the studio, Greer hadn't moved. He stared at the door. "That little girl. Annalise. Make sure she doesn't give up."

She stopped short. Out of all the things she'd expected him to say, that was nowhere on the list. "What makes you think she will?"

"She said her mother doesn't believe she should be dancing. That 'black girls don't dance ballet.' Tell her that's bullshit and if she loves it and wants it, she can ballet as well as any white girl. Tell her to dream big, and never let anyone—not her mother or anyone else—tell her she can't." He shifted his gaze to the wall of photos. "It's what Mom would have said to her."

Holy shit. Had Larissa's stories about his parents gotten through to him? The Greer she'd known a few days ago wouldn't have cared about a little girl's hopes and dreams. He'd been too focused on revenge. Was he changing his mind?

She cleared her throat, made sure her voice was light. "Yes, her mother's a piece of work. Her father travels too much for his job, so Larissa has custody. Kind of like—" She cut herself off and mentally kicked her own butt.

"Like?" he prompted.

She'd been so careful not to mention her nephew. Now what did she say? If she deflected the conversation, he'd know something was up. Better to keep it casual. "Uh, like Andy. His mom walked out and left him with my brother, who isn't what you'd call a…stable person. My parents have full custody of him."

He faced her. "I'm not going to harm the kid."

"I can't know that for sure."

"Don't trust me?" If he was hurt by her doubt, he didn't

show it. Not that she expected him to. Nope, he was back to his old unreadable self. Amazing this was the same man who had played with Annalise minutes ago.

She lifted one shoulder in a helpless shrug. "What do you expect? You told me you plan to kill someone, Greer. Whether or not he deserves it is moot. Anyone who can kill another human like you're talking about—"

"Is not a good person?" he finished, jaw tightening, a muscle jumping below his temple. He strode for the door. "Yeah, well, I already knew that about myself. Time you learned it, too."

"Greer."

He paused but didn't look back.

Dammit. She hadn't meant to call out and searched for something more to say. "You are a good man, Greer. If you weren't, you wouldn't care about Annalise. You wouldn't care about keeping me or your brothers safe. You just...need help."

He left without so much as one of his usual grunts.

Natalie let her bag fall off her shoulder. It hit the studio's wood floor with an echoing *thunk* a second before the downstairs door smacked shut. She closed her eyes and rubbed her hands over her face.

She'd told him the truth. She didn't see a bad man when she looked at him. What she saw was a man spiraling. A man who needed help. But she couldn't do a damn thing until he admitted it. A desperate man, on a desperate quest—and that was the crux of the problem. Desperation drove normally good people to do horrible things, and she didn't know how to stop him. She doubted even his brothers could talk him out of it now.

With a sigh, she scooped up her bag and hit the studio lights. On her way out, she passed the wall of photos, and stopped next to the magazine cover featuring his mother. A woman she'd never known, but hugely respected.

She touched the frame. "How do I help him, Meredith?"

Of course she didn't get an answer. Only silence. Shaking her head at herself, she locked up the studio.

Apparently she was on her own.

# Chapter Twelve

He should be dead.

*It was Greer's first coherent thought as he peeled his eyes open and saw the world had exploded around him. His ears rang. A coating of dust covered him, rattled around in his lungs, and made his tongue stick to the roof of his mouth. There was no ceiling on the building anymore—nothing but a sky heavy with dust and death. Fires from around the war-torn city licked at the undersides of dirty clouds.*

*He absolutely should be dead right now.*

*The fact he wasn't came as both a shock and a disappointment. Dead would be easier—but he wasn't, so he had to move. Just keep moving, like he always did.*

*He clambered to his hands and knees, rubble and concrete dust falling off him like a fine snow. He was bleeding. A thin, hot line leaked from a small entry wound low in his chest. He vaguely remembered taking the bullet in the millisecond before he blew the shooter's head off. He didn't think it had hit anything major, but it had definitely done some damage to his ribs. Every breath caught in his throat and sent pain singing through his chest.*

*He could lie back down. If he stayed here long enough, maybe he'd bleed out. Or die of infection. Or thirst. He was so damn thirsty.*

*But that was too close to surrender. And surrender was not a Ranger word.*

*He started a staggering crawl forward as the ruins of what had been a CIA safe house crumbled around him in large puffs of dust.*

*Had he been alone when the world exploded? His head was so muddled, he couldn't recall. But as he moved, new pain sliced through him, and with it came a bright sense of clarity. He spotted an arm, limp underneath a pile of concrete.*

*He hadn't been alone.*

*In the dim light of gathering dusk, he reached for Sergeant Dustin Williamson's hand and tried to pull the man free of the block of concrete crushing his body.*

*It was a futile effort. He knew it was, but he had to try. He never left men behind.*

*Dustin's hand was limp, slick with blood. Greer wrapped his fingers tight around his wrist and pulled with all he had in him. Something gave with a sickening ripping sound and he fell backward, holding nothing but a detached limb.*

*He stared at the tattoo inked on the arm's inside forearm. The Army Ranger Crest, a blue and green shield bisected by a red lightning bolt, a twelve-point sun in the upper left and a star in the lower right. He had the exact same design on his arm.*

*He remembered now. The mortar bomb had hit Dustin before exploding. The arm was likely all that was left of him.*

Boom!

*The building shook. Debris fell. Gunfire ripped through the street below, sounding like fireworks.*

*Greer didn't care. He sat there, staring at the arm, and all he could think was,* it should have been me.

# Chapter Thirteen

It should have been him.

Greer bolted upright from his bedroll on the floor of his apartment, sweat pouring off him. He still felt Dustin Williamson's dismembered arm in his hand. Felt the thick, dusty air rattling around in his lungs. Felt the flames licking at his skin and the agony of a bullet wound in his side. The sick-sweet stench of death surrounded him.

No. He wasn't there anymore. He was home, and he'd only had a dream. All just a dream. Another fucking one.

Greer scrambled for his phone, scrolled through the names, and nearly hit send when he found Seth Harlan in his contacts. Seth, his youngest brother's best friend, had seen some shit overseas. He'd come back from it damaged, and for months he'd been Greer's sympathetic ear on nights like tonight. Seth knew what it felt like to wake up with your heart pounding out of your chest and a cold sweat soaking your bed. He knew what it felt like when the nightmares got too fucking real.

Except now...Seth was healing. He had a good thing

going and had a good woman by his side to help him through the rough nights. Calling him, dragging him back into the darkness, seemed like an act of cruelty.

Greer set the phone down. He didn't need to call for help. He'd handled everything in his life on his own, and he could handle this. It was just a nightmare. Just. A. Nightmare.

He squeezed his eyes shut, but the image of Dustin's arm was right there, burned on the back of his eyelids. The limb had been surprisingly light, no more than ten pounds.

Shit.

He had to talk to someone, even if only to take the tremble out of his hands, and it sure as shit wasn't going to be his brothers. Or Natalie. He grabbed his phone again, scrolled past Seth's name, found another contact, and hit send.

A slurred voice answered. "Yeah?"

Greer checked the time on his phone's screen. Nearly six in the morning, so on the West Coast it was closing in on three a.m. "Did I wake you?"

"You fucking know the answer to that," Zak Hendricks grumbled.

Yeah, he did. A resounding no. Zak slept about as much as he did, and these late-night chats were getting to be all too common between them. "How's the leg?"

Zak gave a laugh tinged with bitterness. "It's still gone."

Christ, it killed Greer that he hadn't acted soon enough, had obeyed orders for too long, and because of that Zak hadn't made it home in one piece. The image of Dustin Williamson's detached arm came with such clarity it was like he was in Syria all over again, holding the limb in his hand. He shuddered. Jumped up from his bedroll and paced the length of his room.

The walls were closing in on him.

He threw open his balcony door and stepped outside into the chill spring morning. He gulped in several deep breaths until the image faded from his mind and he found his voice again.

"Is—" Was that his voice, all thin and reedy? He cleared his throat. "Is it healing okay?"

"Feels like it's still there," Zak said. "It itches, and I can't fucking scratch it."

"Is that why you're drinking?"

"No. I'm drinking because the world doesn't suck as much when I'm drunk." Bottles clanked in the background. "Are you gonna lecture me about it?"

"Will it do any good?"

"Fuck no."

"Then I won't waste the breath."

Silence stretched across the line for several beats.

"I'm assuming you didn't call in the middle of the night to ask about my leg," Zak said finally.

To be honest, he wasn't sure why he called Zak of all people. The guy was miserable, and talking to him always hurt. Maybe he was a masochist at heart, who got off on the guilt every conversation stirred up. "I was just thinking about you, man."

"You've been thinking about me a lot in the middle of the night. And I'm flattered, but…" Again, that bitter laugh. "Even if I was into guys, I'm not interested in sex anymore."

Greer froze. "At all?"

"My sex drive was located in the leg I lost. Who knew?"

He didn't know how to respond, but Zak sure as hell wouldn't be talking about it so openly if he wasn't three sheets to the wind. If Zak remembered this convo in the morning, it'd probably embarrass him. Or piss him off. Or both.

Greer let his gaze travel to the balcony next door. He remembered Natalie all soft and willing underneath him, and his body stirred. For those few moments with her, his mind had cleared, settled. He'd relaxed for the first time since…he couldn't remember. But she'd given him a precious moment of peace.

And Zak didn't even have that to help him deal with his demons.

"Uh, have you talked to your doctors about it?"

"There's no point. Even if my body is still able, I don't care. I'm…numb," Zak continued with an odd note of hollowness in his voice. "I can't bring myself to care about anything. Just flat all out of fucks to give. You should've left me over there, man. At least then I'd have died a hero and not a crippled drunk who can't even pop a boner."

Maybe he was right. Dying in Afghanistan would have been easier for him. Just like it would have been easier for Greer to take that mortar round in the chest instead of Dustin.

*It should have been me.*

"Zak." His voice came out strangled. "Do you…think about ending it?"

A pause. "All the time."

Greer swallowed hard, his throat so tight he was barely able to form words. "Yeah. Why don't you?"

Zak exhaled a soft half laugh. "Same reason you don't."

"Yeah," he said again, even though he was struggling to remember what that reason was. The more he thought about it, the more the pros outweighed the cons.

"Listen," Zak said. "I'm gonna go. I'm not nearly drunk enough to sleep yet."

The line went dead, and Greer slowly lowered the phone, setting it down on the wide concrete railing of the balcony. He flattened his hands on either side of the device and stared at it. Except he wasn't seeing a phone. In his mind's eye, he saw himself vault over the railing and free fall to the pavement below. The fall was only two stories, and it probably wouldn't kill him. But it was such a vivid image, and brought on such a rush of relief, he had to force himself to uncurl his hands from the railing before he tried it.

"Greer?"

Natalie. He closed his eyes and cursed softly. If he didn't respond, maybe she'd go away.

Ha. Right. This was Natalie, after all. As stubborn as she was beautiful.

She called his name again. He grabbed his phone and took a step back from the ledge, both physically and mentally, before facing her.

She stood just outside her balcony door, arms wrapped around herself, the light breeze rustling the fringe of her shawl around her bare legs. She was in a sleep shirt with little frogs on it, and her hair was damp, spiky from a recent shower. The berry scent of her shampoo carried across the ten feet separating their balconies and teased his senses.

"What are you doing out here?" she asked, and there was no mistaking the concern in her voice.

The stirring when he'd thought of her earlier suddenly became an all-out need. He wanted her. But more than that, he wanted to shut his mind down. He wanted the peace being with her gave him.

He drew a breath, let it out slowly. When he spoke, his voice was still hoarse with emotions he didn't want to feel. "Can I come over?"

Her brows drew together. "Of course." She backtracked to the door. "C'mon, I'll let you in—"

Greer didn't think. Or he did, but his only thought was he had to get to her now, because if he stayed by himself a second longer, he might lose his mind. He climbed up on the railing and heard her sharp intake of breath as he jumped across the space between their balconies. Being in the air, it was freeing, much like he imagined it would be, and he suddenly very much wished he'd jumped down instead of across.

He landed hard, jarring his battered body, and the pain

shocked some sense into his head. He was spiraling down a very dark hole, but he had a mission to complete before he reached the bottom. He couldn't forget that.

"Oh my God!" She rushed to his side, her berry scent enveloping him as she knelt to help him up. "Greer! Have you lost your mind?"

Yes. Yes, he was very much afraid he had.

He needed something—someone—to ground him. To remind him why he was alive, or else he might forget. And if he forgot, he would take a flying leap off the balcony just to make all the noise in his head stop.

He grabbed her, pulled her to him, and sucked her lower lip into his mouth. She drew in a quick breath, and he swept his tongue into her sweet mouth. For a split-second, she melted against him, but then she flattened her palms on his chest and pushed.

"Greer. Wait. Stop. Talk to me."

Groaning, he lifted his head and stared down into her worried eyes. "Please. Talk later. Right now…" His voice rasped against the emotion lodged in his throat. "I need this."

Her gaze dropped to his lips. "What do you need?"

"You." He backed her against the side of the building and lifted her until her legs wrapped around his waist. Pain sizzled through his side, but it only added to his need for her. He'd lived with pain for so long, and the reminder of it increased the pleasure he knew he'd find in her soft, sweet body.

"Let me in, Natalie." He traced his lips down her neck, pulled her nightshirt off her shoulder, and flicked his tongue across the tendon. "I need to be inside you."

"Oh, yes." She arched back and rubbed her sex against his straining erection. "Let's go inside. I have condoms."

He fumbled for the slider and walked inside with her still wrapped around him. "Where?"

She squirmed. "Let me."

Setting her down, losing the little bit of intimate connection they had, was torture. She disappeared into another room and came back with a string of condoms. He took it from her, unwrapped the first in the line, shoved down his boxers, and rolled it on.

Still holding his cock in one hand, he gazed up at her. "Undress."

She shivered visibly and peeled her nightshirt off over her head. She wasn't wearing a bra, and her small breasts stood at rosy peaks. She was wearing panties—a little lacy scrap of nothing that showed the bare folds of her sex.

He caught his breath, tightened his hand around his cock. "Touch yourself."

A flush filled her chest with color, but she dropped her hand to her stomach, slid it slowly down past her navel, and under the edge of her panties. He watched her fingers dip in and her head dropped back.

"Are you wet?"

"Oh, yes."

His control snapped. He crossed to her in two strides, picked her up, pushed aside the scrap of fabric between them, and slammed her down on his cock.

"Greer!" She threw her head back, and her body clenched around his like a fist, milking him with each roll of her hips.

It wasn't enough. He needed more. Deeper. Harder. Still pumping into her, he walked over to the couch and laid her across the back. The height was perfect. He looped her legs over his shoulders, and drove into her with the desperation of a starving man at a feast. Her breasts bounced with each thrust, and the skin on her chest and neck flushed bright pink. The little gasps and moans she made incited something raw and possessive in him. He needed this woman in his bed, in his life.

Desperately. Always.

Natalie clawed at the side of the couch, leaving finger marks on the plush microfiber. Her eyes closed and her body tightened, and she lost herself in orgasm.

It was a beautiful thing to watch, he decided. The color seeping into her cheeks, her mouth parting in a gasp that morphed into a low moan sounding a lot like his name.

Oh, how he loved when she said his name like this.

He scooped her up again and moved around the edge of the couch to sit down. She straddled him, her eyes unfocused, her hands on his shoulders, keeping her steady. Her eyes cleared, and she finally realized he'd switched their position. She gasped and trembled as he rolled his hips and filled her all the way. "Oh, God."

"Take control." He urged her to move with his hands on her ass. She quaked all over. It gave him a savage satisfaction to have pleasured her already, because they weren't even close to done yet. "Ride me, Natalie."

• • •

By the third time, they ended up in her bed, and he continued to blow her mind with orgasm after orgasm after orgasm. Didn't take her psychology degree to realize he was deflecting, using sex to put off talking about whatever had him out on his balcony this morning looking pale as death. And, well, she wasn't going to complain about his distraction techniques when he'd given her the most satisfying sexual experience of her life. She figured he'd eventually run out of steam, and then they could talk. But until he did, she'd enjoy the ride.

It was early afternoon before Greer finally collapsed. She'd lost count of the number of times and ways they'd made love, but she was pretty sure she'd be in pain while teaching her next dance class.

So worth it.

She smoothed a hand down Greer's chest. He had to be hurting, too. His injuries were just barely starting to heal, and he'd performed the kind of sexy acrobatic feats found only in the Kama Sutra. "Are you okay?"

He grunted. Typical Greer.

"Will you talk to me now?"

Another grunt.

She propped herself up on her elbow and scowled down at him. "Either you talk to me, or you don't get to touch me again."

His hand tightened possessively, almost painfully on her hip for a second. Pushing out a long breath, he released her and opened his eyes. "What do you want to talk about?"

Oh, where to start?

"Let me help you find Andy. He'll be more receptive if I'm there. He'll talk if I'm asking the questions."

He closed his eyes again. "He'll talk either way."

*That's what I'm afraid of.* She hid her wince against his shoulder. "You said you wouldn't hurt him."

He was silent for a moment. "There are plenty of ways to make a guy talk without resorting to pain. I need to find Mendenhall, and Andy's my only link."

God, he had a one-track mind. Which made for a great lover, but the focus he had on revenge was terrifying. "What makes you so sure this Mendenhall guy killed your parents? What proof do you have?"

He said nothing for a handful of heartbeats. "My mom kept journals. She was always writing everything down. Last fall, I found one of them while looking for a family heirloom necklace to give my sister-in-law Libby for her and Jude's wedding. Mom mentioned Mendenhall in her last few entries. He was practically stalking her in the days before she was murdered."

"That's not proof."

"It's good enough."

"No, it's not."

"It is for me. I know in my gut it was him. The police never looked his way. They never knew to."

"So take what you know to the police. Ask them to investigate. Do it the right way. The legal way."

He grunted.

She propped herself up on her elbow again and studied his carefully blank expression. She knew a mask when she saw one. She also knew under that mask was a whole lot of fury, and she couldn't remember a damn thing from her psych classes about how to help someone through that kind of anger. "Is there another reason you're so intent on killing this man instead of going to the police?"

Greer looked away and her heart surged upward, blocking her throat. She gripped his face in her hands and made him look at her. "Why?"

Jaw set in stone, he held her gaze. "The legal way will take too long, and I can't die without knowing he's been punished for hurting my family."

"What do you mean you can't—" *Die.* The word sunk in, and she sat upright, stared down at him in disbelief. Had he recently received a terminal diagnosis? Was that why he'd disappeared on his brothers? And why he was taking reckless chances like the balcony jump? She pressed a hand to her chest to keep her heart from leaping out. "Are you sick?"

But, no, that didn't make sense. Save for his injuries, he appeared completely healthy. He was strong and fit.

He rolled away from her and sat up on the edge of her bed. Sunlight pooled around him, warm and bright from a beautiful spring afternoon. He seemed not to notice. "I'm not sick."

"Then why—" A possibility worse than terminal illness slithered through her mind, leaving a chill in its wake. She caught her breath. "Are you saying you *want* to die?"

He breathed raggedly and stared hard at his hands fisted on his knees. "I…can't live. Not with…everything I've done."

"Everything you've done?"

"Natalie—" His voice cracked. "I'm basically a loaded gun. The government aims me and—" He stopped.

"And you fire," she finished softly.

He closed his eyes. Nodded. "For years, I told myself I was working for the Greater Good. That I wasn't a bad man because I took out other men who were way worse. But what happened in Syria—" He stopped again, cleared his throat. "I don't know if I'm working for the Greater Good anymore."

She sat up and wrapped her arms around him from behind. She kissed his shoulder. "What happened in Syria?"

"Carnage," he whispered. "We did the job we were there to do, but someone sold us out while we were waiting for extraction and a good man died. I tried to save him. All I found was his arm. I held it in my hands…" He opened his hands. Stared at them like he'd never seen them before. Slowly closed his fingers into fists. "I don't want to live with that image in my head for the rest of my life. That, and so many others like it. Do you know what it's like to meet someone new and already know what they'll look like dead?"

Goose bumps prickled across her skin. "No. No, I don't." She'd never even been close to a dead body before—her grandparents were still alive and her family had never experienced any tragic deaths. She held him tighter. "And I have no doubt it's a horrible thing to live with, but killing yourself is not the answer."

He shoved to his feet, leaving her arms cold. He paced, all of his hard muscles flexing in the sunlight with each restless step. "My mind's made up, and you're not changing it. I didn't tell you so you could shrink-wrap me."

She pulled the blanket up and tucked it around her body.

Although he seemed not to notice his own nudity, she'd rather not have this conversation with her breasts hanging out. "I'm not a shrink."

"You have the degree, don't you?" he snapped.

Patience, she reminded herself. She drew a breath to dispel her rising temper. Normally, she didn't have a problem keeping herself calm, but Greer had a knack for getting under her skin like nobody else. "I do, but I'm not talking as a psychologist. I'm talking as a friend. As your lover." She paused and drew another breath because now nerves danced in her belly. "And as someone who has been where you are."

He stopped pacing and turned slowly toward her, his face shrouded in shadow. "What?"

She wrapped her arms around her middle, hunched her shoulders. Rehashing this part of her past always brought back ugly memories. Sometimes the darkness still snuck up in her weaker moments. Part of her feared talking about it aloud was like flinging open her internal doors and inviting the demons back.

Stupid, she knew. Talking about it was a big reason she'd been able to heal and move on.

And still. It never got easier.

She drew a breath, let it out slowly, and lifted her gaze to his. "When I found out my dance career was over, I took an entire bottle of Oxy. I thought if I couldn't dance, there was no point to living. I was wrong, and lucky enough to have a friend find me before it was too late. That's why I majored in psychology. That's why I volunteer at the suicide hotline. I lived and saw firsthand how my actions affected the people closest to me. Suicide doesn't take away your pain. It just transfers it to your loved ones. You don't want to do that to your brothers, Greer."

He shook his head. The stubborn man. "They're better off—"

"Without you?" Textbook suicidal thinking. Her stomach twisted. "Have you asked them about that? Because I bet they'll tell you just how fucking wrong you are."

He was still shaking his head, so she added, "What about me? Will I be better off without you?"

"Yes," he said without a shred of doubt in his voice. "Look at all the trouble I've brought to your doorstep. You can't tell me you were better off when you didn't know me."

"You're wrong," she said softly. She was surprised at just how wrong. "I care about you, Greer. More than I probably should, but the feelings are there and real. I want to help you—not only because of Andy, but because I can see how much you need to find the man responsible."

He said nothing and didn't move for a long time. "You're not going to stop me from doing what needs to be done."

*We'll see about that.*

She held out her arms. After a beat, he came to her, wrapping his arms around her middle and resting his head on her chest. She kissed the top of his head and cradled him, needing the contact as much as she suspected he did.

They lay there together in silence as the sun streamed through her lace curtains, casting pretty patterns of light and shadow on the floor. His breathing evened out, and his body relaxed. Good. He needed all the sleep he could get. She suspected while left to his own devices, he wasn't getting enough.

She stroked a hand up and down his back, enjoying the feel of him in her arms. She couldn't let him kill anyone. It would do him nothing but harm, shove him over the edge he was already teetering on. She had to stop him.

Even if it meant breaking this fragile bond forming between them.

She buried her face in his hair and squeezed her eyes shut against the burn of tears. God, losing him was going to break her heart, but having him hate her was better than him ending up in prison. Or worse.

But how did she stop him?

Whatever she did, it would have to be soon. And she'd have to fit it in around her work schedule…

She froze.

Work. Duh. She had thousands of listeners every night. There had to be a way to use her audience to her advantage. If enough people tuned in…

Yes. She could stop him, or at least make him think twice before he acted, without going to the police.

A plan began to form.

# Chapter Fourteen

Greer was alone in the bed when he woke late in the evening, and the surge of disappointment at finding Natalie gone took him by surprise. He'd slept all day, and so deeply that he hadn't noticed her leaving, which was also a shock. Lately, sleep was hard to come by for him—except, it seemed, when he was with her. Why was that? Why did she calm the storm inside him? What was it about her that brought him peace?

Something to think about. But not before coffee.

In the kitchen, he found the maker ready to brew and a note from Natalie saying she'd gone to work and she'd be on air at 7:30 p.m. if he wanted to tune in. He checked the time. It was already 7:45. He hit the button on the coffeemaker to start the pot, then spotted the radio on her counter and switched it on. It was already tuned to her station, and he smiled a little as she soothingly talked a caller through divorce woes.

At the sound of Natalie's voice, Jet trotted into the kitchen, plopped down beside him, and pressed up against his leg. Smiling again, he rubbed the dog's head. Jet's tongue lolled out and his eyes all but rolled back in his big head. He was the picture of doggie bliss, and it reminded him of…

Rocky.

Oh, he'd forgotten about his childhood pet. He'd had a dog just like Jet when he was little—really little, like preschool age. Reece had been a toddler and the twins weren't born yet. Rocky had been an old dog, as gentle and patient as they came. He remembered using Rocky's big furry body as a pillow while he lay on the floor and watched cartoons.

And then one day, Rocky disappeared. Dad said he had gone away to live on a farm and wasn't coming back. Looking back now as an adult, he knew the dog had died and his parents had been too heartbroken to tell him the truth. They'd never gotten another dog.

Greer dropped to his knees in front of Jet. He didn't know why and would have felt ridiculous if anyone had been around to witness it. But it was just him and the dog, all alone. With Natalie gone, the peace she'd offered was dissipating. He remembered how much comfort Rocky had given him and needed the contact with another living thing…so he hugged the furry beast.

Jet's tail thunked against the tile floor, and he furiously tried to lick the side of Greer's face.

Laughing, Greer shoved his big head aside. But the hug worked—he felt light again. Whatever magic Natalie possessed obviously extended to her doofus of a dog.

The coffeemaker beeped, and he gave Jet's head one final rub before standing to pour himself a healthy dose of caffeine.

Maybe he should get a dog like Jet and Rocky. Then when this thing with Natalie came to its inevitable conclusion, he'd still have a companion to get him through the cold, lonely nights—

Wait. No. He set the pot down hard and coffee sloshed out onto the counter. What the fuck was he thinking? A dog? He didn't plan on living long enough to take care of a dog.

Natalie was getting inside his head, despite all the blocks he'd thrown up to keep her out. He wasn't going to rethink his plan. He'd accomplish his mission and then check out. Game over. He was done with this clusterfuck of a life.

He reached to turn the radio off because the last thing he needed was her disembodied voice weaseling its way into his subconscious. She already took up too much room there.

The commercial break ended, and Natalie's voice flowed from the radio: "It's time for *What Would You Do?* our weekly call-in segment where I pose a hypothetical question to you, our listeners. Tonight's question poses an interesting moral dilemma."

He wasn't sure what made him pause, but suddenly alarms were clanging in his head, loud as church bells on Sunday morning. Instead of turning the radio off, he increased the volume.

She was up to something. He didn't know what but knew better than to ignore his internal alarm system.

"What would you do," she continued, "if someone you know—maybe even someone you love—tells you they plan to kill another person? Do you contact the proper authorities and possibly get them arrested? Do you try to talk them out of it? Do you laugh it off and hope they're bluffing? Do you offer to help? What would you do? We'll find out after the commercial break."

Greer stood there for a moment, frozen, staring at the little radio until a seething heat rose up inside him, hotter even than the fever that had tried to kill him. He swung out an arm, knocking the radio off the counter and startling Jet, who let out a sharp bark and scampered away. He paid no attention to the dog and took three steps toward the door before he caught himself. The radio station was a twenty-minute drive. By the time he got there, she'd have moved on to something else. He backtracked to the bedroom and grabbed his cell phone from where it had been charging on the nightstand. She'd left the number for the station on a Post-it for him, and bitterness coated his tongue as he jabbed it out.

Betrayal. That was the taste in his mouth. She'd fucking betrayed him.

He gave his father's name to the man who answered the phone and was placed on hold. He waited, staring hard at the radio on the floor as she came back on air and debated with other callers about when murder was justified.

Finally, she said, "Next up we have David. Hi, David, you're on *Talk to Tally*. What would you do if someone you knew told you they wanted to commit a murder?"

"I'd mind my own business."

. . .

Natalie froze, her mind going blank and the radio going silent for several long seconds. Here it was. She'd had butterflies zipping through her belly all night, waiting for this moment, wondering if he'd even be listening or not, terrified of how he'd react.

And, shit, now that it was here, she wished nothing more than to rewind the last few minutes and take it all back.

She realized there was nothing but dead air and switched on a commercial break. She grabbed the handset for the phone. "Greer, it's just a talking point."

"My life," he said slowly, "is not just a talking point."

Oh, God. This was a mistake. A stupid, desperate mistake. "This is what I do. I take things I experience or hear or see or read and talk about them. Have you ever tried talking for four hours straight? You run out of things to say! And this... it's been weighing on me. I don't know what to do about you and this suicide mission you're on and—"

The dial tone filled her ear, and she slammed the receiver

down, then picked it up and slammed it down again just because it felt good. He hadn't even given her a chance to explain. And now the jerk was probably going to do something stupid, and she couldn't leave the studio until the morning show DJs arrived.

Someone needed to go to him. And if it couldn't be her—

She launched off her stool and grabbed her bag from its usual hook on the wall, dumping the contents out on a table. She had it in here somewhere…

There.

She picked up Reece Wilde's card and her cell phone, then stepped out of the sound booth to make the call.

It was way past time the rest of the Wildes found out what their brother was up to.

Despite the late hour, Reece answered on the first ring and he sounded wide awake. "Goddammit, Vaughn, I told you—"

"Uh," Natalie said in surprise. "Not Vaughn."

There was a pause. Some shuffling. She imagined him pulling the phone away from his ear and checking the number on screen.

"Shit," he said after another second. "Natalie. Sorry, I thought you were my brother calling again."

"It's okay." She hesitated, not sure how she should go about dropping her bombshell news. Finally, she decided to just spit it out. Like ripping off a bandage, fast was always better. "Greer's been staying at my place for the last few days."

Reece said nothing for a moment. Then he sighed. "Yeah, I know. Vaughn told me you admitted to having contact with him, so I figured that's where he was. Why hasn't he called us?"

She swallowed. Now to drop the other bombshell. "He's… planning something. He didn't want you guys to know."

"What is it?"

"It's bad. He says he's going to kill someone. He's after the person who murdered your parents."

Silence. Then, softly, "Jesus Christ."

She couldn't help the sudden rush of tears flooding her eyes, clogging up her throat. "I don't know what to do, Reece. I thought I could talk some sense into him, but he won't listen to me. I don't know how to stop him."

"Where is he now?" Reece asked. She heard him moving around, probably getting dressed. A woman's voice said something indecipherable in the background, and he answered her away from the receiver before coming back. "Is he still at your place?"

"If he is, he won't be there for long. I pissed him off." *On purpose*, she added silently. She'd done it with the full knowledge that this…thing sizzling between them probably wouldn't survive her actions tonight, but if she managed to save him from himself, it would be worth it. "He's probably going to try to disappear, but you can't let him. If he does, we'll never see him again."

"You care about him," Reece said softly. A statement, not a question.

She wanted to cry, so she laughed instead. "He doesn't want to let me in."

"Yeah." He sighed. "We Wilde men have a bad habit of doing that. Don't give up on him."

"I'm not planning on it, and neither should you. He needs his brothers right now, Reece. More than he needs me."

"Not so sure about that." In the background, a car door opened, then shut. "I have to call the twins and Jude. Stay in touch, okay?"

# Chapter Fifteen

It had to be tonight.

Natalie's little stunt had blown up any chance he had of doing this covertly. He had to find Mendenhall tonight and end it.

If only the bastard would show his face.

He staked out the bar, waiting, praying Mendenhall would put in an appearance. Right before closing, just as he was about to give up hope, a shadow darted around the corner and slipped in the side entrance. Greer sat up and watched the mouth of the alley. The figure reappeared moments later, carrying a brown paper bag. He stayed close to the shadows but crossed under a street lamp while scampering across the road like the rodent he was. Yellow light reflected off his sweat-slick bald dome of a head.

*Gotcha.*

Greer followed, keeping a distance for fear of his bike's throaty growl drawing attention. Mendenhall was headed away from his flophouse, toward a decent neighborhood full of white picket fences and minivans. It was the kind of place that had a neighborhood watch and HOA, but the house he scurried to was a rundown piece of shit. Rich Mendenhall and this house were probably the community pariahs—the guy parents warned their kids away from and the house kids dared each other to walk up to.

Greer waited a beat after the front door closed behind Mendenhall. A neighborhood like this had too many watchful eyes, too many nosy, well-meaning neighbors to point in his direction once a body turned up. But fuck it. Why did he care about stealth now? No point since Natalie had aired his dirty laundry to the whole goddamn city on the radio.

Betrayal was a bitter coating on his tongue. He shouldn't have trusted her. Shouldn't have told her his plans. If he'd been in his right mind that first night, he wouldn't have, but the fever had gotten the better of him.

He strode up to the house and didn't bother with knocking. One strong kick had the rickety door flying open. Mendenhall was in the process of guzzling down his new bottle of vodka and choked on it when he saw Greer storming toward him.

"We have a score to settle, Rich."

Mendenhall held up shaking hands and stumbled backward. Greer grabbed him by the neck and shoved him up against the wall. "Thought you got away with it, didn't you?" He drew his gun, pressed it to Mendenhall's forehead. "Betcha never thought one of the kids you orphaned would come after you."

Mendenhall whimpered. "I-I didn't…"

"You didn't what? Kill my parents? That really the lie you want to go with when I have my finger on the trigger?"

"I-I loved your mother. I wouldn't hurt her. Never. I couldn't!"

"Yeah? So what happened, Rich? Huh? You decided to take Dad out and she got in the way?"

"I swear. I wasn't there. I didn't hear about what happened

until the next day." He shook his head hard and his bladder let loose, staining the air with the pungent odor of urine. "Y-you have to believe me."

"Why should I believe you? You stalked my mother, terrified her in the last days of her life."

"I-I'm not a killer."

His finger tightened on the trigger. The gun clicked. Mendenhall squeaked and jerked his head away.

"There wasn't a round chambered, but there is now. This is your one chance to clear your conscious. Why did you kill them?"

"I didn't!" Tears and snot streamed down his face. "I swear to you I didn't. I stalked your mom, yes, but David warned me away from her two nights before they died! He threatened me with a shotgun. He said he'd kill me if he ever saw my face near his house again. I knew he was telling the truth. I knew what he did for a living. I stayed away from her after that. I swear it." He whimpered and raised his hands, shielding his face as if that would protect him from a bullet. "Please. Greer. We played football in your backyard when you were little. I sneaked you candy. Please don't kill me."

Greer didn't want to believe him. He wanted to pull the trigger. Wanted this to be over. His gun hand shook, and after a vicious internal battle, he lowered it. "Shit."

The man was a coward. He didn't possess either the balls or brains to kill two people and get away with it for twenty years.

All of this had been for nothing.

"Fuck!" He thumped the wall beside Mendenhall's head with the palm of his hand. He'd been so certain Richard Mendenhall had been the guy. He'd *wanted* Rich to be the guy. He'd wanted justice. Peace.

And now he was back at square fucking one.

Mendenhall's sweat was overpowering with the stink of

alcohol, and Greer took a step back. "No, you're not a killer. But you *are* the creep who stalked and terrified my mother, so you're going to sit your ass down in that chair"—he motioned with his weapon and Mendenhall scrambled to obey—"and tell me everything you remember from those months before her death."

Snot oozed down Mendenhall's face. "You want to know who killed her?" He swiped at his nose, leaving a trail of green slime up his arm. "I'll tell ya. It was your father."

Greer raised the gun again. "Bullshit. I should shoot you for suggesting it."

Mendenhall cowered back in the seat but didn't stop talking. "Truth hurts, doesn't it? It was David. Whether or not he actually pulled the trigger, he killed her. It was the shit he was doing in the military. The stuff he knew. That's what got her killed. Lucky he didn't get you boys killed, too. It was an assassination, plain and simple. If you want to interrogate someone about that night, you go point your gun at Bruce Chambers. He knows what really happened."

Bruce Chambers.

The news didn't surprise him. In fact, it was what he'd suspected all along until that diary turned up...in a box that Bruce had conveniently found in the old storage unit he'd once shared with Dad.

Greer finally holstered his weapon. "One last question, Mendenhall. That night at the bar, did you hire those kids to jump me?"

Mendenhall's face twisted in real disgust. "If I had wanted to knock you around, I'd have done it myself, and you wouldn't have walked away."

Doubtful, but yeah, it was exactly the answer Greer had expected from him. All bluster and ego, but not a real threat. Mendenhall was innocent. To a point. And he'd almost put a bullet in his brainpan.

He needed to regroup. Get his shit together.

Greer realized his hands were shaking and grabbed the bottle of vodka on his way out the door, ignoring Mendenhall's screech of dismay.

If he hadn't been so focused on the diary, he'd have realized he was chasing a wild goose. Hiring kids to do the dirty work wasn't Mendenhall's style. Nope. That was one hundred percent Bruce Chambers's modus operandi.

Bruce fucking Chambers, the man behind the curtain. He enjoyed pulling people's strings and enjoyed it even more if those people were kids he could mold to his will.

Greer knew all about that from experience.

But why use Andy Taggart? It wasn't a random choice or coincidence. For one, Greer didn't believe in coincidence. For another, Bruce was a calculating bastard. He needed a plan. Bruce wasn't someone he could go at on a whim. Man was too smart for that, too calculating, and he'd be one step ahead the whole time. If Greer was to succeed, he needed to out-think a master strategist.

Fuck.

He couldn't confront a powerful man like Bruce until he knew all of the facts, so it all came back to finding the kid. And the quickest way to do that was through his aunt.

Natalie.

Damn, there was that bitterness again. He swallowed some vodka to rid himself of the taste, then stuffed the bottle into a saddlebag before straddling his bike.

If he had to work with Natalie, fine. He could manage. If he were honest with himself, it wouldn't be a chore. Despite everything, he wanted to see her again. He was an idiot for trusting her, for letting her get so close, for letting himself get too close. He couldn't trust her again. And still, anticipation zinged through him at the thought of seeing her.

Christ. At this point, his name had to be listed in the

dictionary as a synonym for masochist.

He needed time to think. Needed a quiet place to figure this shit out…and maybe polish off the vodka Mendenhall had so generously donated to him. He couldn't go back to his apartment. Natalie might be there. Couldn't go to the Wilde Security office, either, because the likelihood of running into one of his brothers was better than good. They all kept strange hours depending on the cases they were working, and the office was rarely empty.

There was only one place that came to mind. Even though it was now ash, he turned his bike and pointed it toward the only place he'd ever considered home.

He let his mind shut down and relied on instinct to take him where he needed to go. So he was halfway up the drive before he realized someone else was already there. Someone who drove a shiny, newer-model Escalade.

Reece.

He slowed and turned the bike to head back down the drive, but Reece jumped in front of him. There was no way he'd be able to make an escape without knocking his brother over.

"Move."

Reece crossed his arms over his chest and held his ground. "No. Not until you talk to me."

"What the fuck are you even doing here? The house is gone."

"I'm well aware. Shelby and I were in it as it was burning down."

Greer's heart gave a little jump of panic, and he couldn't help but glance over at the pile of ashes. Reece and Shelby had been *inside* when it happened? Holy shit. "You're okay?"

"Yeah, we both made it. The house didn't." His gaze also traveled over to the burned-out shell of their childhood. "We're talking about rebuilding it, making it a home again."

Greer's throat closed up at the thought. "Mom and Dad would have liked that."

"I know." Reece returned his attention to Greer. "Natalie said you might show up here. Guess she was right."

Anger burst inside him with the destructive force of a bomb. And like that, all the tender feelings he'd been feeling toward his brother went up in smoke. "Natalie needs to mind her own fucking business."

"So you said. Quite publicly, as I understand it." Reece moved forward, giving him no choice but to meet his brother's gaze. "Where have you been, bro?"

"Hell."

"Yeah? What were you doing there?"

"What I had to."

Sighing heavily, Reece dragged both hands over his face. "What's going with you? How could you just disappear on us for four months?"

Nosy little brother. He tried to steer the bike around him. "Didn't know I had to report my every move to you."

Reece caught his handlebars. "You owe us an explanation. Jesus, Greer. We thought we were looking for a body."

"Well, now you know I'm alive." For a little while longer, at least. "Let go of my bike."

As the engine rumbled impatiently, Reece held on. "Natalie told me what you're doing and why you're doing it."

Goddammit. Of course she had. She was good at sticking her nose where it didn't belong. "It doesn't concern you."

"The hell it doesn't. They were my parents, too."

"You can't be involved." Not if Bruce was the killer. Things were about to get ugly, and he had to know his brothers were safe.

"Greer." Reece said his name on a drawn-out sigh. "You're not a fucking island. You have brothers and sisters-in-law, who all want you home. Come back to Wilde Security with me. Talk to us. Whatever this is, you don't have to do it alone. You yourself once said that's not how this family works."

He *had* said that, and it sucked to have his own words thrown back at him. "I don't want you involved."

"Well, that's bullshit." Reece still held the handlebars of his bike, forcing him to either knock his brother over or stay put and listen. He didn't want to listen.

"Let go of my bike."

"No. The twins, Jude, and I all have just as much right to know who killed our parents as you. We either do this as a family, or we don't do it at all."

He ground his teeth. "Don't make me hurt you, Reece."

"Yeah? Try it."

"Remember you asked for this." He hauled back a fist and slammed it into Reece's jaw. Reece reeled backward, stumbled, and landed on his ass in the mud.

He revved the bike's engine and swung it wide around Reece and the SUV, then gunned it down the driveway. In his mirrors, he saw Reece stagger to his feet and rub his jaw. He would not feel bad. If punching Reece was the only way to keep him safe, he'd do it a thousand times over.

Because the absolute last thing he wanted was for his brothers to wind up in Bruce's crosshairs.

# Chapter Sixteen

As soon as her shift ended, Natalie raced over to Wilde Security, hoping the brothers had good news. Instead, she found Reece reclined in one of the office chairs, his wife Shelby furious over a nasty bruise on the side of his jaw.

"Oh no." She dropped her bag just inside the door and crossed the room to him. "Did Greer…?"

"Yeah." Reece took the cold compress from Shelby and held it to his jaw. "He didn't pull his punch, either."

"The bastard." Shelby paced, fuming, then instantly returned to her husband's side when he sat upright and winced. "You need to have your head checked out. Pretty sure you have a concussion."

"Jesus," one of the brothers said and pinched the bridge of his nose. "Greer's lost his fucking mind."

Oh, they didn't even know the half of it. Natalie glanced over at the speaker. He had a stud in one ear and a tattoo sleeve up one arm. He wasn't one of the twins, so she guessed this must be the youngest Wilde, Jude. "You're right. He's not in a good place."

Vaughn scowled. "What do you mean by that?"

How much should she tell them?

She studied each of the brothers and their wives. Jude and Libby couldn't be more different. She was as tidy as a schoolmarm, her blond hair tied back into a neat ponytail, and he was all bad-boy swagger with roguishly long hair he'd recently finger-combed.

Reece and Shelby were an odd pair as well—he was the kind of guy who ironed his pants and wore his shirt buttoned all the way, while her hair was stop-sign red. She had a matching nose ring, and colorful ink covered most of the skin on her small body.

Then there was Cam and Eva, who looked like they fit together, two pieces of the same whole. They even dressed alike in jeans, leather jackets, and boots—the only differences were her jacket was a navy blue while his was brown and her kickass boots came up to her knees while he only wore one well-used work boot. On his other foot was a cast covered in colorful drawings.

Vaughn and Lark also looked like they belonged together, but in a different way. She was classically beautiful and dressed the part of a trophy wife, but there was something calculating about her, a weariness in her eyes, an edge that matched Vaughn's.

And despite all their differences, together, they were a family, the bond between them tangible in their shared concern for Greer.

She had to tell them, she realized. They had to know just how far down into the depths of depression Greer had spiraled. It was the only way they'd be able to help him. The only way she'd be able to save him from himself.

She drew a breath and let it out slowly. "I believe he's suicidal. No—more than believe. I know he is. He's told me as much."

The room exploded with shouts of disbelief, denial. Natalie waited silently through it all, keeping her face calm despite the deep ache in her heart. It wasn't an atypical response. Family members never wanted to believe their loved one wanted to die.

"No." Vaughn's voice rose above the rest of them. He broke free of his wife's soothing grasp and strode forward, got in Natalie's face. "No fucking way. Suicide's the coward's way out, and Greer's not a coward."

"He's not a coward," she agreed, holding her ground. "Furthest thing from it. He's the bravest man I've ever known. But because of that bravery, he's done things, seen things that weigh heavily on him, and he doesn't think he can live with them anymore. He doesn't think he's a good man. We need to prove to him that he can, and he is."

Cam got up and used his crutches to hobble over to his twin. He put a hand on Vaughn's shoulder, and the gesture seemed to have a calming affect. Vaughn backed off a bit.

"He's still working for the military, isn't he?" Cam asked.

She blinked. She hadn't realized they were unaware of that fact. "Um…yes."

"Shit." Cam squeezed his eyes shut. "I wondered."

Reece frowned. "No, he's out. I've seen his discharge papers."

"Paperwork means jack shit," Jude said. "Any idiot with a computer can whip up discharge papers. If they wanted him off the books, they could've easily made it look like he's no longer employed by the good old U.S. of A."

Vaughn's scowl darkened. "So what do they have him doing? Black ops?"

*I'm basically a loaded gun…*

No. She wouldn't tell them that. There was a line between spilling some of Greer's secrets for his own safety and completely violating his trust. A thin line, admittedly, but one she wasn't willing to cross.

She shook her head. "All I know is he still works for the military. He hasn't told me more."

"He wouldn't," Jude said softly. "He'd want to protect her, guys. That's what he does."

Murmured agreements came from everyone in the room.

Cam sighed and rubbed at the back of his neck. "Dammit, I knew something was wrong."

All eyes turned on him.

"Wait, what?" Jude said. "You *knew*?"

"I…" Cam trailed off. His shoulders slumped. He looked miserable. "No, I didn't know. 'Suspected' is the better word."

"Come on, get off that leg." Eva stepped up beside him and placed a hand on his back, guiding him over to a seating area comprised of a couch and a couple of deep chairs. He settled onto the couch. Eva sat beside him and laced their fingers together in a touching show of solidarity. "Now," she said softly, "you need to tell them."

He seemed to draw strength from her touch and straightened. "Yeah. All right." He met his brothers' gazes one at a time. "Greer's been having panic attacks. I first noticed it at Jude and Libby's wedding, and I wasn't the only one. Seth Harlan saw it, too. Like recognizing like, I guess. I figured then that Greer was probably still working for the government because PTSD doesn't usually take years to manifest."

"And why the fuck didn't you say anything before now?" Jude asked, incredulous.

"What was I going to say? 'Oh, hey, by the way, our missing brother is suffering from PTSD?' C'mon. What was that going to help? I figured we'd find him first, then deal with the rest of it."

"He's right," Natalie said because she could tell Cam's brothers were spoiling for a fight, and they didn't have time for a sparring match. "That information wasn't going to help you find Greer. If it wasn't for him being mugged and me finding him in the hallway in front of my apartment, I very much think we still wouldn't have found..." She realized all eyes had turned to her and trailed off.

Reece pinched the bridge of his nose as if trying to relieve a headache. "He was mugged?"

Ah, crap. She probably shouldn't have told them that. She swallowed hard and nodded.

"Our Greer?" Vaughn asked incredulously. "You're talking about the guy who could kick any one of our asses without breaking a sweat. How the hell was he mugged?"

Yeah, she definitely should have kept her mouth shut on the subject, but the cat was out of the bag now, and she wasn't about to force it back in. "He was already hurt. Shot. They caught him by surprise, really did a number on him."

"Whoa, whoa." Jude held up both hands in a halt gesture. "Shot? When was he shot?"

"I don't know. I found him that way. The wound had already been stitched and bandaged, and he had an infection." She absolutely was not going to tell them about Syria, or what Greer had done while he was there. It wasn't her place, and she suspected it was information she shouldn't even know to begin with.

"Jesus," Cam said. "This keeps getting worse."

And they didn't even know it all. She steeled herself. This next part was not going to go smoothly. "It was my nephew."

Again, all eyes focused on her.

"Andy was one of the kids involved in the mugging," she continued. "That's why I need to find him before Greer does."

Silence.

"Well, shit," Cam muttered at the same time Vaughn said, "Fuck."

Libby pressed a hand to her stomach. "Oh, God. Greer wouldn't hurt a kid, would he?"

Jude slipped an arm around her waist and kissed her temple, but he didn't leap to Greer's defense like Natalie expected.

Nobody did. She stared at them in wide-eyed disbelief. Did they really think so little of him? Granted, she had thought the same at first, but after watching him interact with Annalise at the studio, she knew better. And so should they. "Of course he wouldn't!"

"You said he's behaving erratically," Reece said slowly.

"Because he's hurting! He needs help. He needs you— needs *us*—to believe in him because right now, he's not able to believe in himself."

"He doesn't want our help," Reece pointed out. "He made that quite clear when he punched me."

"Well that's just too damn bad. He needs it."

Another beat of silence.

"So," Cam said finally, "where do we start?"

Natalie released a soft breath of relief. With the Wilde brothers on her side, she had a better shot of making sure everyone she cared about got out of this mess unscathed. "We start with Andy. It doesn't make sense to me that he got involved. He's not a bad kid. Mischievous, but until a few days ago, I would have said he didn't have it in him to hurt a fly. He's kind of a geek. A computer whiz."

"Sounds like Reece when he was a teenager." Jude elbowed his brother. "He's a geek."

"And you're a pain in the ass," Reece said, but there was no heat behind it. If anything, the comeback was instinctual.

She turned to Reece, because, yes, she had the sense he and Andy were kindred spirits. "I swear Andy's a good kid. He's been in trouble a couple times for hacking—that's it. We need to find him, hear his side of the story. I'm not excusing what he did to Greer, but there has to be a reason he did this."

"Do you think someone hired him to do the mugging?"

Cam asked.

She nodded. "I don't know why Andy would accept such an offer, but it has to have something to do with Greer looking for your parents' killer. It's the only thing that makes sense."

"So someone out there wants Greer hurt, if not dead." He turned to his brothers. "Ask me, that's reason enough to search for Andy. At the very least, we can keep him from trying again."

Eva set a hand on her husband's shoulder. "I can help. I'll go into work, see what I can dig up in the old police files."

Cam nodded. "That will help. I, uh…" He fumbled. "I tried to read the case file once and couldn't do it. The pictures, descriptions…it was too much."

"Nobody blames you for that. It'll be easier for me. Plus, fresh eyes never hurt." Eva kissed him softly then left her seat and moved toward the door, a woman with a mission. "I'll call if I find anything. You do the same, especially if Greer turns up. I want to be here for that."

"You plan to kick his ass?" Cam asked.

"Or hug him. I haven't decided. Probably both." The little bell on the door jangled with her exit.

Vaughn walked over to his computer. "I still have the program running, tracking Andy's phone."

Reece followed him and studied the screen over his shoulder. "What program did you use?"

"Just the find my phone app he already had installed. I hacked his account, and once I knew his password, I activated the app and the rest was easy."

Reece gave his shoulder a friendly shove. "You're getting better at this."

"Your Hacking 101 classes have helped," he said distractedly, then banged his fist on the desk. "Fuck me. The kid knows something's up. He keeps changing his password, and now he has me blocked."

"Let me have a go," Reece said.

Vaughn relinquished his chair and Reece slid into it. His fingers flew over the keyboard, barely pausing. Vaughn watched over his shoulder, sometimes nodding, sometimes frowning. They'd occasionally carry on a short conversation that sounded like a foreign language to Natalie.

*Andy would like these guys.*

The thought made her heart ache. She hoped they'd get this mess all cleared up and he'd have a chance to meet them. He'd enjoy talking with people who not only understood his computer-speak, but loved it as much as he did.

"I'm gonna make some calls," Cam said after several beats of silence and got up on his crutches again, hobbling over to his own desk. "I still have contacts on the street. If there's a hit out on Greer, I'll find out."

God. A hit? Did Andy really attack Greer just for money? It didn't make sense.

The remaining Wilde women — Shelby, Lark, and Libby — had gathered in the seating area together, but Natalie didn't feel like it was her place to join them, so she stayed where she was.

Jude started pacing. He didn't strike her as a man who liked sitting still, which Libby confirmed by saying, "Jude. Pacing's not doing any good. Why don't you walk Natalie home and see if Greer shows up? I'll call you as soon as Vaughn and Reece have something."

He stopped moving, looked at his wife, then over at Natalie. They all knew the suggestion was little more than busywork — Greer wasn't going to show — but Jude looked desperate enough to get out of the office that Natalie didn't protest. She could use a change of clothes anyway, and Jet probably needed a walk.

"I wouldn't mind the company."

Jude nodded once and stopped beside his wife to drop

a kiss to her forehead. Then he led the way out and held the door open for her.

Jude didn't say anything at first. He seemed to be stewing. They were across the parking lot and entering the small park that separated Wilde Security from her building before he finally spoke: "Reece says you care about Greer."

She should probably deny it, but what was the point? "Yes, I do."

"Good. He needs someone."

"From what I can tell, he has more than someone—he has you, your brothers, your wives."

"It's not the same. He needs a woman in his life." Jude kicked at a pebble on the path. "If he's suffering from PTSD, he needs someone beside him when he wakes up from the nightmares. Someone to remind him the flashbacks are past, and the future is bright."

"Sounds like you're speaking from experience."

"In some ways, I guess I am. My best friend had a really hard go of it when he came home from Afghanistan, until he found his girlfriend and she helped him cope. If Greer's going through the same thing, he needs that. He needs you."

Her throat closed. "I don't know if he'll let it be me after tonight."

"Yeah, you pissed him off."

"I was just trying to help. Just trying to…" Frustrated, she flopped her hands. "I don't know. Save him from himself. He's so bent on revenge—"

Jude threw out an arm, stopping her in her tracks. "Revenge?"

She opened her mouth but closed it again without uttering a sound. Right. She had told Reece about the revenge scheme, not Jude. Apparently Reece hadn't had the chance to share that tidbit of information with his brothers. "Greer plans to kill the man he thinks is responsible for your parents' murders. He thinks he needs to do it before he…"

"Before he what?"

"Takes his own life."

Anger flashed in Jude's bright blue eyes, followed quickly by sorrow. He dropped his arm. "He's really hurting, isn't he?"

"He's carried a lot of weight. A lot of guilt. I think it's just gotten to be too much for him."

Jude was quiet until they emerged from the park into the parking lot right below her apartment. She didn't blame him for needing the moments of silence. She'd dumped a lot on him in the last few minutes.

"Brothers," he finally muttered with a shake of his head.

She thought of her own—all the times she'd covered for Mathew when they were kids, all the times he'd let her down—and sighed. "Tell me about it."

Jude pulled open the apartment complex's front door and waited for her to pass. "You have a brother?"

By unspoken agreement, they headed toward the stairs. The elevators in this building were notoriously slow and unreliable. She went up ahead of him. "Yes. Mathew. He's six years older than me, and he was my hero until…one day, he wasn't. He got into drugs when he was sixteen and was never the same again."

"That sucks."

"It did. My parents turned a blind eye to his problem for a long time. It wasn't until Andy came along four years later that they finally admitted he needed help." And, God, she hoped Andy wasn't following in his father's footsteps. Her worst fear was discovering Andy had attacked Greer due to drugs. "I wanted my big brother back and tried to help Mathew as best I could, but I was so young and my parents were all but enabling him. He didn't want to admit he needed help."

"Like Greer."

She shook her head. "I think Greer will seek out help

when he's ready. Mathew never did."

"Where's your brother now?"

"No clue." She raised a shoulder and stopped in front of her apartment door to grab her keys from her purse. "He's been in and out of rehab more times than I can count. He'll do okay for a while, then slip right back into his old habits." As soon as she had the door open, she froze. Jet wasn't there to meet her.

Jude didn't notice. He was digging for his own keys to Greer's place. "I'll meet you in a few. I want to take a look around."

Greer wouldn't be there. Maybe he had been recently, but he wasn't any longer. Nope—he was somewhere in her apartment. She didn't see him in the kitchen or living room and set her purse down on an end table before continuing to the bedroom.

And there he was, propped up in her still sex-tousled sheets, one hand buried in Jet's golden fur and the other wrapped around a half empty bottle of vodka. His gun sat within reach on the nightstand, and her heart gave a little jolt of panic when she spotted it.

She stepped over the threshold but didn't move any closer than that. If he was on the edge, she didn't want to do anything to inadvertently push him over. Jet's tail thumped a couple times, but he otherwise didn't move. Smart guy knew Greer was hurting and needed him to stay put. Good dog. She decided right then Jet deserved all the bacon he could eat from here on out.

"I heard Jude's voice," Greer said with a dull hollowness in his tone. His expression was closed off, unreadable, and his bleary eyes focused on the empty space over her shoulder. "Why is he here?"

"Because he's worried about you," she answered softly. "We all are."

"I'm not worth worrying over."

"I think that's our decision to make, don't you?"

"You wouldn't be saying that if you knew what I did tonight."

Oh, God. Had he gone through with his revenge plan? Had he killed someone? Her stomach jittered, but she somehow managed to keep her voice neutral, her body language calm. "What did you do?"

He took a large swig from the bottle. "I was going to kill an innocent man." He snorted. "Well, not innocent. He's a creep, and I'm sure he's stalked and terrified other women like he did my mom, but he's not a killer. I wanted to kill him, though. There's this anger inside me—it's lived there since that night the police came to the house and told us we were orphans—and when I was holding the gun to Mendenhall's head, it was right there at the surface, straining against the chains I've kept it locked up in. Even though everything he said rang true, and I knew he wasn't the man who killed my parents, I still wanted to pull the trigger." He lifted the bottle to his mouth but stopped before it touched his lips. He finally met her gaze directly. "It scared the hell out of me, Natalie."

She released a soft breath of relief. If he was this torn up about threatening the wrong man, there was still hope for him. She ventured a step closer. "Is that why you came back here?" When he didn't respond, she added, "I thought you'd never want to see me again after last night."

"I didn't but can't seem to stay away."

"I only said what I did because I care about you. I don't want to see you arrested or worse. I don't want you to carry more death on your shoulders."

He nodded, raised the bottle again, and took a long drink that had his Adam's apple bobbing in his strong neck. "Something's missing in me, a piece that's broken off and gotten lost somewhere along the way—I know it, I accept it, and I've dealt with it just fine until I met you. With you… I don't know. You make me want to be…whole again. For maybe the first time in my adult life, and I don't—I don't want to lose that. You."

He was drunk. There was no way he'd be saying such things sober. Still, her heart gave a happy leap. He cared about her, too. It scared him, but the feelings were there and just as strong as hers.

They'd get through this. It wouldn't be easy, but they'd get through. Together.

She crossed to the bed and sat down, taking the bottle from his hand before he could drink more. She set it aside, laced her fingers through his. "Let me help. Let your brothers help."

He stared down at their entwined hands. "I miss them."

"We've missed you too, bro," Jude's voice said from the doorway. "Where have you been?"

# Chapter Seventeen

Greer gazed up at the door. His youngest brother stood there, backlit by the living room lights, a battle of emotions raging across his expression. Anger. Fear. Grief. Jude never had been one to hide his emotions.

They were going to have it out, right here, right now.

At his side, Natalie shifted as if she was going to excuse herself. He refocused on her, keeping a tight grip on her hand. She couldn't leave. Facing his brother would be the most terrifying thing he'd ever done, and he was so fucking tired of always putting on a brave face when inside he was little more than a frightened teenager, alone in the world and unsure of how to keep his family together. He needed her for this. He was beginning to suspect he needed her for a lot of reasons.

*Stay*, he pleaded silently.

She searched his eyes. He didn't know what she saw there, but she nodded slowly and squeezed his hand.

Several moments passed in silence. He didn't know where to start, or even how. Eventually, Jude saved him from having to figure it out.

"You've missed a lot." He sighed and dragged a hand through his perpetually tousled hair. "Reece and Shelby nearly annulled their marriage."

Greer winced. "I told him not to."

"And he listened. They worked things out, and she opened a coffee shop in the empty store beside Wilde Security."

This, he could do. This small talk, catching up. He needed this easing into brotherly interaction again, before they went near the big stuff. "I'm glad the building's getting more use."

Jude nodded. "Reece has a crew coming in to see about renovating the rest of it. He's thinking we'll rent the other spaces out for retail or offices. It'll generate extra income."

"He always has been good at generating income."

"Yeah, he has us operating in the black now. He partnered us with Tucker Quentin, and we've been doing a lot of personal security for Tuc's Hollywood friends. It's a pretty cushy gig, and the pay's unbelievable compared to what we were making chasing down cheaters. Libby and I can finally afford a house. We've been shopping around."

Just as he suspected, his brothers were absolutely fine without him. In fact, they all seemed to be doing better since he left. "That's good. We were hemorrhaging money before, but I knew Reece would figure out a way to turn it around."

Natalie squeezed his hand, and he winced a little. Somehow he was screwing this up, but every time he looked at his brother he remembered his dream—the grown man with the ten-year-old's voice, accusing him of everything that he had done. "Uh, congrats on the house."

Jude lifted a shoulder. "We're going to need the extra space. Libby's pregnant. Seven weeks."

All the air left Greer's lungs, and for a long time he forgot how to breathe. It wasn't until Natalie started rubbing circles on his back that he remembered how the whole suck air in, blow it out thing worked.

"Pregnant," he breathed. Greer closed his eyes as his throat constricted painfully. A baby. There hadn't been a baby in the family since Jude was one. And now he was going to have his own. Wow.

*Maybe it'll finally be the girl Mom and Dad always wanted.*

The thought made his gut cramp with dread. If something happened to Jude and Libby, that child would grow up broken, a half-finished human being like him.

No. That couldn't happen. It was all the more reason to keep Jude away from Bruce Chambers.

He swallowed to ease the sensation that he was being strangled. He couldn't have a panic attack now. "Congratulations."

For the first time since Jude walked into the room, he smiled. No, more than smiled. He beamed. "She's due in November. If it's a girl, we're naming her after mom. If it's a boy, we're thinking of naming him David Greer Elliot Wilde."

With his breathing under control again, he nodded. "After both of your dads. It's a great idea."

Jude's brows cranked down. "No, not after Dad. I mean, yeah, he'll share Dad's name, too, which is a bonus, but… Greer, I want to name my son after you."

Natalie let go a surprised huff of air, and her fingers tightened around his. But if she was surprised, he was flabbergasted. Nothing Jude could have said would have shocked him more.

"Why me?"

"You honestly have to ask that, bro? I was only ten when Dad died. My memories of him… Well, I don't have very many and the few I do have are fuzzy, like a dream. I know I loved him, and he loved me, but he wasn't there for me when I needed a dad."

Greer nearly choked on the fist that had taken up residence in his throat. "Not because he didn't want to be."

But because Bruce fucking Chambers took him away from his kids. If nothing else, Jude's words solidified his mission in his mind. He was going to get justice—if not for his parents, then for the little boy who still carried the weight of their deaths like a cross even though he barely remembered them.

"Jesus," Jude muttered and started pacing. He dragged both hands through his hair, then spun around. "That's not what I meant. Dad... I'm not blaming him for not being there. I know he would've been if he could've. What I'm saying is he wasn't the one who helped me with my homework." He smiled a little. "Or yelled at me when I didn't do my homework. He wasn't the one who gave me The Talk, the one who waited up to make sure I was home by curfew. He wasn't the one who made sure my childhood was as normal as possible. That was you, Greer. And that's why I want to name my son, if I have one, after you."

There were no words. He honestly didn't know what to say, how to react. Natalie nudged his shoulder, and he glanced over at her. She nodded toward Jude, silently telling him to move, to go to his brother.

Yeah. He could do that. Part of him was ashamed he hadn't thought of it first. He wished he could blame it on the vodka he'd stolen from Mendenhall making him slow, but it wasn't. The caring man Jude described—well, boy, really—had died in Syria. Now bridging the gap between them seemed nearly impossible. Each step he took toward his youngest brother made him more nervous. He'd been avoiding this moment, this confrontation, since returning from Syria. What was Natalie expecting him to do? What did Jude expect?

He reached out and rested his hand on Jude's shoulder. Jude blinked hard and closed the remaining distance between them, grabbing him in a rib-crushing hug. It hurt like hell, but he suddenly didn't care.

This was right. This was home. How could he have forgotten this?

He held Jude just as tightly and remembered doing the same to the devastated ten-year-old boy that horrible October night twenty years ago.

"Do you blame me?" Jude whispered. "I was the reason Mom and Dad were out that night. I know Reece and the twins don't, but...do you?"

Greer set him back and stared into his eyes. "Jude. Christ. Why are you still carrying that weight? It wasn't your fault."

"They wouldn't have been at that gas station if they hadn't been out looking for me. If I hadn't snuck out—"

"I don't think it would have mattered."

Jude went very still. "What?"

"I've been looking into their deaths, searching for their killer almost since we buried them. It's always been in the back of my mind. The whole 'random act of violence' thing didn't sit right with me. Dad knew how to defend himself."

Jude shook his head. "That doesn't mean anything. I knew plenty of guys overseas who were equally capable of defending themselves, and that didn't stop them from dying."

"That was war. There's a difference, and you know it."

"Are you saying...?" Jude broke away and started pacing again. "Are you saying Mom and Dad were targeted?"

Greer glanced back at Natalie. She nodded encouragingly. He drew a breath. "You don't know what Dad was." *Or what I am.*

"Dad was a Ranger, like you."

He lifted a shoulder, trying to play it off. He really didn't want to go into the details. Especially not now that he knew Jude had a case of hero worship when it came to him. "Rangers make enemies."

"But those enemies have never singled out one particular Ranger for revenge. They can't, because they only ever see a unit, not—" He stopped and even though he was facing away, Greer could almost see him connecting the dots. He turned slowly, and his blue eyes were flinty, his jaw set. "What aren't you telling us?"

Greer heaved out a breath. A small hand touched his arm, and he glanced down to find Natalie beside him. She traced his arm with her fingers until she found his hand. "It's time to tell them everything."

"I don't want them to hate me."

She shook her head. "They won't."

He wanted to kiss her. Maybe it was the alcohol in his system, but he wanted it more than anything else at that moment. He lowered his head, pressed his lips to hers. She smiled, accepted the kiss, returned it. Moments later, when he straightened, he found Jude watching them with an odd expression on his face. Part surprise, part curiosity, part amusement.

"What?" he said, a bit defensive.

"Nothing." A slow smile spread across Jude's lips. "I've just never seen you kiss anyone before."

The back of his neck heated, but he didn't release Natalie. "We should call the twins. And Reece," he added, though the thought of facing Reece again after their last blow-up sat like a rock in his gut.

"We don't have to." Jude nodded in the general direction of Wilde Security. "They're all at the office."

That rock became a hot coal. He squeezed his eyes shut. Why did the idea of going to the office he'd set up with his brothers scare him so much?

Natalie's arms tightened around his waist. That little reassuring squeeze was exactly what he needed.

"Okay." He opened his eyes and looked at Jude. "We should go over. I'm ready to talk."

# Chapter Eighteen

They walked back across the park in silence, Jude leading the way.

Wilde Security.

Greer hadn't been there since January, and at the moment, he would have preferred returning to Syria or shipping off to Nigeria over walking through that door. At least in war zones, he knew what he was, what his job was, how to deal. He was a killer. He killed. And he locked everything away so he didn't have to deal.

This shit, though? This reconnecting with family and forming new bonds with Natalie…it was so far out of his realm of comprehension. Killers didn't have family connections. They didn't fall in love.

And yet here he was.

Natalie still held his hand. She hadn't let him go, which was probably good because he'd never wanted to run from anything more in his life.

Jesus. He was more than half drunk. He should wait until he sobered up. What if he told them too much? What if he laid open his soul and they saw him for the monster he was inside? Jude wouldn't want to name his son after him then.

He stopped moving. Natalie stopped beside him, but she didn't say anything. Just waited patiently.

He shook his head and tried to pull his hand free from hers. "I can't do this now."

"Why not?"

"I'm drunk. I'll get in there and open my mouth and all sorts of shit I never want them to know will come spilling out."

She pressed her lips together. "You're not drunk. And you're not going to say anything you don't want to. They're not going to force anything out of you, I promise. They want nothing more than to help you, and if letting you keep your secrets helps, they'll accept that."

Up ahead, Jude disappeared around a bend in the path, but losing sight of him didn't calm his jangling nerves.

"But," Natalie said after several beats of silence, "in my experience, keeping secrets has never helped anyone heal."

"What if I don't want to be healed?"

"If that were true, you wouldn't have come this far." She dropped his hand and took several steps in the direction Jude had disappeared. "It's your choice. You can go back, but that's not where your future is."

His future.

Breath stalled in his lungs. When he came back from Syria, he hadn't wanted a future. Then, suddenly, there she was. His angel dancing her way into his heart on pointe. He fleetingly wondered if this was what it had been like for Dad when he first met Mom. A staunch, in-it-for-life military man like David Wilde probably hadn't expected to fall for a ballerina, either.

Natalie stared at him now with worry in her big melted-caramel eyes. The morning sunlight set off the gold in her hair, and the light breeze kept pushing a strand over her forehead.

She held out a hand to him.

His future.

He could almost picture it. Waking up every morning with her by his side. Walking Jet together. He'd watch her dance. Maybe he'd even see a shrink like she'd suggested, get his head on right, and do volunteer work with her.

For the first time in a very long time, he saw a future that was more than death and despair and soul-crushing secrets. It could be a good life. All he had to do was accept her hand and face his brothers. It would be easier to go back, go to Nigeria, play his part like a good little killing machine until he figured out a way to end Bruce.

But that wasn't what he wanted. Not anymore. He wanted Natalie. Nothing in his life had ever been so clear to him. He wanted the future, and if the only way he'd have a chance with her was to tell his brothers the truth, he'd do it.

He reached for her hand, closed his eyes when her fingers slid through his and locked in place. She closed the distance between them and raised up on her toes to press a gentle kiss to his mouth.

"You can do this," she said, and the conviction in her voice convinced him that she was right.

It was going to suck. His brothers were going to be angry. But as long as she stayed by his side, he'd get through.

"Okay." He nodded. "Let's do this."

Jude was not waiting for them in the parking lot. He must have already gone inside. As the two of them approached, he allowed himself a moment to admire the changes since he'd last seen the place.

Last fall, a bomb had destroyed part of the old strip mall, but now there was little sign of the damage. The parking lot was clean, and already filled with cars. As he watched, a woman got out of one of the cars and walked toward the storefront beside Wilde Security. She drew his gaze to the colorful sign over the door: The Bean Gallery. So that must be Shelby's coffee house. It appeared to do brisk business.

Good for Shelby.

The office had also gotten a facelift. The plate glass window in front had been frosted a snowy white. A good idea, since many of their past clients had wanted to maintain their privacy. WILDE SECURITY was printed in black lettering across the center, along with a...logo? A black W with a gold S, set inside a shield. Huh. That was new. Most likely Reece's idea. He'd built his own software company from the ground up, so he knew a thing or two about branding and marketing.

It looked respectable now, like a real business, no longer the half-assed, slap-dash, semi-formed idea of one. It was exactly what he'd hoped it'd be when he dreamed it up a little over two years ago—a solid, steady source of income for his brothers.

He supposed he had Libby's father to thank for that. If Elliot Pruitt hadn't been so set on hiring Jude to protect her from a stalker last year, Wilde Security may have never gotten off the ground.

Jesus. His eyes were watering. And he was standing here at the door like an idiot. He blinked the blurriness from his vision and glanced over at Natalie. There was no judgment or condemnation or impatience in her eyes. She could have a short fuse—he'd seen it a time or two—and she definitely lost her patience with him more often than not, but now she was all quiet understanding. Like she knew how fragile he felt at the moment. He appreciated her more with each passing second.

Hell, that might even be love. He wasn't sure, but it was unlike anything he'd ever felt before.

She smiled. "Okay?"

"Yeah." And for once, he wasn't lying. He wasn't one hundred percent yet, but he might be on his way. At least, he was closer than he had been in a long time.

He pushed open the door and found the office's interior had been repainted a soft, welcoming blue. The trampled industrial-gray carpet had been switched out for newer stuff a few shades lighter. The dented metal desks were now wood and had legitimate computer systems at each station. There was a comfortable waiting area, a couch and a couple chairs, underneath the window, and that was where he found his family. Well, part of it—the women were missing, leaving only his four younger brothers.

At the sound of the bell on the door, Reece stood. A bruise colored one side of his jaw, and dammit, the sight of it had anger tightening Greer's throat. Not anger aimed at Reece, but at himself. He'd vowed over his parents' graves to protect his brothers, and instead he was picking fights and running away from them.

What the hell had he become? He didn't recognize himself anymore.

Cam also stood up from his seat on the couch, despite the cast encircling his leg. When had that happened? And why the fuck did his brothers keep breaking bones?

Vaughn, on the other hand, didn't move. He glared, a scowl darkening his expression. Out of the four of them, Vaughn would be the hardest to apologize to. Under his gruff exterior was a carefully guarded sensitive soul. He was probably most hurt by Greer's disappearing act, and the man held grudges like a champ.

"Well?" Vaughn finally demanded after the silence went on too long. "Are you just gonna stand there, or are we going to sit down and figure out how to fix this dysfunctional family of ours?"

"Hey," Jude said mildly. "We put the fun in dysfunctional."

Leave it to Jude to try to lighten the mood. Greer finally moved, dropping into the deep, cushioned chair closest to him. To his relief, Natalie didn't try to use the lack of other women as an excuse to leave. Instead, she perched on the arm of his chair like she had every right to be there.

And, if he was honest with himself, she did. She'd somehow become his lighthouse in the violent storm that was his life.

He let out a long breath and shook his head. "I don't know where to start."

# Chapter Nineteen

"How about with why you disappeared?" Vaughn demanded.

"Or," Cam said, lowering himself carefully back to his seat, "why you lied about your discharge from the Army?"

They were both good questions, and ones he wanted to answer, but they were also more complicated than his brothers realized. When he opened his mouth, no words formed.

Natalie stroked her fingers over the back of his hand, drawing his attention. "Start at the very beginning."

Yeah. The beginning. He wouldn't be able to explain it all unless he started with the night their secure, upper-middle-class lives fell apart.

He drew another breath and tried again. "The night Mom and Dad died, I realized it'd be up to me to keep us together. If we wound up in foster care, they'd have broken us up, and I couldn't allow that. You know I filed for and got emancipation. What you don't know is the state wasn't going to give me custody of you. They said I was too young. I couldn't properly care for four young boys when I was just barely sixteen."

Reece frowned and slowly returned to his seat, his brow

furrowing in thought. "But you did get custody."

"Not at first. They were going to ship you all away, sweep you up in the system, and I was so afraid I'd lose you. I promised Mom and Dad I'd take care of you—" He paused to clear the rocks out of his throat. "So I sold my soul to the devil."

"What the fuck?" Vaughn said.

Jude held up a hand. "Are we talking figuratively or like crossroads demon, occult-type shit?"

Greer snorted. Given what he now knew, Bruce Chambers could very well have been a crossroads demon. "I went to one of Dad's colleagues for help. Bruce Chambers. He had the connections and pulled the strings to make sure you all could stay with me…on the condition that I joined him in the Army once Jude graduated high school. I agreed, and he paid for the housekeepers, groceries, bills. What I didn't realize then was every dollar added another year to my sentence."

Vaughn didn't bother hiding his doubt. "Sentence? You're saying you were his prisoner?"

*More like slave.* But, no, he wasn't going to tell them Bruce basically owned his sorry ass. "As soon as I got through basic training, he scooped me up for his little pet project."

Still skeptical, Vaughn raised an eyebrow. "Which was?"

And here it was. Moment of truth. "Black ops. Assassinations, mostly. My most recent job was…" He trailed off and looked at Natalie. She knew some of this already, but he hadn't told her the worst of it. "Two weeks ago in Syria. The guy they sent me after—he was bad news. I haven't lost sleep over him. But my orders were to take out his family. Wife, children. And so I did."

Other than Cam's whispered oath, the room was dead silent.

Tears trailed from Natalie's eyes. She leaned over and rested her cheek on top of his head. "It's okay."

No, it sure as fuck wasn't. He didn't even know what his body count was at this point.

Reece leaned back and took off his glasses, rubbing at the center of his forehead. "So you weren't ever a Ranger?"

"Officially, I am. I went through Ranger School and have done the job. Unofficially, I'm a ghost. I don't exist."

Cam released a long breath. "Was Dad…?"

He wished he could lie. Well, he could, but what was the point? They'd find out sooner or later—hopefully sooner since he fully intended to expose Bruce for the monster he was. "Dad and Bruce ran the ops together. The squad didn't start off as what it became, and I think that's why Dad was killed. I think he wanted out and Bruce wasn't going to let him leave because he knew too much. Once he was gone, Bruce filled the empty spot he left with me."

"Why didn't he ever tap any of us for his little assassin squad?" Vaughn asked. "We've all had extensive military training."

"That was part of our agreement. He wasn't allowed to recruit any of you. He had to leave you alone, or I'd blow the whistle on him."

Vaughn's anger finally boiled over, and he popped to his feet. "For fuck's sake, Greer. You threatened this guy, even when you knew he killed Dad for doing the exact same thing?"

"He didn't know," Natalie protested, but he laid his hand over hers, stopping her. He tried to convey with his eyes that he had this. His message must have gotten through, because she relaxed. Marginally.

He refocused on Vaughn. "I only just started putting the pieces together last night. Bruce knew I'd resumed my search for Mom and Dad's killer, so last fall he sent me on a wild goose chase by giving me a diary of Mom's that pointed to the wrong guy. When he first gave me that diary, right around Jude and Libby's wedding, I didn't act on it. I'd almost convinced myself to let it go. Jude, you were happy with Libby. Cam, you and Eva had finally stopped circling each other. And then that insanity with Reece and Shelby eloping in Vegas…and it seemed everyone was over it but me. I finally started to think it was best to leave the past alone.

"Then, four months ago, Bruce sent me to Syria. The more I think about it, the more I wonder if it wasn't a panic move on his part. After we completed our mission, we were attacked at a CIA safe house." He let go of Natalie's hand and lifted his shirt to show them the bullet wound. "Nobody should have known where to find us, but they came right at us. One of my men lost his life and I barely made it out."

Jude flinched. Greer knew this had to be hitting all of his youngest brother's exposed nerves the wrong way, but he was way past sugarcoating things now. "Bruce set me up. He hoped I wouldn't survive Syria, but I did, and now he's already pushing to send me off to some other war zone in Africa."

"Sounds like he's scared of you," Natalie said.

"Yeah, well, if he killed our parents, he ought to be."

"Why didn't you tell us any of this before now?" Cam asked.

Because he was ashamed of the things he'd done, but he wasn't ready to burden his brothers with that yet. He'd already dumped a lot on them. "I wanted you to have what I had…a normal childhood. But I also wanted you to have what I didn't get…a normal high school experience, where your biggest concern was girls or homework."

"You think we didn't worry?" Reece shook his head. "Of course we did. Why do you think I worked my ass off building DMW Systems? I wanted us to have money, so you could leave the military, meet someone"—he nodded toward Natalie—"and finally have something approaching a normal life. I thought I knew how much you gave up for us, but I had no clue."

"None of us did," Vaughn said and gravel coated his voice. "Holy shit, bro."

Greer couldn't speak. If he opened his mouth and said anything more, he'd dissolve into a blubbering mess. And yet, he no longer felt like he was shattering under the weight he'd been carrying for so many years. Like dropping a rucksack after a twenty-mile forced march.

Beside him, Natalie sniffled, which drew Vaughn's attention to her. His brows slammed together. "I still don't get how any of this has to do with her nephew."

She sniffled again and wiped at her wet eyes. "We don't know, either. That's why we need to find him. Did your search on his phone turn up anything?"

"No. Dead end."

Reece added, "We think he ditched it."

She sighed. "He would know enough to."

"But we already know Bruce Chambers is involved," Jude said, "so why do we need the kid? Let's just take the bastard down and be done with it."

If only it were that easy. "Bruce has powerful friends and a long reach. We can't touch him until we have all the facts."

"So let's do it. We have some powerful friends, too. HORNET, Tucker Quentin. Between them and the five of us—"

Greer's heart gave a painful thump. Christ, no. This was exactly what he hadn't wanted. "I didn't tell you this so you can put yourselves at risk."

"Oh, you told us so we could sit back and watch you put yourself at risk?" Jude snorted. "Fat chance, bro."

"Jude, you're going to be a father. You have your child to think about now."

He spread his arms. "All the more reason we need to do it now. I don't want my kid coming into a world where

Chambers is still free to ruin teenagers' lives. What if he or one of his lackies comes after my kid in sixteen years?"

"They won't. I'm going to handle it."

Jude crossed his arms over his chest and scowled. It wasn't an expression he wore often and looked odd on his usually smiling face. "You're going to handle it by getting yourself killed? Yeah, well, I'm not letting you fulfill that death wish. I want my kid to grow up in a world with all of his or her uncles."

He scowled right back until Natalie stepped between them, hands up as if she intended to push them apart should they try to go for each other's throats. The mental image was funny enough that it distracted Greer from the stare-down. Both he and Jude had a hundred pounds on her, easy, and yet he had no doubt she would successfully break up a fight between them if she had to.

"Guys," she said soothingly. "We've all had a very long night. Let's take today, relax and let everything settle before any decisions are made."

"What about your nephew?" Vaughn asked with an underlying note of hostility in his voice.

She sagged a little. "I don't think he's in immediate danger. Or any danger, to tell the truth. Knowing everything I know now, I'm starting to suspect he's running because he's afraid of being punished for what he did to Greer. Wherever he is, he'll be okay for another day."

"It's a good plan," Cam said after a beat. Always the levelheaded one, always the peacemaker. The water to his twin's flame.

"No," Vaughn said. "I wanna find this kid and—"

"We need time to process—"

"Fuck that."

"Twins," Greer said on an exasperated sigh. "Enough."

"Don't call us that," they said at the same time.

"We hate that," Cam complained.

"You know our names," Vaughn added. "Use them."

Greer smiled. Couldn't help it. Christ, he had missed his brothers. The twins, so very much alike and yet different. Jude, the perpetual joker. Nerdy, pragmatic Reece.

He hadn't realized how much he'd missed them until now.

"Listen," he said to smooth the waters. "Natalie's right. I'm not in top form right now." The vodka was making its presence known in the pounding behind his eyes. He nodded toward Reece. "And Reece looks about ready to collapse. Let's get eight hours and meet back here to come up with a game plan."

His brothers eyed him.

"You're not gonna do anything suicidal, are you?" Vaughn asked. Nobody could ever accuse him of being too subtle.

Greer winced, but Natalie spoke before he managed a reply. "I won't let him."

They studied her for several seconds, then all four of them started nodding like bobble heads.

"Yeah, I believe her," Jude said.

"She'll keep him in line," Reece agreed. And, okay, after taking a punch to the face, he was entitled to that little dig. Greer had been out of line, after all.

"Make sure he takes those eight hours," Vaughn said, and there was no mistaking his meaning. Sleep, not sex.

"And he needs to eat something," Cam added.

Greer ground his teeth together. "Stop it. I don't need a babysitter."

All gazes focused on him with varying degrees of dubiousness. Even Natalie, who looked the most doubtful of them all.

"All right." He held up his hands in surrender. See, he could admit defeat. Sometimes. "Yeah, I deserve that." He'd done nothing lately to earn their trust, but, as he gazed around the room at the people who meant the world to him, he realized he'd have to fix that.

Because maybe he wasn't as ready to leave this world as he thought.

. . .

"I'm proud of you."

Several steps in front of Natalie on the stairs to their floor, Greer froze and half turned to look at her over his shoulder. If she had to put a name to his expression, it'd be "utter disbelief." It'd also be "exhausted."

The man had been through the ringer tonight, no doubt about it.

And yet he was shocked that anyone could be proud of him? Ego was certainly not one of his flaws.

She closed the distance between them and kissed his cheek as she passed. He didn't move until she reached the top of the stairs, pushed open the heavy metal door, and raised a brow at him.

He took the stairs two at a time and caught the door just before it fell shut. "Why would you be proud of me?"

"Why wouldn't I?" She stopped in front of her door and fished in her coat pocket for her keys. By unspoken agreement, they had decided he'd be staying at her place for the day. He didn't even glance at his apartment door.

Jet greeted them enthusiastically, tail smacking back and forth between their legs like a happy whip. If he didn't calm down, they'd end up with tail-shaped bruises on their calves.

Absently, Greer reached down to give the dog an ear scratch. Jet plopped his butt on the floor, his eyes all but rolling back in his head at the attention.

Greer didn't take his gaze off her. "I've done horrible things. You know it all now. You should be horrified, not proud."

"I'm both," she admitted and grabbed Jet's leash from the hook by the door. "Not horrified at you, but at what was done to you. A lesser man would have cracked under the pressure, and you were only a kid."

He winced. "Don't do that. Don't put me up on a heroic pedestal. It's bad enough to know that Jude sees me—saw me as some kind of superhero."

"Everyone looks up to their older brother. I did—"

"Until you didn't," he interrupted.

She shook her head and bent down to clip on Jet's leash. "That's different. Mathew's never sacrificed anything for anyone. His own son barely knows him. He's lived a life driven by selfish impulses. He's nothing like you."

"I don't want the responsibility of being anyone's hero." He took the leash from her hand. "I'll walk him."

Straightening, she blew a wayward stand of hair out of her eyes. "Are you sure?"

"Yeah. I need…" He trailed off as if unsure what he needed. After a visible struggle, he finished, "Some time alone."

Given how unpredictable he'd been lately, the last thing she wanted was to let him have time to brood. But nor could she follow him around and mother over him for the rest of his life. Heck, she didn't want a relationship she had to mother over. She wanted a partner, and she wanted that partner to be Greer. At some point, she had to trust that he'd be okay by himself, or their relationship wouldn't survive.

She gazed down at her dog. The only sign of Jet's impatience to get on with his walk was his brown eyes bouncing back and forth between them, like he was watching a ping-pong match. She rubbed his head. *Take care of him, buddy.*

As if Jet heard her silent plea, his tail thunked twice. Then he sprang to his feet in full doggie excitement mode when Greer reached for the door.

"Natalie…" He paused, seemed to search for the right words. "I couldn't have done what I did today, couldn't have faced my brothers like that, without you by my side. Thank you."

Her throat tightened. "You're welcome."

"When I get back, we should talk about us. I want there to be an us."

Oh, God, she was going to cry. Her chest was so tight each thundering beat of her heart felt as if it would crack it open. "I want that, too."

"Okay. Good." He opened the door and Jet zoomed out into the hall, nearly dragging Greer off his feet. And he laughed. "Okay, we're going!"

She drew a full, shaking breath as she watched him and her dog disappear down the stairs. She'd been so afraid that when this was over, he'd wash his hands of her. Why would he want her around to remind him of the hell he'd been through these last few weeks? The heartbreak might have destroyed her, but she'd have dealt with it if it meant Greer would go on to live a happy, healthy life without her.

But he was going to be okay. And he wanted "us."

She should make him breakfast. Knowing him, he probably hadn't bothered with eating since she last feed him. But, crap, what did she even have to make? She used up all her eggs last time and hadn't gone grocery shopping since.

Maybe pancakes?

Mind on her kitchen pantry, she started to shut the door when the sound of the elevator opening stopped her. People who lived in the building knew better than to use the elevator unless they really had to, so she waited a beat to see if Mrs. Chan needed help with anything. But it wasn't Mrs. Chan, or Todd and Elena, the young couple with the six-month-old baby who lived next door to her.

It was Eva Wilde, and she was in a hurry, each thunk of her boots on the thinly carpeted floor ringing with urgency. Spotting Natalie in the doorway, she faltered and almost dropped the folder she was carrying. Her dark hair spiked from a bun that was falling out and tension had carved lines into her forehead and around her pretty, lipstick-free mouth.

"Natalie…" She fumbled, glanced around. "Is Greer around?"

"He'll be back soon. He took my dog for a walk. If you need to see him, we can go down to the park and—" She was already reaching to close the door behind her, but Eva stopped her.

"No. It's actually you I needed to see."

She froze. "Me? Why?"

Eva wet her lips and handed over the folder. She hesitated before accepting it, terrified of the blue file folder for reasons she couldn't begin to understand. "What is it?"

Eva opened it for her. She saw what looked to be a copy of a police report. Eva pointed to a highlighted name and her heart hit the floor.

Mathew Taggart.

She slowly took the report, but none of the words around her brother's name were making sense. "What…?"

"This is the report filed by the first officer on scene when David and Meredith Wilde were murdered. Your brother was there, Natalie. He worked at the gas station and was the only other person there that night. He was considered a suspect in the murders. Technically he still is because they were never able to prove or disprove his involvement. All they know is he was there."

Dazed, she gazed up into the other woman's worried eyes. "Have you told Cam about this yet?"

Eva shook her head. "I came here first, but I'm not going

to keep this from my husband or his brothers. I just wanted to give you a heads up before I said anything to them. This isn't good, Natalie. They're not going to take it well. Greer…won't take it well."

She stared down at the report, but her hands were shaking too hard to read the words. "He said he wanted there to be an us," she whispered, more to herself than Eva. Tears blurred her vision and two escaped to run down her cheeks and splatter on the paper. She didn't bother brushing them away.

Eva set a hand on her shoulder. "I'm so sorry."

No. This couldn't be right. Before the drugs, her brother had been a good kid. A solid high B student, who loved music and sports and didn't mind his little sister tagging along with him and his friends. He'd only lost himself after he became addicted…

Her gaze finally focused and she searched for the date of the report. October 10, 1994. Mathew had been sixteen. She didn't remember anything specific happening that day — she'd only been eight — but that was right around the time her brother began to change. He'd grown sullen and impatient with her when he never had been in the past. Early the following year, barely six months after the murders, he'd been arrested for the first time for buying heroin.

Oh, God. She had to talk to her parents.

# Chapter Twenty

She had to drive by the burned out husk of the Wilde family home to get to her parents' house. It made her sick, and by the time she pulled into the driveway behind Mom's Camry, her stomach was churning. She glanced over at the folder on the seat beside her.

They couldn't know. There was no way her parents knew. They were good, law-abiding people, and if they thought their son had killed two people, they would have turned him in. Unless they thought he was innocent.

Would they have sheltered him then?

They had always made excuses about his bad behavior and drug use. "He'll grow out of it," and "he just hasn't found his way yet," were two of their favorite lines.

Gulping down a surge of sickness, she grabbed the folder and shoved open her door.

Holly Taggart was already opening the front door, brows drawn together. "Tally, honey, are you okay?"

She shoved the folder at her mother's chest. "Did you know about this?"

Holly caught the folder before it crashed to the porch and her eyes narrowed. "Excuse me? Know about what?"

"Who is it?" Carl Taggart came to the door behind her mother. Dad always looked exactly like what he was—a college literature professor—and today was no exception. He wore corduroy pants that bagged on his thin frame and a wrinkled button-up under an ugly sweater vest, which was his favorite. Next to Mom's tidy slacks, pressed blouse, and perfectly coifed hair, he looked as if he'd just rolled out of bed.

"Tally?" he said, glancing back and forth between his wife and daughter. "What's going on? Are we scheduled for brunch today?"

Dad was scatterbrained and too mild-mannered to be the disciplinarian in their household. It was Mom who ruled this roost, so she ignored Carl and focused on Holly. "Did you know the police think Mathew killed two people?"

Holly's face lost all color, and she dropped the folder, scattering the police report. Natalie didn't know how it was possible, but her face turned an even whiter shade of pale upon seeing the documents. Carl's eyes bugged behind his thick glasses, and he made a choking sound as if he swallowed his tongue.

"H-how did you find out about this?" Holly stuttered.

"The hard way." She bent to pick up the report, held up the first page and pointed to the names of the victims. "I'm seeing—was seeing," she corrected because with the way this conversation was going, it was looking more and more like the cops' suspicions were correct. "I was seeing the son of this couple."

For a split second, her mother's eyes lit with interest. "You're dating someone?" But that spark immediately fizzled out. "You're dating…one of the Wilde boys?" She pressed a hand to her chest, smoothed it down over the front of her blouse. "Oh."

*They know who the Wildes are.*

Natalie squeezed her eyes shut as a wave of horror washed over her. She swayed a little on her feet and thought for a moment she was going to toss her cookies all over her mother's shiny, three-hundred-dollar ballet flats.

*They. Know. The Wilde family.*

"Oh my God, Mom. Dad. How could you?"

Holly reached for her. "Honey, come inside."

"No!" Horrified, she backed away. These weren't the parents she knew and loved. "How could you excuse this?"

"He's our son," Holly said firmly. "Your brother. It doesn't matter what he did or didn't do. We don't know the specifics, and it doesn't matter. It's our job as his parents to protect him."

"We'd have done the same for you," Carl said, his eyes glistening. "Family is—"

"Everything?" she repeated the line she'd heard over and over again while growing up and thrust the police report at them. "What about *their* family? Five young boys were orphaned."

"And they've been provided for," Holly said primly.

"What?" She hadn't thought she could be more horrified, but nope, she was wrong. "You sent them money? As if a few bucks makes up for them losing their parents?"

"Natalie Leanne Taggart," Holly snapped. "That's enough. We're done talking about this."

"Oh, no. We're not even close to done. Where is Mathew? And, come to think of it, Andy. You're protecting him, too, aren't you?"

Carl stepped forward. "Now Andy didn't do anything."

"He beat up on an injured man!"

Carl's lips thinned. "He thought he was protecting his father."

How could they be so callous? So cold? "Where are

they?" she demanded. "If you don't tell me, I'll go to the police and tell them everything I know."

"Tally…" Her mother's voice lost its authoritative edge and became pleading. "Don't do this."

With tears streaming from her eyes, she straightened her shoulders and squared off in front of her parents. "Where are they?"

• • •

Greer sat in Natalie's apartment, waiting, his ears still ringing from the impact of Eva's news.

Natalie's brother was the only suspect the police ever had. So, after everything, it was only a random act of violence. A sixteen-year-old kid had taken out his father, had shot his mother, and left her to bleed out on the pavement, while he stole their car.

Jesus.

A mortar round had just exploded through his life for the second time in less than a month. The first had killed his friend. The second…

His future.

All of it slipped away before his eyes. That pretty picture of him and Natalie together… Fantasy. Nothing more. Nothing that could ever be.

It didn't matter. He didn't need a future. He'd had it right from the start. All he needed was revenge.

The front door opened, and Jet jumped up to greet Natalie as she appeared in the hallway. When she spotted him on the couch, she hesitated, the dog dancing happily around her legs.

"Where did you go?" Holy shit, was that his voice? It sounded so…hollow. Dead.

She set her keys down on the kitchen counter. "I was trying to find out the truth."

He shoved out of his seat. "The truth is your brother killed my parents."

"We don't know that for sure. All we know is he was there that night."

He snapped up the copy of the police report Eva had given him. "I read the damn report. They dragged him in for questioning multiple times, but they had to let him walk because he wouldn't say a goddamn thing."

She said nothing in response, but tears glistened on her cheeks. Even through his anger, the urge to go to her and brush away those tears was nearly overpowering. Which just pissed him off all the more.

"Where is he, Natalie?"

She rolled her lips together, shook her head. "What will you do if I tell you?"

"You know damn well what I'm going to do!"

She blinked and more tears cascaded from her eyes. "Then I won't tell you. What he did was so wrong—but killing him won't bring them back. It won't make any of this hurt any less."

"What the fuck do you know about pain?" he demanded and watched anger flare in her. She straightened her shoulders and walked toward him like she wasn't half his size. She shoved his shoulder surprisingly hard, and he had to back up a step to keep his balance.

"What do I know about pain?" she parroted back, fury making her voice higher than usual. Her tears flowed freely now. "I lost my family today, as surely as if they had died. My parents have been lying for Mathew, enabling him, all of these years. I had to force his location out of them, and my dad— my sweet, mild-mannered, English professor dad disowned me. This is destroying my family and ripping my heart in two. I've been falling in love with you a little at a time since I first moved in next door. Every time you grunted a hello at me, I fell a little harder. And when you showed up on my doorstep, bleeding, all I wanted was to help you slay this demon of yours. But your demon is my brother. My family. So don't you *dare* act like you're the only one hurting here. I'm being pulled in two fucking directions, and until I talk to Mathew and find out the whole truth, I'm not going to let either you or my parents bully me to choose a side."

Greer opened his mouth but found he had nothing to say in response. On the floor at his feet, Jet whimpered. The poor dog looked frightened, and honestly, he couldn't blame him. Natalie was feral right now, her teeth clenched, her eyes showing too much white. She shoved him again and kept shoving him until his back hit the edge of the still-open door.

"Leave," she commanded.

He backed up a step before the slamming door hit him in the face. For one hot moment, his temper boiled over and red hazed his vision.

*I've been falling in love with you a little at a time since I first moved in next door...*

And like that, his temper cooled. It didn't disappear, still simmered underneath his skin, but his anger had shifted away from her. He didn't know who or what he was angry at—the universe, maybe, for its fucking twisted sense of humor—but it wasn't Natalie.

*I'm being pulled in two fucking directions...*

She was right. She was in an impossible situation.

Christ. He rubbed his hands over his head and locked them behind his neck as he stared at her door. He was tired. So fucking tired of fighting. With her. With his brothers. With himself. Hadn't he already fought more battles than any one man should have to? When would it end?

He raised a hand to knock but dropped it again a beat later. A knock could be ignored easily enough. He tried the knob, but she'd locked him out.

Damn. He'd deserved to be thrown out. He'd acted like a complete jackass just now. His mother would be so ashamed of him.

He walked over to his own apartment but didn't bother going inside. There was nothing he wanted in there. Everything he wanted was behind that locked door across the hall. He lowered himself until his ass hit the floor. His cell phone dug into his side, so he lifted a hip to pull it from his pocket. He had several missed calls from Bruce Chambers and voice messages about needing him to call back, ASAP. The guy probably wanted to ship him off to Nigeria. All of his old suspicions swirled to the surface, but he shook them off.

He was done. If finding his parents' killer meant he was going to lose Natalie, he was so done with it all. Because she was right. Whether or not he got revenge, the pain of losing his parents wasn't going to stop.

He tossed the phone aside and settled in. He'd just have to wait her out. She had to leave the apartment eventually.

# Chapter Twenty-One

He was still out there, standing guard.

Natalie checked the time on her phone. She was running late, and she feared Mathew would bolt if she didn't meet him at the designated place on time. Her parents had given her a phone number to contact him, and it was all she had. If he disappeared, Andy would make sure he'd have a new phone, and her parents wouldn't give her the number a second time.

The call was one of the hardest things she'd ever done. Their parents had told him not to talk to her, but after much coaxing, he'd finally agreed to meet her at the old gas station and walk her through what had happened between him and the Wildes that October night.

She dreaded it, but not as much as she dreaded not knowing. She couldn't give Greer his revenge, but she'd at least get him answers.

But first, she had to escape him.

• • •

The stairway door opened, and Greer glanced over without much interest. His ass was going numb and he was starving, but nothing was going to pry him away from her door.

Mrs. Chan bustled in carrying several bags of groceries. She stopped when she saw him. "Greer. What are you doing out here? Did you lock yourself out?"

"No. I'm waiting for Natalie."

Mrs. Chan fumbled one of her grocery bags, and a can of soup rolled across the floor to bump against his foot.

Okay, maybe there was something that could pry him away from his vigil for a second. Dad had raised him too well for him to ignore an old woman juggling grocery bags. He grabbed the can of soup and stood, shaking out his legs one at a time. They'd both gone to sleep, and pins and needles prickled painfully under his skin. He ignored it and limped over to take the bags from Mrs. Chan.

She beamed at him. "Thank you! You're such a nice young man. Here, let me just get my keys…"

He followed her around the corner to her door. Sighed when she produced a key ring fit for a janitor and started shuffling through the multitude of keys. This, he decided, was his good deed for the year.

As Mrs. Chan took her good old time looking for her apartment key—why on earth did anyone need so many other keys?—he stared at the ceiling and strived for patience. Then he heard it. A sound like a dog snuffling at the bottom of a door. The same sound Jet made anytime Natalie left.

He looked at Mrs. Chan. "You."

She smiled placidly and took her grocery bags back. "I told her I'd distract you, and I have." She tilted her head toward the stairs. "Now go get your girl and apologize for whatever the hell you did to piss her off."

"Mrs. Chan." He dropped a kiss to her forehead. "You're a meddling old witch."

Her cackles followed him all the way down the stairs.

Following Natalie's Prius was easy enough with his bike, and soon enough, he didn't have to follow because he knew exactly where she was going. Every muscle in his body tightened with dread.

The gas station.

Was she meeting her brother there? Would her brother hurt her? She'd said many times that Mathew was unstable. What if he decided the easiest way to keep her quiet was to kill her, too?

Shit.

He poured on the speed, no longer caring if she saw him. If she did, maybe she'd rethink this ridiculous plan. He could call her, threaten her brother. Then she'd definitely not go to the meeting for fear of leading him to Mathew. It was a solid plan, except he'd left his damn cell phone sitting on the floor in front of his apartment.

Up ahead, her car slowed as she neared the abandoned gas station, and his heart started doing corkscrews that put roller coasters to shame.

*No, Natalie. Please, don't stop. Keep driving. Finding out the truth isn't important enough to risk your life.*

She didn't listen to his silent plea. She turned into the gas station's parking lot.

No.

He was right behind her, pulling up just as she got out of her car. There wasn't another car in the lot, but a twitchy, rail-thin man waited against the graffiti-adorned concrete wall. That must be Mathew. Beside him was a boy who looked to be a younger, healthier version of the same man.

Andy. The boy with the peach-fuzz mustache.

Greer threw off his helmet, jumped off his bike, and stalked toward them.

"No!" Natalie shouted behind him. "Please, Greer, don't

hurt them!"

Hurt them? Fuck that. His only goal here was to keep them from hurting her. Five feet in front of them, he stopped. Andy went wide-eyed and ghostly pale. Mathew cowered against the wall like a child expecting more abuse from his father.

*This* was the man who killed his parents?

Uh-uh. No fucking way. This was all wrong.

"Greer!" Natalie reached his side and pulled on his arm in a panic. "Please. Don't. He's my brother."

He held up a hand, staving her off. "Do you know who I am?" he asked them.

They both nodded.

"I-I'm sorry," Andy said in barely a whisper. "I-I didn't want to hurt you, but he said he'd come after my dad, and my grandparents, and Aunt Tally if I—"

"Who said that?"

Andy looked at his father, who hunched even farther in on himself.

"Matt…" Natalie slid a step closer. "Who is Andy talking about?"

Mathew wouldn't look at either of them. "The man who was there that night."

Greer's entire world ground to a halt. "The night my parents died?"

Mathew nodded once, jerkily.

Natalie breathed out a slow breath. "You didn't kill them?"

Finally, he straightened. He looked at his sister, and his gaunt face softened for an instant before he shifted his gaze to Greer. "I didn't kill them, but I was here. I saw what happened." He swallowed, his Adam's apple bobbing visibly in his neck, then he lifted one needle-scarred arm and pointed at the spot that used to be gas pumps. Now there was nothing left but the chipped concrete slab the pumps had once sat on. "They drove in and filled up. They were both very upset. Said they were looking for their youngest son. They seemed like a nice couple, so I took down their phone number in case I spotted him. Another car pulled in and the woman went back out. The man paid for their gas. We heard the shots just as I handed him his change. Four shots. *Bang bang bang bang.* He turned and yelled for his wife and someone appeared in the doorway. Didn't say anything, but I could tell your father knew who it was. And then another shot. So loud." Mathew curled his hands over his ears as if trying to protect them. "He died, right there. I thought I was going to be next, but the man appeared and just said if I told anyone…anyone…" Straightening, his gaze traveled into the distance over Greer's shoulder and his complexion turned to ash. "He'd kill me and everyone I love. So I never said anything. All this time, I never said anything. I let my parents and the cops think I was the killer because I knew he meant it."

Natalie gasped. "Greer…"

All the hairs on the back of Greer's neck prickled. He didn't need Natalie's warning or the look of pure terror on both Mathew's and Andy's faces to know someone was holding a gun on him. Instinct and years of training told him that much. He lifted his hands and turned slowly.

He wasn't the least bit surprised to find Bruce Chambers with a pistol aimed directly at his head. "Nigeria, huh?"

Bruce lifted a shoulder. "I gave you an out. Should've taken it."

"So you could try to kill me there like you did in Syria? I don't think so."

"What happened in Syria—" He broke off. His eyes were shot through with red as if he hadn't slept and wetness spiked his lashes. "I didn't want it to come to that, but you couldn't let it go. You just had to keep digging, like a damn dog with a fucking bone. You're just like your father."

"So now what? You gonna shoot all four of us? This place doesn't have enough blood on the ground for your liking?" Greer scoffed at himself and dropped his hands to his sides. "I should've trusted my instincts from the beginning. I knew you'd do anything to protect your little assassin squad."

Bruce's features showed something closer to resignation than guilt. "I did what I had to. He called me that night to help him look for Jude, and I saw my chance. He was going to ruin everything we'd worked for."

"You should have let him," Greer said. "Hell, you should have helped."

"No. I couldn't. All the good we've done—"

"What good?" Hatred, dark and bitter, threatened to choke him. "You took desperate, struggling kids, and turned them into killers. Now Dustin Williamson is dead, Zak Hendricks is drowning his nightmares in a bottle, and I—" His voice caught. "I've sat with a gun to my head, finger on the trigger, and the only reason I didn't pull it is cause I knew my parents' killer was still out there. So fuck that greater good bullshit you spoon-fed us. I don't see any good. Where I'm standing, all I see is damage."

Bruce straightened. "I did what I had to do."

"And Mom? You had to kill her, too?"

Something flickered in his eyes, there and gone before Greer could identify it. "Your mother was just collateral damage. Wrong place, wrong time."

"No. No, no, no," Mathew muttered, but Greer didn't dare take his eyes off Bruce to see what was going on.

"Shut up!" Bruce commanded and the gun wobbled in his hand.

Wobbled? Greer stared in disbelief at the shaking gun. Bruce was one of the steadiest shots he knew. His hands never wobbled when there was a gun in them.

Something was wrong here. A piece of the puzzle was missing.

"No!" Mathew shouted. "No, I'm done shutting up. I shut up for too long. That's not how it happened." He pointed at Bruce. "He was there, but he didn't—"

Greer saw the gun recoil in Bruce's hand before he heard the deafening blast of the shot. The bullet blew past, close enough that the heat of it seared his shoulder, and hit its target.

Mathew gurgled, staggered sideways a few steps, and collapsed. Natalie screamed and rushed to her brother's side. Andy's eyes rolled back in his head, and he passed out in the spreading pool of his father's blood.

"Jesus!" Greer held up his hands in a halt gesture—not that it was going to do much if Bruce started picking them all off. "Enough death. Enough killing. Bruce, enough!"

Bruce looked at him, eyes wet. "You really were like a son to me," he said and lifted the gun to his own head. "All I ever wanted was to protect you. A man protects those he loves."

He pulled the trigger.

Stunned into immobility, Greer stared at his mentor's body. His parents' killer. Dead in the same place they had died. Killed, not by Greer, but his own hand.

*What the fuck just happened?*

The first wail of sirens filled the afternoon sky and, finally, other details started to register through the fog of shock. The scent of iron and death hung heavy in the air. Natalie was sobbing.

*Natalie.*

He whirled around, searching, and found her on her knees beside her brother. Mathew wheezed and gurgled with every breath. Andy was still passed out cold.

Greer suspected there wasn't much he could do for the older Taggart, so he checked on Andy first and found his pulse strong. The kid would wake up with a headache and a shit-ton of bad memories, but no serious injuries.

His father, on the other hand…

Greer knelt beside Natalie and lifted Mathew's shirt, searching for the wound. The man was all skin and bones, and the bullet had torn a ragged hole through his middle.

"Oh." Natalie shuddered and pressed her small hands against the wound, trying to keep deep red blood from pumping out of the hole. "Oh, Matty. Hang on."

Wincing, Greer gently removed her blood-covered hands and lowered the shirt again. Even with his extensive battlefield medical training, the wound was beyond his skills. In truth, it was beyond even the most gifted trauma surgeon's skills. Mathew's complexion was already taking on the waxy sheen of death, but how could he tell Natalie that?

He wrapped an arm around her and did his best to calm her wracking sobs. "Shh, angel. It's okay. Hear those sirens? Help's coming. Help will be here soon." Even as he said the words, he watched life begin to drain from her brother. Mathew reached out blindly, groped the air, and Greer caught his hand, gave it a squeeze. "Hey, you're okay, man. You're okay."

Mathew's eyes fluttered, and his lips moved. He seemed to be trying to say something. Greer leaned closer, and with his last breath, Mathew Taggart managed four little words.

"He was not alone."

# Chapter Twenty-Two

*He was not alone.*

The words echoed in Greer's head as he watched the coroner drive away with both Mathew's and Bruce's bodies in the belly of the white van.

What had Mathew meant by that? He was half-inclined to brush it off as the incoherent ramblings of a dying man, but something niggled at the back of his brain. A thought or a memory flitting around the edges of his consciousness, an annoying fly he couldn't swat away. A missing puzzle piece.

This wasn't over.

Would it ever be?

His legs no longer wanted to work, the adrenaline having drained out of him, leaving him shaky and exhausted. He lowered himself to the old concrete slab where the gas pumps once stood.

His mother had been shot four times right here.

He stared at the cracked pavement in front of him. It seemed like it should be marked somehow, stained by the violence that had taken a mother from her sons, but it wasn't.

It was just a parking lot.

Someone called his name, and he lifted his head, searched the crowd of cops and medics, then the reporters and lookie-loos gathered on the street, kept back by sawhorses. Eva was there on the sidewalk, flashing her detective shield to one of the uniformed officers. Cam was right behind her, hobbling on his crutches. Reece and Shelby were behind them. Jude and Libby. Vaughn and…some woman he vaguely recognized but was too exhausted to try putting a name with her face. But for the first time, he noticed the ring on Vaughn's hand.

*Vaughn* was married?

Wow. He *had* missed a lot these last few months.

Eva reached him first. "What happened?"

He gazed up at her, then over at Cam and the rest of his brothers. "Mathew Taggart was only a witness. Bruce Chambers killed Mom and Dad to keep his assassin squad a secret and then threatened to hurt Mathew's family if he ever talked."

*He was not alone.*

Cam sagged on his crutches. "So we finally know what happened."

Vaughn gazed down at the pavement under his feet and scowled. "It doesn't help. I always thought knowing would help, but —"

"It doesn't," Cam finished.

"Bruce is dead," Greer told them. "After he confessed, he shot Mathew and then himself."

Cam stilled and his head turned slightly to one side as it always did when he was mulling something over. Then he asked, "Why?"

"Why what?"

"Why would he kill himself?"

And that's where Greer was stumped. In all the years he'd known Bruce, he'd never been able to dissect what went on in his head. His motives were always his own. But he did know one thing. "Men like Bruce need command like they need air. He wouldn't have survived prison."

"So why didn't he run?" Vaughn asked. The twins always operated on the same wavelength, and he must have figured out where Cam was going with the line of questions. "If he knew the jig was up, why not take off? He had the connections to disappear."

*All I ever wanted was to protect you. A man protects those he loves.*

*He was not alone.*

Yeah, there was more to this. "Can I leave?"

Eva glanced around. "There's Captain Ortiz. He's probably in charge. Hang on, I'll go find out."

Greer propped his elbows on his knees and shoved his hands into his hair. He didn't want to wait. He wanted to get the hell out of here. If Bruce had a partner, his family still wasn't safe. His brothers weren't safe. *Natalie* wasn't safe.

Who else had been there that night?

He wracked his brain, trying to come up with a name. Anything—or anyone—who had a stake in whether his parents lived or died. Nothing popped. Bruce wasn't like Richard Mendenhall. He hadn't been around all the time while Greer was growing up. He hadn't come to holiday barbeques or played touch football with the boys in the backyard. In fact, Greer remembered seeing Bruce only a handful of times before the night his parents died. His father had been very careful to keep that dangerous part of his life separate. He had no idea where to even start looking for Bruce's accomplice.

Jude sat down beside him. "So this is where it happened?"

He glanced over in surprise. "You've never been here before?"

Jude shook his head. "It was a no man's land to me. I

demonized it. Never wanted to see it." He studied the old concrete building with its graffiti painted sides and boarded-up windows. "But it's…just an old gas station. They died at a gas station." His voice hitched. "All because I wanted to see *Jurassic Park* and snuck out of the house."

"Hey." Greer grabbed his shoulder, waited until he turned back. "They would have died whether or not you snuck out. If not that night, then another. If Bruce planned it, he would have found another opportunity."

"None of us blame you, Jude," Reece said. "So stop blaming yourself."

Nobody spoke again until Eva returned.

"You're free to go, Greer," she said. "They'll want to talk to you again, but for now, you can go home."

He stood but didn't move.

Home. He didn't really have a home anymore, did he? His apartment was empty. His parents' house in ashes. He searched the gathered crowd again, but there was no sign of Natalie. He didn't blame her. She'd just held her brother while he died. She probably wanted nothing more to do with him at this point.

Feeling more alone than ever, he followed his brothers and their wives. Such was his lot in life.

"Greer!" Andy's voice carried across the parking lot, and he turned to see the kid running after him.

Still no Natalie.

"What do you want?" He knew he was sneering, but his mood was too dark to attempt anything approaching civility.

Andy didn't shrink away. He stood his ground, shoulders back, chin lifted. His father's blood still stained his shirt. "I need to apologize. I didn't want to hurt you."

"Then why'd you do it?"

Andy swallowed so hard his Adam's apple bobbed. "That man tracked me down after school one day and said he'd hurt my dad if I didn't, so I asked some friends to help. Well, not really friends. Gang members. I did some…IT work for them once."

IT work? Yeah, right. From what Natalie had said about him, the kid probably hacked something for the gang. "What happened to the one I stabbed?"

"You didn't kill him," Andy said quickly. "You just got him through the leg."

Why that came as such a relief, Greer couldn't say.

No, actually, he could. He didn't want any more death in his life. No more nightmares to add to the ones that already kept him up at night.

Andy's shoulders sagged, and he suddenly looked every bit the child he still was. "I should've gone to the police or something. I watch enough cop shows to know Bruce wanted me to leave my DNA behind."

That was likely exactly what Bruce had planned. He enjoyed using puppets to carry out his misdeeds, and Andy had been the perfect one. He'd wanted to have the boy finish the job his other puppets started in Syria, which would have left DNA evidence behind that in no way implicated his assassin squad.

"I did everything wrong," Andy said.

"Yeah, you did." He wanted to hang on to his anger, nurse it, savor it. But it took guts to tell someone you were wrong, and it took balls to own up to your misdeeds. Besides, the kid looked so earnest. "Apology accepted." He realized he was grumbling and tempered his tone. "And I'm sorry for your loss today."

Andy's lip trembled, but he didn't break down. "He wasn't a good dad…but he was mine."

"Kid…" Greer cleared his throat, searched for something to say. He saw his brothers standing several yards away, watching the exchange, and nodded toward them. "One of my brothers is a genius with computers. Maybe you can come by the office after school a few times a week, learn a thing or two from him."

Andy's eyes widened. "You'd let me?"

"Will it keep you out of trouble?"

He nodded hard, doing a fair impression of a bobblehead. "Reece Wilde is legendary. I'll literally do anything to learn from him. Can I start tomorrow?"

A legend? Greer looked over at Reece again—tall, skinny Reece with his glasses and penchant for ironing his pants—and snorted. "Yeah, sure, kid."

He walked over to his brothers, and Reece glowered at him. "Tell me you didn't just volunteer me for babysitting duty?"

"Hey." Greer clapped him on the back. "He thinks you're legendary."

Jude guffawed. "Reece? A legendary what? Stick in the mud?"

Libby smacked her husband's arm. "Stop it. Every kid needs a hero."

"Besides, I think it's sweet," Shelby added and laced her fingers through Reece's. "It'll be good practice for when we start having kids."

Reece grumbled under his breath as the others continued to tease him. Greer glanced away from the four happy couples, scanning the crowd again. No Natalie, but Andy still stood where he'd left the kid, phone out, thumbs tapping a text with all the speed of a concert pianist.

Greer returned to his side. "Hey, kid. Have you seen Natalie?"

"Uh-huh." He finished with his phone and looked up. "She just texted. Said she had something important to do at her dance studio, and asked if I was okay. She left in a hurry as soon as the cops let her." His brow wrinkled. "Do you think I could have a ride home?"

*He was not alone.*

Shit.

He pointed Andy at his brothers. "One of them will take you." Without waiting for a response, he sprinted toward his bike, scooping up his helmet from the pavement where he'd dropped it earlier.

*He was not alone.*

• • •

There were no classes scheduled today, and the studio was dark. Natalie used her key to let herself in and hurried up the stairs, her heart thundering too loudly in the quiet space.

She just needed to see one thing—

"Oh my God." She halted in shock at the top of the stairs. All the photos had been ripped off the walls and thrown about like a tornado had howled though the space. Frames broken, glass shattered, pictures torn.

She picked her way carefully through the debris. The stand of dance magazines she'd been aiming for was upended, the volumes spilled and trampled. She knelt down, sifted through what was left, looking for...

There.

She pulled the magazine from the rubble and gently dusted off bits of glass. On the cover was Meredith LaGrange-Wilde mid-leap. She righted one of the chairs and sat down, spreading the magazine out on her lap. She'd read the article a few weeks ago and had even considered giving it to Greer so he'd at least have a piece of his mother. The pages were full of glossy photos of Meredith—little instances of her life, frozen forever. On one page, she danced on a stage in New York, all glamour and grace. On the next, she held a tiny baby in a carrier on her chest while she tried to corral her other four sons into a dance lesson.

Natalie bit her lip and ran her fingers over the photo. When she'd last looked at this picture, she hadn't known the brothers, but now she could tell who was who—well, except for the twins. As toddlers, they had looked so much alike— unruly dark hair, blue eyes, and mischievous grins—it was a wonder their parents had been able to tell them apart. Greer couldn't have been older than five, but he dutifully mimicked his mother at the barre while Reece sat on the floor with crayons and a pad of paper and the twins chased each other around the studio. This very same studio.

She flipped the page…

And there it was—a small insert among the bigger article. It showed two young girls, both barely teens, their thin arms slung around each other's shoulders.

*Despite their friendship, the women admit they have been rivals at times.*

*"There's competition," Larissa Schaffer says. "Of course there is. Ballet is a small world and we both audition for the same roles."*

*"But it's friendly. All in good fun. No matter what happens, we're like sisters and we'll always support each other. We're more alike than not," Meredith adds with a laugh.*

*"That's true. We both have a thing for military men. Except…" Larissa elbows her friend. "Mine's hotter."*

Oh, God. Larissa.

The moment Bruce showed up, the pieces started falling together for her. She'd recognized him when she caught a glimpse of him at the military base as Greer had dragged her out, but she didn't place his face until he appeared at the gas station. Larissa kept a picture of him in her office drawer. Younger, but definitely him. He had a slightly crooked nose that was unmistakable. When she'd asked about his picture, Larissa called him "the one that got away."

"What happened?" Natalie had asked.

Larissa had smiled sadly and tucked his picture back into the drawer. "I made a horrible mistake and he couldn't forgive me enough to marry me. He still looks out for me, though. Even to this day. I like to think part of him still loves me, despite everything."

*A horrible mistake.*

Oh, God.

Meredith Wilde hadn't been collateral damage. She was shot first, and four times. That was an act of simmering rage. She'd been the target, and her husband had been the collateral damage.

A crash sounded from the office and Natalie jumped. Her heart practically performed a grand jeté out of her chest.

*He was not alone.*

It was almost as if Mathew was here, whispering those words in her ear. She swallowed to moisten her parched throat and slowly closed the magazine.

She needed to leave. Right now. Take the magazine to Greer and his brothers and let them figure out what to do.

Careful not to make any noise, she stood and backed toward the door. Slowly, slowly. Just as she was about to turn and bolt, her shoe crunched down on a piece of glass. There was another crash in the office, and then fast footsteps across the floor of the studio. Larissa appeared in the waiting area, dressed in a leotard and tights, the laces of her pointe shoes untied and dragging behind her. Strands of hair fell out of a topknot, and she was wobbling on her feet as if she'd been drinking. She held a gun loosely at her side.

"Bruce?" Her voice was hoarse. "Is it done?"

The room closed in around Natalie, and her legs turned to gelatin underneath her. Running was out of the question. She didn't dare attempt it when there was a gun in the mix. Even drunk, Larissa could get off a lucky shot.

Natalie hid the magazine behind her back. She cleared her constricted throat, but it still took a solid second before she was able to push words out. "Uh…it's me, Larissa." Feigning confusion, she took a small step forward, even though all she wanted to do was flee in the opposite direction. "What happened?"

"Oh." Larissa looked at the mess and waved the gun dismissively. "Just…an accident. What are you doing here?"

"Nothing." It was hard not to look at the gun, but Larissa seemed unaware she was holding it, and Natalie wasn't about to draw her attention to that fact. "Nothing important. It can wait."

"Then go home."

"Okay." She took a step backward, and then spun for the door. She was almost to it when Larissa spoke again.

"*Oh*." Disappointment dripped from that one word. "Oh, Natalie. You had to go and get involved. How many times has your mother told you not to meddle?"

Shit. She'd seen the magazine with Meredith on the cover.

Natalie felt more than saw Larissa level the gun on her. Second time today someone had held her at gunpoint. That was a new record, and one she hoped she'd never break. Drawing in a deep breath, she turned back and faced the threat. "You killed Meredith and David Wilde."

"Uh-uh." She shook her head. "I killed Meredith."

"Why? She was your friend."

Larissa laughed. "Meredith was no friend. She pretended, but she was only ever interested in herself. When I got pregnant, she took all my roles. Nobody wanted me after that. My body wasn't perfect like hers anymore. But, oh, they all wanted her, even when she kept popping out kids left and right. All I could do was teach, and you know what she told me? She said maybe teaching would be good for me. I was a *natural* at it. It was my *calling*. She tried wrapping it up in encouragement, but I knew what she meant. That old saying, 'those who can't do, teach.'" She scoffed. "She was wrong. My calling was the stage. I busted my ass for years to be on stage, but it all came so sickeningly easy to her. She was a perfect dancer with a perfect life and a perfect husband and perfect kids."

Larissa grabbed one of the photographs of Meredith still hanging crooked on the wall and sneered at it. "I wanted so badly for Meredith to fail at something, but she had everything going for her when I could barely afford to feed my son. Those last few years, I couldn't even stand to be around her."

There was so much bitterness and hatred in this woman Natalie wondered how she'd never seen it before. Never even caught a glimpse in all the years she'd trained with Larissa.

"Then, out of the blue, she told me she needed to sell our studio. She couldn't do it all anymore, and something had to give. And of *course*, she had controlling interest." She danced her fingers over the photo. "Oh, she offered to sell her share of the business to me, but how was I supposed to afford that? I was a single mother. And she didn't care." She flung the photo to the floor, the frame cracking, glass shattering. "The selfish bitch didn't care!"

Natalie edged away. Reasoning with this woman wasn't going to work. Neither would playing the sympathetic shoulder. If her eight years of psych classes had taught her nothing else, it was how to spot a person on the brink of insanity, and Larissa was there. Her only option was escape, but she'd have to keep Larissa distracted and talking as she eased away. "You killed her…for the dance academy."

"It was all I had and she wanted to take it from me! We had it set up so it would come to me if something happened to her. So I made 'something' happen." Larissa sucked in a shuddering breath, and smiled. It was ugly and twisted, more sneer than smile. "I saw my chance when she called and said her youngest son was missing. Of course, I put on a sympathy act, but I was ecstatic. Finally, something was going wrong for her."

She stepped on the photo, grinding the point of her slipper into Meredith's smiling face. "Bruce and I drove to the gas station to help them search. When we got there, she was standing by the pump, and she looked so calm. Her son was missing, and she was fucking *calm*. She wasn't wrecked. No, she was smug, so sure she'd find him if they just kept looking." With a huff of disbelief, she swung her arm out, indicating all the ruined photos and magazines with the gun. "I had hoped she'd be hurting, and—and I was so angry. Angry she was taking the studio, angry she wasn't hurting, angry that, yet again, everything would work out for Little Miss Perfect."

Her smile turned bitter. "Bruce kept a gun in the glove box. Nobody else was around. It was so easy to make it all go away."

Every muscle in Natalie's body trembled, but she had to hold it together. Had to figure a way out of this mess. Had to—

Behind her, the stairs creaked. She chanced a quick glance backward and saw Greer at the bottom. He pressed a finger to his lips and made a rolling motion with one hand.

Keep her talking. Keep her distracted. Okay. She could do that.

Larissa took a step forward. "What are you—?"

"You killed Meredith," she prompted quickly, forcing herself to look away from Greer. But behind her back, she made her finger into a gun, warning him of its presence. "But what about David? You would have gotten the studio even if he'd lived."

Larissa shook her head. "Bruce needed David gone, and we couldn't leave him to point a finger at us. He walked into the store and killed him to cover for me." Again that ugly smile appeared. "He's always covered for me. He loves me, and I've kept him on a tight leash. My own personal attack dog. He's out there right now fixing this. He's going to kill the only witness who can point to me."

"My brother," Natalie whispered.

"Yes," she said like she was talking to a stupid child. She pointed at Natalie with the muzzle of the gun. "I recruited *you* to the academy so I could keep an eye on your family. You weren't a dancer. You didn't have the body or the talent for it, but I needed to make sure your brother never talked, so I convinced your mom you could be the next Meredith LaGrange. And who better to train you than Meredith's grieving best friend?"

The words were like needles piercing through to her soul. She'd always been told she didn't have the body for dance — she was too tall, not leggy enough. Larissa had always told her they were wrong, encouraged her to prove them all wrong. And she had. She'd made a name for herself, but to hear those same horrible words now from Larissa dropped a bomb right where all of her personal demons lived.

She fought back tears. It didn't matter. Her dance career was over anyway and had been for a long time. Larissa was just being cruel, trying to get under her skin, but she wasn't going to allow it. Greer was only a few steps below her and knowing he was there gave her strength.

Besides, now she knew right where to strike to hurt Larissa the most. "Bruce is dead."

The gun wobbled. "Liar."

"Turn on the news. He killed himself. He saw your house of cards tumbling and left you to deal with the fallout alone."

Without warning, Larissa charged. "You lying little bitch!"

There was no possible way to dodge the angry woman, so she braced for impact. Larissa hit her hard, but it was the wall they both collided with that really hurt. The floor disappeared from under her feet. She fleetingly caught Greer's expression of horror, saw him reach for her as they both tumbled down the stairs past him.

And then she wasn't aware of anything but the fall. She flashed back to the day she first injured her knee. She'd known mid-jump that something had gone wrong. She'd lost control and wasn't going to land right. She'd seen her entire career flash before her eyes and had already given up on it in the seconds before she hit the floor.

This time, though, it was her life. And she sure as hell wasn't going to give up on that.

She hit the bottom feet first and her ankle cracked, her bad knee blazed with pain. She collapsed forward onto her belly and tried not to throw up.

Larissa landed beside her and groaned. She still clutched the gun in her hand and raised it, turning it toward herself.

No! They weren't both going to escape through suicide. Someone had to be held accountable for Mathew. And for Meredith and David.

Natalie lunged over and grabbed the gun, yanking it sideways just as Larissa pulled the trigger. The crack of the weapon firing left her ears ringing, and the slide sliced open her hand, but the bullet burrowed harmlessly into the floor between their bodies. She wrenched the weapon away, and handed it to Greer, who skidded to a stop beside them.

He immediately turned it on Larissa. "Don't you fucking move."

She didn't. In fact, she whimpered and curled up into the fetal position. Coward. Her and Bruce both. They had deserved each other.

Greer stared down at the other woman, and that old remoteness flooded back into his eyes. Hearing the details of his mother's last moments must have hurt. Natalie ached from it, and she hadn't even known Meredith.

Wait. Oh, God. From the beginning, he'd wanted revenge. Now he had the perfect opportunity. And when he tightened his grip on the gun, she knew he was going to take it.

"Greer, no. Don't." She sucked in a deep breath and shoved herself to her feet. The pain was intense and made her gasp, but she kept her gaze fastened on Greer. "It's done. Let's end the killing right here, right now."

"She killed my parents, tore my family apart, all because she was jealous and wanted money." His muscles trembled under the hand she laid on his forearm.

"From what I've seen, your family is pretty damn united."

He shook his head. "It doesn't matter. For what she did, she doesn't deserve to live."

"That's not your call to make. You're not in Syria." She winced inwardly as the words left her mouth. They'd hurt him, but she had to make him understand. "Do you want more blood on your conscience?"

He flinched, and she forged on, praying that something she said would penetrate his anger. "The things you've done — they were sanctioned by our government. I get it and I don't blame you for it. I'm proud of you because a lot of men can't handle that kind of pressure. But, think about it, somewhere overseas, there's a family and *you* are their Larissa. You're their boogeyman. And remember Annalise? If you kill her grandmother, you'll be her boogeyman. When does it stop?"

He blinked several times, but his gun hand didn't waver. She was getting through, but not enough. Desperation rose inside her, closing up her throat. What did she have to say to —

On the floor by her foot, she noticed the magazine. She scooped it up and rifled through the pages until she found the picture of Meredith and her boys. She shoved it at his face. "Look at her, Greer. Your mother wanted you to dance. Not kill."

He grabbed the magazine with his free hand, his gaze all but devouring the photo. Finally, he lowered the gun and released a shuddering breath filled with emotion. "I loved her so much."

Eyes burning with tears she wasn't ready to shed, Natalie wrapped an arm around his waist and leaned into his side. "I know you did. And I know she loved you." *Just like I do.* She didn't say that last part out loud. It didn't seem appropriate. At least, not now. "We should call Eva and have her arrested—"

As if on cue, the front door burst open and Eva swung inside, gun aimed, followed by another plainclothes cop and several in uniform.

"Speak of the devil." Greer raised his hands, the gun dangling from his index finger. "How'd you find us?"

"Andy told us, and knowing you Wilde boys like I do, I figured something was going down and grabbed back-up." Eva accepted the gun and handed it off to another officer. Then she holstered her own and assessed the scene with hands on her hips. "What happened here?"

Greer nodded toward Larissa. "Bruce Chambers had an accomplice. She admitted to my mother's murder and then tried to kill Natalie."

Eva arched a brow, then said over her shoulder, "Miguel, care to do the honors?"

The other detective, an older Hispanic guy with a bit of a belly, grinned and grabbed handcuffs from his belt. "Oh, yeah. Gladly. This case has haunted MPD for years."

As he cuffed Larissa, Eva returned her attention to them. "Are you guys okay?"

Even though her leg felt like it was on fire, she opened her mouth to lie. "I'm—"

Greer sent her a sharp look. "Don't finish that." He scooped her up into his arms. "Natalie fell down the stairs."

Eva nodded and was already reaching for her cell phone.

"I'll call an ambulance."

"No, I'll take her," Greer said. "Can I borrow your car?"

"Sure." Eva shrugged and tossed him her keys. "I'm going to be here for a while anyway. Cam's with Vaughn and Lark. I'll have them swing by and pick me up."

Greer said nothing more as he carried her out to Eva's car and settled her in the passenger seat. He said nothing when he slid behind the wheel and drove out of the lot that was fast filling with police. And he still said nothing when he pulled up in front of the emergency room two minutes later. He just got out of the car and came around the hood to help her.

Was he mad at her for stopping him from killing Larissa? His face was a blank mask, and she had no way to gauge his emotions, but he still kept mum even when the doctors wheeled her away. He only stood there and watched her go.

Yep, she thought with a wince that had nothing to do with the pain in her leg. He was definitely angry.

# Chapter Twenty-Three

Natalie was sound asleep by the time Greer convinced himself to go up to her room and see her. The doctors had explained that because of her history of blood clots in her bad leg, they were keeping her overnight for observation, but otherwise, she was lucky. The fall hadn't re-injured her knee. As it was, she only had a fractured ankle and would be sporting a cast to match Cam's for the next few weeks.

Even after the doctors told him he was free to visit her, he didn't move from the chair in the waiting room. It wasn't until his brothers showed up and started nagging on him that he finally worked up the nerve.

And here she was, sleeping.

Probably for the better. He was ashamed of himself for losing his cool like he had, for making her talk him away from the edge when she was the one in pain.

He was so fucking sick of living one step away from that edge. He needed help. If he had any chance of a shot with her, he needed to get right.

Christ, he wanted that shot. He couldn't ever remember

wanting anything so badly in his life.

He loved her.

And that scared him more than anything else. Could he give himself over to another person that completely? Would she even accept it if he did? She'd seen him at his worst. Lower, even. Why would an intelligent, independent woman like her want to tie herself down to a headcase like him? He turned away from her bed.

"Greer, where are you going?"

Shit. She was awake. He was tempted, so tempted, to pretend he hadn't heard her. To keep walking and just… disappear again.

"You're going to run off, aren't you?" she said softly. "Where? Nigeria? Some other war-torn country?" She sniffled, and he squeezed his eyes shut.

"Don't cry."

"Why not?" Her voice wavered. "The man I love finds it easier to be a soldier than to talk to me."

"That's not true." He finally faced her. She was sitting up in bed, her bruised arms wrapped around her knees, tears falling freely from those lovely caramel eyes.

"Bullshit." She laughed, but it was low and harsh. "Don't you stand there and tell me you weren't thinking of taking off."

He winced. "I was, but—I wouldn't have."

"I don't believe you."

He took a step toward her. Stopped. "What do you want me to say? I'm screwed up. You know that better than anyone else in my life. Yes, going to war is easier for me. Yes, I'm better at killing than talking things out. I don't know how to… love you."

She blinked. "You don't have to know how. You just feel it."

He moistened his lips. "What if I can't?"

She flinched as if he'd struck her. "You can't love me back?"

"If I let myself love you, I'm opening the door to everything else I've kept locked up."

"Maybe that door needs to be opened."

He didn't know how to respond to that, so he said nothing.

Natalie sighed. "You need to make a choice. I love you, and I can't do this by half measures. If you want to go back to your old life, I'm not going to stop you. But if you want there to be an us…" She lowered her legs and smoothed the sheet over them, then patted the bed next to her hip. "All you have to do is let me in and I'll help you fight your demons."

He hesitated. His arms ached to hold her, but his brain was still throwing out all kinds of warning flares. If he went to her now, there'd be no turning back. If he walked away, they were done. He saw that clearly enough in her eyes.

What was more frightening? Opening his heart to her or losing her?

Fuck it. When he peeled back all the layers of bullshit he'd wrapped his heart in, there was no contest. He took a step, and then another, and another. He was done looking back. She was his future.

Relief flashed across her face, and then he had her in his arms. Her fingers curled into his shirt at the small of his back, and she buried her face against his neck. He held her tightly, and the tension that had been knotting his muscles since he saw her tumble down the stairs finally eased.

"Natalie, I—"The words stuck in his throat, but he had to get them out. "I do love you. I don't know when it happened, didn't know it was possible. But when I was at my lowest, you were my angel. You brought me back to life when I didn't even know I wanted to live."

And there it was. He hadn't only opened the door to his heart—he stuck a stick of C4 under it and blew it to pieces.

She pulled out of his arms and cupped his face in her hands. "Listen to me. You are a warrior, and depression is a war. You can win, and I promise I'll be right there fighting by your side every step of the way."

"Yeah." He swallowed hard. Thought of his buddy Zak Hendricks, drinking way too much and basically biding his time until either the alcohol or something else killed him. Thought of Jude's best friend, Seth Harlan, and how hard he'd fought to heal himself. He wanted to be Seth, not Zak. He wanted to heal. "I don't want to end up a statistic."

"That's half the battle." She smiled and wiped at the tears on his face. "We will get you through this. We will win."

A few weeks ago, he wouldn't have believed her. But maybe there was a shot. He finally saw light at the end of the tunnel, and his angel was standing there with open arms.

He leaned in, brushed his lips lightly over hers. She opened her mouth, inviting him to take the kiss deeper and he did. He shoved his hand into her hair and sipped from her mouth like a man dying of thirst. He wished he could take her home, take her to bed, and get lost in her.

"Whoops!"

At the sound of Jude's voice, Natalie broke the kiss.

He missed the contact immediately and scowled over his shoulder. "Go away."

"No," she said patiently and patted his cheek. She smiled at the crowd in the doorway. "You can come in, guys."

"How are you?" Reece asked as the brothers filed in.

Jude rolled his eyes. "Obviously, since she was just sucking face with Greer, she's fine. The more important question is…" He produced a handful of bright markers and grinned. "Do you have a cast?"

"Don't let him near it," the twins said at the same time.

"Actually…" She pulled back her sheet, exposing the plain white plaster wrapped around her ankle. "I do. Have at it."

Jude sent a smug look toward the twins, then got to work creating his newest "casterpiece," as he called them.

Greer leaned over and kissed her temple. "You're probably going to regret this."

"Nah." She picked up one of the markers and sat up to draw a heart on the top of her foot. "I told the doctors to give me a white cast for just this reason."

Jude paused in drawing long enough to press a hand to his chest. "After my own heart. If I wasn't already married, I'd make an honest woman out of you."

"Good thing you're already married," Greer said mildly, "or I'd have to kill you."

Natalie elbowed him.

He frowned at her. "What? Just stating a fact."

"Okay." Jude jabbed the tip of a blue marker at him. "*You* make an honest woman out of her."

"Give me that, you little shit." He snatched the marker away, and, with Natalie smiling knowingly at him, he picked up her hand and drew on a crude ring. "I plan to."

His brothers all went still.

Reece blinked several times behind the lens of his glasses. "Did you just propose?"

"Sure looks like he did." Jude grinned and finished his drawing. He stepped back and motioned to the cast with a hand flourish. "Voila!"

Everyone leaned in, but there was no crazy drawing this time. Just a simple message in a script too elegant to have possibly come from Jude's hand.

*Welcome to the family.*

"Hey!" the twins said in unison.

"How come she doesn't get doodles of rainbow-farting unicorns?" Vaughn asked.

"Or happy dancing dicks?" Cam demanded, pointing to a

way-too-detailed drawing on the side of his cast.

Jude shrugged and capped his marker. "'Cause I like her."

The twins looked at each other, communicating in their freaky non-verbal way. Then they nodded.

"Dead man?" Cam asked.

"Oh, yeah," Vaughn said.

"Jude, I'd start running if I were you," Greer advised.

"Psh." Jude waved a dismissive hand. "I can outrun Hobbles McGee."

Cam pointed to Vaughn with one of his crutches. "But not his twin."

Jude glanced back and forth between them. "Ohhh, shit. Bye, Natalie! Feel better." He scrambled for the door as Vaughn took off like a rocket after him. Cam followed at a more leisurely pace, laughing and calling taunts at Jude.

"Brothers." Reece heaved out a sigh and also went to the door. "I'd better make sure they don't get themselves kicked out of the hospital. We're here way too often to risk banishment."

Greer watched them go and shook his head in amazement. "They're never going to grow up."

"Oh, admit it." She rested her head on his arm. "You don't want them to."

"You're right. I don't." They had lost so much of their childhood, and it was good to see them screwing around. It healed some of the wounds that had festered inside of him for twenty years. The rest of the wounds—the ones his brothers hadn't been able to touch, the ones he'd hidden from them for fear of exposing too much of himself—Natalie would help heal.

And he loved her for it.

He lifted her hand and kissed her ring finger.

Her smile faded a little as she gazed down at the drawn-on ring.

He winced. "It's not very good, is it? Reece and Jude got all the artistic skills in the family."

"Did you mean it?"

Still holding her hand, he slid off the bed and got down on one knee. If he was doing this, he was doing it right. "Yes. I mean it with every beat of my heart."

A slow smile spread over her face, and she picked up the marker, turned his hand over, and drew a band around his finger. Under it, she wrote three letters.

*Yes.*

# Epilogue

*November*

"The Dance of the Sugar Plum Fairy" played over and over in Greer's head. It was stuck there and wouldn't fucking leave. He kept catching himself humming it while he finished up at the office, and he'd never hummed anything in his life. All because today's bodyguard assignment had forced him to attend the Washington Ballet's presentation of *The Nutcracker* with a French businessman's ten-year-old daughter.

It wasn't the first time the Frenchman and his family had used their services—both Cam and Jude had accompanied the girl in the past. And, while the Wilde brothers had all loved their mother dearly, and they all adored Natalie, none of them particularly loved sitting through a ballet, so they'd drawn straws.

He'd come up short.

What he wouldn't tell his brothers was that, really, it hadn't been so bad. He'd actually enjoyed himself. The little girl was amazingly bright and had a near-encyclopedic knowledge of ballet. When she found out he was the son of Meredith LaGrange and married to Natalie Taggart, she'd been starstruck. After seeing her safely home, he'd given her father Natalie's card. He had no shame when it came to drumming up business for his wife's new dance academy.

Now if only he could get the damn song out of his head.

Humming—again—he closed up the office and walked past the dark windows of Shelby's coffee shop, which was closed for Thanksgiving. He paused at the next door down and smiled at the script painted on the door: The LaGrange-Wilde School of Dance.

As soon as Natalie's ankle healed, they'd knocked out a wall between two of the empty stores in the old strip mall, and she quit her radio job to pour her soul into converting the space into a dance studio. Now it was just about finished, and they'd scheduled a grand opening for the beginning of January.

Greer pushed through the door, and "The Dance of the Sugar Plum Fairy" assaulted his ears. *That* was why he couldn't get it out of his head. The music must have carried through the building's ventilation system into the office.

Natalie glided across the studio floor like she was weightless, each movement precise, and yet still graceful. He was no expert—and yeah, he was more than a little biased—but he thought she performed the dance even better than the woman had on the stage tonight. He couldn't take his eyes off her. She was mesmerizing.

He'd always known she'd been good before her injury. He'd just never realized she'd been...a star. If fate hadn't intervened so cruelly, she would have had a long and illustrious career. For the first time ever, he realized exactly what her knee injury had taken from her. She'd lost her entire identity and had to rebuild herself from scratch.

Christ, she was so much stronger than he was.

He winced and rubbed a hand over this jaw. Admittedly, he'd been bad about attending his therapy sessions. He hated talking about…things. It was easier to find excuses why he had to cancel. But no more. If Natalie could get through the destruction of her entire former self, and come out better on the other side, he could damn well face his demons, too.

The song ended. Natalie dipped her head and bowed as if she was performing for a real audience, so he thought it was only right to applause.

She spun. "Oh." She placed a hand on her chest, which rose and fell from the exertion of the dance. "You scared me. Are you all done over there?" She walked over to the towel she'd dropped over the barre. "How was the ballet?"

"You dance it better." He watched her dab the towel over the tops of her breasts. She wasn't wearing her usual one-piece leotard, but a sports bra and small spandex shorts that showcased her leanly muscled legs.

Sweat glistened on her skin as she bent to scoop up her water bottle. "And you're biased." She pointed the tip at him before opening it with her teeth and taking a long drink.

Desire rose in him like a summer storm, quick and hot and violent. The intensity of his need for her had frightened him at first, but now he was starting to like it. Especially when she stopped mid-drink and her eyes brightened with lust.

She pulled the bottle from her lips and pressed a hand to his chest to slow his approach. "Uh-uh. Reece and Shelby are expecting us for Thanksgiving dinner, and I still need to shower."

He leaned in, trapping her between his body and the barre. "They can wait." He dropped his mouth to hers and felt her resistance drain away under his kiss. Her hands slid up his shoulders, circled to the back of his neck.

"Okay," she breathed when they came up for air. "We can get away with a quickie in the shower."

He growled and spun her so she faced the mirror behind the barre, nipping at the tendon where her neck met her shoulder. "I don't want to wait."

"Oh…" She tilted her head, giving him better access to the side of her neck. "Greer."

It drove him wild when she said his name like that, all breathless and needy, and she'd even used it against him a time or two. But not this time. This time, he was one hundred percent in control.

He guided her hands to the barre. "Hang on."

She shivered but did as he commanded, wrapping her fingers around the smooth wood. Her shorts rode up, giving him a glimpse of the tantalizing globes of her ass. She wasn't wearing anything under that spandex, and his cock stirred as if he didn't spend a good portion of his nights buried balls deep in that gorgeous little body. It didn't seem to matter that he'd taken her multiple times last night, and once just hours ago before he left for work. He wanted her again. With that single-minded goal in mind, he stripped off her spandex and unzipped his pants. She glanced back, a small smile curving her lips as he wrapped a hand around her hip and drew her back against his erection. She wiggled her ass teasingly, squirming away just as he was about to shove into her, and laughed when he groaned.

"Tease." He gave her ass a punishing little smack. She sucked in a sharp breath of surprise, but it did the trick, distracting her long enough from her teasing that he was able to enter her with one long thrust.

Her gasp morphed into a moan, and she arched against him. One hand uncurled from the barre and slapped against the mirror, holding herself steady while he pounded into her. It was raw, possessive, and when she came hard enough to yank his own climax from him, he was left dizzy and a little stunned.

"Well." Panting, Natalie pressed her forehead against the glass. She huffed out a laugh. "I don't know if I can move."

He wasn't entirely sure if he could, either. His cock still pulsed inside her and his legs shook. "I'm good with not moving." He leaned forward and trailed his lips along her spine. "Let's stay right here."

She laughed, which made her body clench around him. "Your brothers are expecting us, remember? And now I really need a shower."

Holy hell. He was already getting hard again.

He disengaged their bodies and turned her toward him, clasping her face between his hands. He kissed her softly. "I love you."

Smiling, she raised up on her toes to kiss him back. "I love you, too."

Every time she said those words, his chest swelled as if his heart pulled a Grinch and expanded three sizes. Sometimes the sensation was so overwhelming, he feared he might make a fool of himself and break down sobbing. This was one of those times, and he grinned to hide it. "Does that mean I can join you in the shower?"

She laughed again, ducked out of his arms, and backed toward the locker room. "I don't know. Are you a dirty man?"

Yup. Definitely hard again. His cock stood at rigid attention. "Oh, yeah. I'm very dirty."

"Hmm. We'll see about that." Just before she disappeared into the locker room, she glanced over her shoulder and crooked a finger. "You coming?"

No, he wasn't. He stalked after her. But she would be as soon as he got his hands on her again.

· · ·

They were late.

Very late.

Dinner had already started by the time they arrived at Reece and Shelby's newly built house. It wasn't an exact replica of the house that burned down, but they'd designed it to have much of the same Colonial charm. There was also a new tree in the front yard. It wouldn't be big enough for a tire swing for a long time, but Reece had nailed a "no climbing" sign to its skinny trunk. Seeing that, Greer's throat closed up a little.

As if sensing the wave of bittersweet emotion, Natalie closed her hand around his and led the way up the porch steps to the door.

Jude answered with his two-and-a-half week old son, Davey, sleeping in one arm. "Hey! Perfect timing. We just sat down to eat."

Natalie stepped in first and shed her coat. She kind of... threw it at Greer and held out her arms for the baby.

"Uh-uh." Jude gave her his shoulder and tried to swat her away. "He's been passed around like a hot potato, and I just got him back."

"Oh, c'mon," Natalie wheedled, following him to the dining room. "You get him every night. I haven't seen his sweet, smooshy face in like...three days!"

It was weird, Greer thought as he hung up the coats. Seeing Jude with a baby. It worked for him, somehow, but it was weird. He should probably get used to it. The excitement around Libby's pregnancy and Davey's birth had sparked baby fever in the Wilde family. He suspected several, if not all, of his brothers and their wives were now actively trying to start families.

Greer walked into the dining room and found the entire family seated around the table, including Andy Taggart, who spent almost all of his time at Reece and Shelby's. So much, in fact, that when they planned the house, they had given him a room. Over the last year, Andy had been absorbed into the family like a little brother.

Funny how that worked.

Natalie had gotten her wish and was snuggling Davey in one of the corner seats at the table. Beside her, the end seat, the one that had always been reserved for their father during family dinners—his "throne," as he'd called it—was the only empty seat left.

Greer stared at it.

Conversation slowed, then stopped altogether. All eyes turned to him, but he couldn't move. He couldn't accept their father's seat. That would be like…replacing him.

Natalie passed the baby to Libby, then stood and took his hand, pulling him forward. She didn't say anything. Just put his hand on the back of the chair, met his gaze, and waited.

Christ. The woman had the patience of a saint.

He glanced around the table at all the expectant faces. All of them watching, waiting to see what he'd do—well, all except for Andy. The kid was mowing down on his dinner like only a teenage boy could, completely unaware of the sudden tension in the room.

Greer focused on him and the knot in his stomach eased. He sucked in a steadying breath, pulled out the chair, and sat.

Nobody said anything for a moment.

Finally, Cam cleared his throat. "Okay, now that everyone's here, Eva and I have some news."

Vaughn arched a brow. "Yeah? So do Lark and I."

The twins stared across the table at each other, again communicating in their nonverbal way. Then they both grinned and said at the same time, "We're expecting."

"Okay," Libby said and gently bounced Davey as he started to fuss. "That was freaky."

"See?" Jude said and poked his fork toward the twins. "Freaks of nature. I've been saying that for years. And next you'll be telling us you're both having twins."

"No," both Eva and Lark burst out.

"Thank God," Lark added and took a drink of her water. "I don't think the world can handle another set of Wilde twins."

Shelby made a little sound that drew everyone's attention to her.

Beside her, Reece was leaning back in his seat, looking rather smug. "Should we tell them?"

"Shelby?" Eva nailed her sister with a *spill it* look. "Tell us what?"

Shelby all but bounced in her seat as she slid a picture from under her plate and held it up. It was a sonogram, and it clearly showed two little blobs instead of one. "Another set of Wilde twins!"

The room exploded with exclamations of surprise and well wishes.

This was how Mom and Dad would have wanted it, Greer thought as he watched his brothers and their wives. This is probably what they had envisioned their retirement looking like. Their sons, daughters-in-law, and a houseful of grandbabies.

He wished they had lived to see it.

Natalie's hand settled on his leg under the table. He looked at her, saw the understanding and sympathy in her eyes. Of course she'd know what he was thinking. She always knew. He covered her hand with his, gave her fingers a little squeeze to tell her he was okay.

And he was. He was thrilled for his brothers.

"Oh," Libby said when the noise died down, a little misty-eyed. She leaned her head on Jude's shoulder. "Davey will have all kinds of cousins to play with next Thanksgiving."

Jude kissed her temple. "And every holiday after that."

"What about you two?" Libby asked, shifting in her seat

to see Greer and Natalie. "Any plans to add to our brood?"

Greer snorted. "I already raised four brats."

"Hey," his brothers said all at once.

"We weren't brats," Cam added.

"Well," Reece amended, "maybe Jude was."

Jude opened his mouth but snapped it shut again without uttering a protest. "Yeah." He drew the word out on a sigh and poked his fork at a piece of turkey on his plate. "I was. I'd apologize, but I have a feeling my son is going to get me back for it."

Vaughn smirked. "Karma's a bitch like that."

"Yeah, it is, and you better hope to hell your kid takes after Lark." Jude returned his attention to Greer. "But, seriously, no kids? You're already a great father. I mean, you didn't kill any of us and we all turned out mostly normal. Except for Reece."

Reece shot him a middle finger.

A fist closed around Greer's throat and squeezed. Hard. For a horrifying second, he thought he was going to lose his shit in front of his brothers. He reached for the glass of water in front of his empty plate to try to ease the tightness.

Natalie patted his thigh under the table, a gesture he found more comfort in than anything else she could have done. Just having her here, having her anchor him to his family—it was enough. More than he'd ever thought he'd have.

"We might try for a baby someday," she told the group. "But for now, we're going to just enjoy being the cool aunt and uncle."

"Whoa whoa whoa." Jude lifted his hands in a slow down motion. "I think we can all agree *I* will be the cool uncle. I'm already the coolest dad."

"Bullshit," the twins said at the same time.

"I design video games for a living," Reece said. "That without question makes me the coolest."

"And I'll definitely be the coolest aunt," Shelby said. She grinned over at Reece. "And mom."

"I don't know about that," Lark responded.

"I can be pretty cool," Libby added. "I put bad guys in jail."

"Hey, I'm a detective," Eva said. "I arrest those bad guys first. Besides, what kid doesn't want to be a cop when they grow up?"

"Uh, I didn't," Shelby said, and Lark agreed by lifting her glass of water and clinking it to Shelby's.

"Can I be a cool uncle?" Andy asked.

Conversations erupted around the table and overlapped as everyone debated just what made a person a cool aunt and uncle, mother and father.

Greer took the opportunity to slip away and stepped outside into the crisp bite of fall. He drew the cold deep into his lungs, held it there, and let it out in a cloud.

A warm, soft hand touched his waist, then slid up his back under his shirt. He gazed down to find Natalie smiling up at him.

"They got to you in there, didn't they?"

"Yeah," he admitted because he could. With her, he could admit anything and would be met with only kindness, acceptance, and understanding. "For a minute there, I thought I was going to bawl like Davey in front of them."

She feigned a shocked gasp. "And lose your man card? Oh, no. We can't have that."

"I love you." He smiled and flicked a piece of hair away from her face before pressing a kiss to her forehead. "Thanks for distracting them. I needed some time to pull myself together."

"They wouldn't have judged you if you had fallen apart," she said softly and snuggled in to his side. "They love you, look up to you, but they know you're as human as they are.

You're not Superman."

"Yeah, I know. It's…old habits dying hard. I've always had to be strong for them and—"

"You don't anymore," Reece said from behind him.

Damn. He hadn't been as sneaky slipping away as he thought. He shut his eyes, shook his head in resignation, and faced his brothers. Without looking, he knew all of them would be there, and sure enough, the twins stood to one side of Reece, and Jude on the other.

Jude nodded. "How about, for once, you let us be strong for you?"

"We know you're struggling with some things we'll never be able to comprehend," Cam said.

And Vaughn finished, "But we do have ears to listen if you need to talk, and shoulders if you need one to lean on."

Greer turned away from them and stared out over the yard, the skinny tree with the "no climbing" sign. He huffed out a breath that clouded in the air and tried to blink the moisture from his eyes. "They'd be so proud of all of you."

"But mostly you," Reece said. "We're a family now because you held us together."

He turned back and slung an arm around Reece's shoulders, another around Cam's. Vaughn and Jude stepped into the circle, and they huddled together like a mini football team for several long minutes. It was something they had done often as boys—their version of hugging each other without seeming too "girly"—but they hadn't done it since their parents died.

Now, Greer didn't want it to end. He sniffled and whispered, "And break."

They all straightened. There wasn't a dry eye among them, but they all pretended not to notice the others' tears.

The women were all gathered in the doorway, and they didn't try to be subtle with their tears.

Greer released a breath and reached out blindly behind him. Natalie was right there, her hand closing around his. He drew her up to his side and knew without a doubt he'd be okay. He had his brothers. His sisters. His woman.

All in all, he was pretty damn happy to be alive.

"All right," Greer said finally. "Let's go eat. I'm starving."

His brothers murmured agreement, sniffled, and surreptitiously wiped at their eyes. They all turned to go back in the house, and Jude patted Reece's back. When he lifted his hand, there was a "kick me" sign taped to Reece's shirt.

Cam noticed it, elbowed Vaughn, and they split up, one flanking Reece on each side.

Oh, shit. Greer saw where this was going, and he opened his mouth to warn Reece, but then…

Nah.

In fact…

He released Natalie's hand, charged forward, and nailed his brother right in the ass with the soul of his boot.

Reece went sprawling.

Cam and Vaughn's jaws dropped.

Jude's expression was so delighted, he looked like a kid on Christmas morning. He held up a hand for a high five. "Dude. You…are my hero."

# Author's Note

Well, here we are. Three years and five books later, we're at the end of the Wilde Security series. It sure had its ups and downs for me, but I really do love these characters. So before we turn the last page on this series, I thought it'd be fun to give you a peek into what writing it was like for me.

Shortly after my first book, *Seal of Honor*, sold, my editor Heather called me about writing another series for Entangled's Brazen line. I was a little apprehensive, to be honest. I'd never written category romance (short, trope-filled romances), and I certainly didn't think I wrote sexy enough for the super hot Brazen imprint. But I sent her a handful of story ideas I'd been playing with, including one about brothers who own a private security company together. She liked it and soon I had the basic plot for *Wilde Nights in Paradise*. (By the way, when I threw out that title during the editing process, I really didn't think it'd actually stick!)

*Wilde Nights* was by far the easiest of the five books to write. Jude was just too much fun.

Book 2, *Wilde for Her*, was harder. Not because I didn't enjoy the characters or story—I adore Cam & Eva—but I was writing the book while coping with the death of a family member, and the words came very slowly.

The hardest to write was definitely number 3. Shelby was an awesome character—but Reece? I struggled with him. I couldn't seem to get into his head. I struggled with this book for a full year before Heather and I realized I couldn't in fact write a Brazen. I enjoyed my suspense plots too much, so we shifted the series over to the Ignite imprint. Once I no longer had to keep the plot suspense-light, *Wilde at Heart* finally came together and became the longest book in the series.

Book 4, *Running Wilde*, was my second favorite to write. Vaughn and Lark just ignited off each other from page one, and the road trip trope was so much fun to work with.

And, finally, this book. It was emotionally draining, especially the epilogue. I spent three whole days on the epilogue, wanting to get it just right, and I hope I did. So far, it's my favorite thing I've written.

Saying goodbye to the Wilde boys is bittersweet. On the one hand, they gave me lots of trouble. A book wasn't a Wilde Security book until I started *headdesking* out of frustration. But on the other hand, they gave me lots of laughs and happy tears. It's kind of like saying bye to family I'll never see again—even now I'm getting choked up at the thought of never returning to the Wilde Security office. But I'm happy the boys got their happily ever afters, and I look forward to seeing where their friends—HORNET, Tucker Quentin, and Zak Hendricks—will take me next.

It's been a wild ride, hasn't it?

# Acknowledgments

Shout outs: Heather Bogucki won a contest several years ago and gave me such a great name for Greer's heroine. It was perfect on so many levels—you have no idea. Thanks, Heather. Marsha Williams, another contest winner who suggested Greer's nickname for Natalie, "angel". I couldn't have picked a better one myself! Linda Clarkson, you rock so hard for suggesting the title of this book!

As always, thanks to my editor, Heather Howland, and the rest of the staff at Entangled. I love you guys!

And my street team, the Honeys—you are my favorite people. *hugs*

# About the Author

Tonya Burrows wrote her first romance in eighth grade and hasn't put down her pen since. Originally from a small town in Western New York, she suffers from a bad case of wanderlust and usually ends up moving someplace new every few years. Luckily, her two dogs and ginormous cat are excellent travel buddies.

When she's not writing about hunky military heroes, Tonya can usually be found at a bookstore or the dog park. She also enjoys painting, watching movies, and her daily barre workouts. A geek at heart, she pledges her TV fandom to *Supernatural* and *Dr. Who*.

If you would like to know more about Tonya, visit her website at www.tonyaburrows.com. She's also on Twitter and Facebook.

*Discover more mystery and suspense titles from*
*Entangled Ignite...*

## UNFORGETTABLE

### an *Untouchables* novel by Cindy Skaggs

Vicki Calvetti thought she made it out of the mob, but when figures from her past crash land on her doorstep, it's clear she's not quite finished. Undercover cop Blake Reilly gets the shock of his life when Vicki, the woman who got away, walks into his club full of drug dealers. Their undeniable chemistry is full speed ahead until someone ends up dead, putting both their lives at risk unless Vicki can remember what she paid to forget.

## BOUND TO SERVE

### a *Dangerous Liaisons* novel by Julie Castle

Condor is Delta Star's ultimate secret agent. Untouchable, unstoppable, and he always nails his targets. New field agent Bridget Jamison will stop at nothing to capture the terrorist Simon Perez. When the Delta Star Director threatens to take the case away from her, she agrees to be Condor's partner to keep her chance for justice. Now they're on a mission to infiltrate a dangerous criminal organization, and they'll have to keep their passion contained long enough not to risk their cover...and their lives.

## Brazilian Revenge
### a *Brazilians* novel by Carmen Falcone

Human rights lawyer Leonardo Duarte wants to destroy Satyanna Darling, the woman who disappeared after a weekend of earth shattering sex…along with his priceless sculpture. But when he finds her in a Brazilian prison a year later he realizes she didn't act alone and blackmails her into helping him find the man behind the theft. But even while things heat up between them, secrets and mistrust threaten everything.

## Secrets and Seduction
### a *Dangerous Desires* novel by Sahara Roberts

Trauma doctor Monica Vasquez agrees to act as an informant for the U.S. government in the cartel-run town of Copas, Mexico. She expects the danger. She doesn't expect the heated rush of desire for Andres Calderon, the handsome horse trainer who lost his family ranch to the vicious cartel. But violence—volatile and deadly—simmers beneath the surface of this small Mexican town. And when it erupts, Monica and Andres will have to decide how much they trust their love…and each other.

*Discover the* **Wilde Security** *series…*